I0615287

The So-Called Trial of the Century

Written by

Stephen P. DeLuca

The So-Called Trial of the Century

Published by Stephen DeLuca
180 W Main St Westminster, MD 21157 USA

ISBN: 978-0-9960905-2-0

Printed in the United States of America by Lulu Press

From the Highbridge Morning Star:

Opening arguments are expected today in the long-awaited trial of alleged murderer, Mark Pitt, who is accused of killing his live-in girlfriend, Evelyn Averdantis, adopted daughter of Mr. and Mrs. Morris Averdantis. Judge Abner Tuilgy will preside. Representing the defendant, who is a well-regarded artist, will be Dick Bright of the public defender's office. Mr. Bright unsuccessfully defended Esther Weingarten of embezzlement charges last year. She is now serving a 10-year stretch in Hazelton. Heading-up the prosecution team is Ambrose Wynn, well-known Assistant District Attorney and husband of nightclub singer, Lynn Maguire. Pitt faces the possibility of life in prison, if convicted.

Pitt has steadfastly maintained his innocence throughout the police investigation and he pleaded not guilty at his hearing. Police and the prosecution have made no statement regarding the means by which Pitt may have dispatched Miss Averdantis. However it came out in Grand Jury testimony that Pitt cannot account for his whereabouts at the victim's time of death. The victim was found nude in the bathtub of the loft she shared with Pitt in the old Excelsior Brush factory in Lingstrome Flats.

This promises to be a colorful trial, at least. This is only the third time since 1892 that a famous artist has faced murder charges in this city.

1. The Prosecution– Opening Argument

Judge Tuilgy looked up from the bench. "Mr. Wynn, are you ready to begin?"

"I am, Your Honor."

"You may proceed."

"Your Honor, ladies and gentlemen of the jury, the State contends that, on the afternoon of the eleventh of May of last year, the defendant, one Mark Pitt, caused the unlawful death of one, um, Evelyn Averdantis. In fact, that he caused the unlawful and *horrific* death of a promising young woman, who was in the prime of her life– a young woman who had everything to live for. In her own odd way, a rather attractive young woman. And a young woman who came from an old and well-established family, I might add."

"I object, Your Honor!"

"To what, Mr. Bright?"

"My esteemed friend, the District Attorney, has no way of knowing if the deceased indeed had *anything* to live for, much less that she had *everything* to live for, as he asserts."

"Overruled. Continue, Mr. Wynn."

Bright started to sit down, but popped back up again. "Another thing, Your Honor. The State claims that the deceased came from an old and well-established family. In fact, her mother married into that family when young Evelyn was three years old, so she's not related except…"

"Overruled. Proceed, Mr. Wynn."

Bright took his seat, but remained perched at the edge of his chair.

"Thank you, Your Honor. Miss, um, Miss Averdantis had everything to live for. She was bright and talented, sort of cute, as I said, a kind and generous young woman who had just begun to come into her own and…"

"I object, Your Honor!"

"What now, Mr. Bright?"

"Your Honor, Miss Averdantis was *not* bright. I have obtained copies of her school records…"

"Mr. Bright, whether or not the deceased was a bona fide genius does not matter. You will stop objecting to the District Attorney's characterization of the victim in these opening remarks. Please continue, Mr. Wynn."

Bright screwed up his face and sat back down.

Wynn glared at Bright for a moment before resuming. "Eleanor was a devoted daughter and loving sister. She was a reliable friend and caring neighbor."

Bright rose again. "Your Honor, I must object again."

"What is it this time, Mr. Bright?"

"Mr. Wynn characterized Miss Averdantis as a loving sister."

"Yes. I don't see anything particularly…"

"Your Honor, Miss Averdantis was an only child."

"Sustained."

Wynn took a breath and continued. "Eleanor…" Wynn's assistant coughed suddenly, scrawled a note and slipped it to him. Wynn glanced at it before continuing. "*Evelyn* was destined to become a shining example of what every girl in this great nation of ours would aspire to be when she grows up: a person of flawless character and overwhelming charm and boundless talents. She would have started a wonderful family and raised her children with the kind of American values we all can be proud of." He paused to let his statement sink in, then he quietly continued. "Yes, she would have become all that and more, ladies and gentlemen, except she met and fell into the clutches of one of Planet Earth's most vile creatures." His voice rose in volume and deepened in tone as he turned toward the defendant. "This so-called defendant, Mark Pitt, so aptly named since he has obviously come up from the very pit of *hell* to practice his frightful talents upon the trusting members of the human race, took poor little Evelyn by her delicate little hand down a depraved road to her doom. When Mr. Pitt had subjected her to all the perverted acts in his copious bag of tricks and he had used up poor Evelyn and left nothing of her once-shining soul, he disposed of her. He discarded her like one would toss away a pork chop that had been picked clean except for the little bit of fatty meat in the corner of the bone that you can never quite reach with your teeth. And in the end, what was left of poor Evelyn was found like a piece of rotten garbage in a rotten alley in a rotten

6

section of this rot– this City. Her lovely young body, once the delicately-curved and graceful expression of youthful womanhood, which should have become the temple of love and the vessel of those never-to-be-born wonderful and well-behaved little children, was defiled in the most nauseating and shocking manner!"

Wynn paused to allow the gasps from the audience subside. He also took a sip of water.

"Ladies and gentlemen of the jury, I am certain that you, having been citizens of our great City, have heard stories of the horrors inflicted upon the innocent. You've no doubt read in our great newspapers stories of atrocities that our decent and trusting citizenry have had to endure at the hands of sickos and perverts like this creature over here. The law enforcement agencies have not always been successful at apprehending these monsters sent to test our spirit. We were lucky this time, ladies and gentlemen. Maybe these monsters are getting too confident. Maybe they are getting careless. In any case, we caught this one, almost red-handed." Wynn walked up to the jury box, placing his hands on the short wall in front of the jurors. He continued his remarks in a more intimate, conversational tone. "Now, I know that some of you will want to give Mark Pitt the benefit of the doubt and look for ways to let him off the hook. That is a noble and generous impulse for you to have and you should be admired and lauded for it. It is, however, much as it pains me to say it, a misguided way to be. It very quickly will become plain to each of you that there is no doubt in this case and that anyone who tells you otherwise is as evil and twisted as the defendant, and is trying to hide something perverted and vile contained in their own soul!"

"I object, Your Honor!"

"To what, Mr. Bright?"

"He is telling the jury that *I* am evil and twisted."

"That is true. Sustained."

Wynn looked at the members of the jury and cocked his head toward the defense attorney, giving a slight chuckle that was audible to the courtroom.

"Your Honor! Did you see that? That's not right!" Bright was livid.

"Mr. Wynn, please refrain from insinuating that the defendant's attorney is as vile a creature as his client. He is, after all, not the criminal on trial here."

His rear had almost touched the chair when Bright realized what Tuilgy had said. "Judge!"

7

"What is it now, Mr. Bright?"

"What is it now? You just called my client a vile creature and a criminal, for Pete's sake!"

"Sustained. Please continue, Mr. Wynn."

"Certainly, Your Honor." Wynn looked smugly at Bright for a long time before resuming his opening statement.

Bright rolled his eyes, then dropped down heavily into his chair.

"All right, all right– I will concede my illustrious adversary's point. It *is* reasonable to have some kernel of doubt in your mind about something of which you have no firsthand knowledge. After all, that's a mature and well-balanced approach to convicting a criminal. None of us– not Judge Tuilgy nor my esteemed adversary, burdened as he is with the regrettable task of trying to get a maniacal killer off scot-free, nor I want you to simply sit here waiting for the final instructions before you vote to execute this creature named Mark Pitt. No, we want you to pay strict attention to each of the witnesses that I will invite to take the stand. Listen to them and hear them as they fill in the awful and sordid details of this Pitt's psychologically malevolent life and actions. You will see very clearly the path that led inexorably to his ultimate transgression against God's law. Listen carefully to the parade of so-called witnesses that my poor friend, Mr. Bright is forced to trot out in his futile and feeble efforts on his client's behalf." Wynn turned toward the defense table. "Look at his sad and hopeless visage– not the defendant's, ladies and gentlemen, but poor Mr. Bright's. He knows it's hopeless..."

"Your Honor, this is too much to bear!"

"See what I mean, ladies and gentlemen? It's too much even for a seasoned attorney such as Mr. Bright."

"How can you let this kind of smear campaign continue, Your Honor?"

"Sustained."

"We will prove– though it hardly needs proof– that this treacherous and evil miscreant did the things that he was accused of and arrested for and will forfeit his life for. He certainly did a lot more than that, but we must limit our attention to the acts he has been charged for in this trial." Wynn casually made his way back to the prosecutor's table. "We will prove, ladies and gentlemen, that Mr. Mark Pitt systematically destroyed the soul, mind and body of the poor victim, Miss Evelyn, uh..." He glanced down at one of the papers lying on the table. "... Averdantis. You will be shown all the horrifying photos of what happened to her once-lovely young physique– the atrocities committed upon her person. You will hear from expert witnesses who will give you their expert conclusions about how poor Evelyn ended up defiled, broken, unrecognizable– in the vernacular: totally trashed." Wynn walked back toward the jury box. "You may not believe what you will see and hear. You may not *want* to believe it. But, you *must* believe it. You will have no choice, my friends. Can I call you my friends? Because I think you *are* my friends. Sure, I've never had you over to the house for dinner and a game of charades afterward. But, you are so much like people who my dear wife and I do have over to the house from time to time that, in these scant few minutes we've spent together, I've already begun to think of you as my friends."

Bright became agitated again and poised to rise to his feet as Wynn went on about friendship.

"Yes, my friends, you and I are of like minds and, as such, we want the same things. You want what I want, which is to put this devil to the torch, just as he deserves. You want to see him struggle to free himself from his bonds and you want to hear his howls of pain as the flames..."

"Your Honor!"

"What is it now, Mr. Bright?"

"Your Honor, the D.A. is talking about flames and howls of pain! Need I remind the court that the defendant, Mr. Pitt, does not face death by burning at the stake? Regardless of the outcome of this trial, he will not face being drawn and quartered or flayed alive or– evidently Mr. Wynn's favorite– burning at the stake or, for that matter, any other medieval punishment. Despite what you desire, Mr. Wynn, we don't put people's eyes out or cut their tongues out, anymore."

"More's the pity, Mr. Bright. More's the pity. Perhaps if there were more..."

"All right, gentlemen. Let's have no more of this discussion. Mr. Wynn, please continue."

"Yes, Your Honor." Wynn looked long and hard at Bright as the latter took his seat. "Regardless of what punishment the defendant is going to receive when he is convicted, I'm certain, my friends, that we are, as they say, on the same page in this matter. He knows it. Look at his face, my friends. Don't be afraid. He can't harm you. We've made sure of that. That's why we have the bailiff and the deputy over there." Wynn pointed to the old ex-cop standing near the flags. "We know that what Pitt really wants to do is spring out of his chair, leap over the table and pounce on you, tearing at your eyes and flesh with his claws."

"Objection, Your Honor. My client does *not* have claws. He has hands and he is not planning to spring and pounce at anybody– *especially* not the fine citizens that have been chosen to ensure his constitutional right to a fair trial." At that, Mr. Pitt leaned over and spoke quietly to his counsel. "Your Honor. Mr. Pitt informs me that he has never had the desire to spring and pounce on *anyone*."

"I object, Your Honor. Counsel is testifying on behalf of his own client."

"Sustained. Please refrain from such interjections, Mr. Bright. Is that clear? Continue, Mr. Wynn."

"Thank you, Your Honor. As I was saying, my friends, don't be afraid of him. Don't *become* afraid of him when you hear all the unspeakable horrors he has committed. Don't let his unfathomable evil intimidate you and prevent you from dispensing justice. Fry him. Fry him just as you would a rasher of bacon or that pork chop we were talking about a minute ago. Fry him because, if you don't, he will ooze his way into some other unsuspecting person's life and you," he pointed authoritatively at the jury, "will be responsible this time. And believe me, you will have a very easy task. We will call to the stand to testify on behalf of our civilization countless legions of decent, law-abiding citizens, each of whom will drive a nail in the coffin of Mr. Pitt with their irrefutable testimony. In the end, he'll have more nail than coffin. And I am very sorry to have to use the word coffin when talking about that monster's fate. I'm sure many of you good friends of mine have heard of demons being vanquished. They wrote about such battles in the Bible. Yet, they never mention in that Good Book that any of those demons got a respectable burial once they had been dispatched from our beleaguered world. No! Indeed, they did not have something so fancy as a coffin to use as a final resting place. Often enough they were torn to pieces and left for the buzzards to fight over. Unfortunately, when you issue the inevitable verdict on the so-called defendant, you will not be able to stipulate that he be dragged through the streets of our Great City. He will instead receive the benefits of the very civilization he scorns and be given a coffin he does not deserve and which he will surely pollute until it and his unholy corpse are both dust. I thank you."

Wynn walked over to the prosecutor's table and sat down. He set his jaw in such a way as to make himself look heroic and waited for the defense to give their opening statement.

2. The Defense– Opening Argument

"Mr. Bright, your opening statement, please."

"Yes, Your Honor." Dick Bright took a deep breath and waited until Wynn had gotten tired of posing– as if for his own civic monument. Finally, when the great District Attorney's jaw slackened a bit, Bright placed the palms of his hands on the table and pushed himself to his feet. He slowly made his way around the table and toward the jury box, making eye contact with one of the jurors, a woman still barely in her child-bearing years who was sitting in the front row. "Are you perfect?"

The woman looked alarmed.

"Your Honor!"

"Yes, Mr. Wynn. Mr. Bright, you will refrain from asking the jurors any questions or there will be dire consequences! Do I make myself clear?"

The juror was crying hysterically into her hands and being comforted by her fellows.

"Your Honor, that was a rhetorical question. I wasn't asking any of the jurors anything."

"Your Honor, he was looking right *at* her when he asked the question."

"Mr. Bright, did I make myself clear?"

"Yes, of course, Your Honor. I really didn't mean to ask anyone– I mean, I *might* have been looking at her, but only coincidentally. I'm sorry if it seemed…"

Amid the hisses and epithets hurled by the crowd at the defense attorney, the juror struggled to compose herself. Once she had ceased blotting her tears, the judge tapped his gavel a few times and ordered the trial to continue.

"Thank you, Your Honor. Let me put it this way– is *anybody* perfect? Well, neither is my client. Is he worse than you or you? Maybe. Maybe not. We know this about my client. He's taller than some of you. He's about the same height as you," he gestured toward one of the jurors in the back row. "But, he's maybe a little heavier." The juror shifted in his seat, cleared his throat and sat up straight. "Mark Pitt wears Converse All-Star sneakers. He puts his pants on one leg at a time and he drinks Tang, though they don't serve it in prison. Before you sits a man who, right at this moment, should

11

be serving *on* a jury instead of being judged by one. Before you sits a man who has done nothing to warrant being incarcerated like some kind of a baboon in a zoo– no, wait a minute– *not* like a baboon in a zoo. They give the baboons a patch of dirt and a handful of female baboons to play with. My sad-faced client has no one to play with."

"Your Honor, if I may interrupt."

"What is it, Mr. Wynn?"

"I'd like to go on record as being completely in favor of allowing Mr. Pitt to have visitation with as many female baboons as he would like." Wynn sat back down to howls of laughter, which Judge Tuilgy tried in vain to quiet. It was difficult for him to suppress his own laughter and the crowded court-room saw it, which brought even more laughter.

Bright waited many long seconds until it had subsided enough for him to be heard, then he bellowed out his first words until the court was quiet. "My esteemed colleague has a very quick wit. He'll need it, just to get through this case when he sees how unreliable and untrustworthy his carload of wit-nesses proves to be. He'll need his sense of humor when his mighty moun-tain of forensic evidence slides like so much muck into the sea. He'll need his sense of humor when the vivid portrait of evil incarnate that he has at-tempted to paint for you starts peeling away to reveal a thoughtful and car-ing human being who has done nothing illegal. And, finally, he'll need that famous sense of humor when Mark Pitt walks out of Judge Tuilgy's court-room, unshackled and free once again to pursue his vocation and the American Dream– just like all of you." Bright paused to put a Certs into his mouth.

"Ladies and gentlemen, you will see for yourselves that Evelyn Averdantis was not the martyred saint that my esteemed colleague has depicted her to be." He crunched his Certs. "She wasn't a *bad* person. I don't want to give you that impression, but I want to make sure that you don't think that any-body who even looked at her cross-eyed should be drawn and quartered. She was a normal young woman– whatever that is. She and Mark Pitt loved each other very much at one time. It seems their love faded over the course of time, and paled next to and eventually may have been somewhat eclipsed by his dedication to the pursuit of the artistic ideal. It cannot be said that Miss Averdantis stood in the way of his art. Nor can it be said that she pro-vided Mark Pitt with any other reason for him to think about killing– or even hurting– her. Sure, you're thinking, 'all couples hurt each other.' I know I hurt my wife. I've never broken any of her bones or ruptured any of her internal organs, but I've hurt her. I admit it. I bloodied her nose one time. It was kind of an accident. I was pushing her and her head hit the wall. She forgave me. I tore out a handful of her hair once. In that case, instead of pushing, I was pulling and so was she. So it was both our faults in a way. And every time I hurt her badly enough, I was man enough to drive her to the emergency room and wait with her until she was seen by a doctor. My point is that people can do things that hurt each other, but that doesn't mean they should be convicted of any crimes." Bright approached the jury box again.

"Look, you twelve citizens will be shown all kinds of reports and charts and graphs, and you'll be expected to make some sense out of them. Forget about it. Even the experts can't make heads or tails out of their own reports. Don't let all those initials after their names fool you. They get up in that box over there and they answer questions and they're faking it the whole time. You can't believe a word they say."

"Your Honor, I must object to the defense attorney's absurd assertion that reputable citizens he has never seen or met will come to your courtroom, swear an oath, take the stand, then try to fake their way through their testimony. That is simply the fantasy of a desperate man who has no defense to offer and who will stop at nothing, including slander, to get his horrid client off the hook for those unspeakable crimes."

"Overruled."

"What?! Your Honor...!"

"Sorry, I meant sustained. Mr. Bright, you will refrain from such slanderous attacks or you will find yourself sleeping in the same cell as Mr. Pitt and subjected to his perverse desires. Do you understand?"

"Yes, Your Honor, though I object to your characterization of my client's desires as being 'perverse'".

"You may continue, Mr. Bright."

"Yes, Your Honor. Where was I? Oh, yes, these so-called experts. I don't know what else to say about these skalliwags that won't ruffle the esteemed District Attorney's feathers, so I will leave you with this caution: Either read all the reports and pore over all their charts yourself or forget that they even exist at all."

"Your Honor, it is not proper for counsel to tell the jury to disregard evidence just because they don't know what it is. They must weigh such evidence as heavily as anything else that is presented to them."

"Sustained."

"Your Honor, how can a juror consider evidence that he or she cannot comprehend?"

"Your Honor, Mr. Bright is conveniently forgetting that we call as witnesses the very people who prepare these reports and charts. They are the most qualified to explain their findings and will do so. Then, our stalwart jurors will know and understand everything that is necessary in order to convict and condemn the so-called defendant."

"Why do you insist on calling him 'the *so-called* defendant', Mr. Wynn? He *is* the defendant, whether you like it or not."

"If you must know, Mr. Bright, one can never be too sure about entities like your so-called client."

"Now he's my '*so-called* client'? What is it with you?"

"Gentlemen! You will cease your bickering in my courtroom and return to the business of the trial. Have you finished your opening statement, Mr. Bright?"

"No, Your Honor."

"Then, please do so. And no more squabbles. You are tarnishing the reputation of this fine institution."

"Thank you, Your Honor." Bright took a deep breath and sighed loudly. "Ladies and gentlemen, you have a hopeless task ahead of you. You don't know any of the people involved in this case. You don't know any of us, despite being considered by the District Attorney as his friends. You don't even know each other. You'll certainly get to know each other by the time this whole affair has run its course. You might even grow to like each other. Who knows? You might despise each other and want to poke each other in the eye or kick each other in the groin. But then again, you might want to sleep with each other or go swimming together. Like I said, who knows? One thing's for certain, though– the entire City will be listening when it comes time for you to speak. And your time will come after all of us lawyers and witnesses have had our say. When will that be? I couldn't say exactly. It might be in a day or two. It might be weeks from now. It might be never. That's right, it might be never. I know I just said that your time will come, but it might not. How can that be? I'll tell you. There could be a mistrial."

"Your Honor, what the– what *is* this?"

"Mr. Bright, do you have a license to practice law in this state?"

"Yes, I do, Your Honor."

"Until I can check into that, I will take you at your word. In the meantime, kindly present your opening argument in the proscribed fashion and let's get on with this trial."

"Yes, Your Honor. I'm almost finished."

"Excellent. Proceed."

"You know, ladies and gentlemen, I was thinking just now of an old Chinese moral tale. It goes something like this:

> An old man is met at a fork in the road by a pigeon sitting on top of a sign nailed onto a fence, and the pigeon is sitting right over it. The pigeon addresses the old man in perfectly good English– only in the original proverb, it would have been perfectly good Chinese. Anyway, this pigeon stops the old man with a wave of his wing and the old man says to him, 'why do you stop me, pigeon? I have much to do today and not nearly enough time to do it all.' So the pigeon says, 'old man, I am lost and you are old and wise and have seen so much in your countless years and many decades in this world.' And he asks the old man, 'which direction must I go to find the best nesting grounds?' And the old man looks at the pigeon and then looks at the sign posted below him. He stands there for a minute and scratches his long white beard. Then he turns his attention back to the pigeon and tells him, 'I cannot help you, my friend, The Pigeon. I am not qualified to advise you.' 'Why the heck not? I can't read because I'm a pigeon, but I'm sure *you* can read. So I waited here for many days perched over this sign because I figured *someone* would come along and just read it to me.' So the old man says, 'it is true that I have lived many, many years in the world and I have seen many, many things during the course of those years. However, it is also true that I am not a pigeon and I have never seen the best nesting grounds for pigeons and wouldn't know which the best were if I saw them.' Well, the pigeon can't believe his ears. 'What does *that* mean, old man? You've seen lots of pigeons in your time and lots of nesting grounds, so I figure you ought to be able to direct me to the best nesting grounds.' But the old man's feathers didn't ruffle so easily. 'My friend, The Pigeon, there are two reasons why I cannot tell you the way to the best nesting grounds. First,

15

few men have ever seen *good* nesting grounds, and *no* man has seen the best nesting grounds.' At that, the pigeon was incredulous. 'That's impossible. How can that be, old man?' 'Because any nesting ground that is a *good* nesting ground lies outside the prying eyes of man.' The pigeon had to hand it to the old man. His point made sense. 'Okay, okay, then let's just skip that part. What about this sign, though? What does it say?' The old man looked at the pigeon and suppressed a chuckle. 'It is indecipherable.' 'Why is that, old man?' And the old man says,'because it is completely covered in your droppings.'

Bright paused for a moment and slugged down a sip or two of water, letting the meaning of his tale sink in for full effect. "Ladies and gentlemen, now you know what you must do."

A few of the jurors looked nervously at each other.

3. The Coroner

"The state calls Dr. Wilbur Guardian to the stand."

A small, balding man, dressed in a conservative suit and wearing horn-rimmed glasses was sworn in and took the stand.

"Dr. Guardian, what is your involvement in this sorrowful case?"

"I am the coroner assigned to this case."

"Tell us what happened on the day of Evelyn Averdantis's death."

"I received the call to proceed to 714 19th Street to attend to a possible homicide. I got to the address at 11:57 am and proceeded upstairs to the apartment. The deceased was found in the bathroom, lying in the bathtub. I pronounced her dead and left the rest of the work to my assistants."

"What was the cause of death, Doctor?"

"Well, you know you can't just look at a body and tell what the cause of death is. We take these bodies downtown and subject them to all manner of insults and examinations in order to confirm our suspicions."

"And what were your suspicions in this case, Doctor?"

"We figured she was murdered by being electrocuted. So, given that as a starting point, we tear the cadaver apart, looking for things to support that assumption."

"And did you find those things?"

"Of course."

"How many years of experience do you have as the City Coroner?"

"Too many. Ha ha! Only kidding. That's a little joke we like to share down in the morgue. Seriously, I've been a Coroner for this City for twenty-six years. Before that, I was the assistant to Dr. Morton for twelve years. Yep, I've been involved in a lot of cases and seen just about all there is to see. Except maybe Niagara Falls. Ha ha! Yeah, Judge Tuilgy and I have sat in these seats many, many times together over the years. Isn't that right, Judge? Yeah, a long, long time."

"So, Doctor, it's fair to say that you know pretty much everything there is to know in your field and a lot of weight should be put in what you have to say about the facts in the case?"

"Yes, I would say so. I doubt my wife would share that sentiment with you. Ha ha! No, but seriously, she loves me. She really does. I *think* she does. She told me she did. Of course that was a long time ago. Ha ha!"

"What condition was the body when you first encountered it?"

"My wife's?"

"No, the deceased– Miss Averdantis."

"Ah, sure. Let's see, she was lying in a tub of water, unclothed– or un-draped as artists are fond of saying. I bet you didn't know that about me, did you?"

"Didn't know what about you?"

"That I am fond of art and such. I've read many, many books in my lifetime about art– the history and the techniques and styles. That's why I'm so glad to be involved in this particular case– because of the artistic angle. I have art books lining my walls. I have books on the Classical Greeks, with those statues. Some of them are nude, you know. Others are draped. So you see, you have what they call draped and undraped. Get it? Yeah, I have some nice books on that modern art stuff, too. Yeah, lots of books. I don't own any paintings or classical sculptures myself, mind you. I mean, how could I, on a Coroner's salary? But I sure have the books. Some of them– a lot of them, actually– I bought used at Stacks 'N Stacks, when they were in busi-ness, you know. I don't know if you remember that place. They were on Concord Avenue. They're gone now, of course. All the old bookstores are gone now. You know, you could go into any of those stores and the guy there would really help you. They knew their business. They certainly did. I know my business, too, Mr. Wynn. Yessirree, I sure do."

"Anything else notable about the condition of the body?"

"Well, let's see. I'm afraid I'm not sure that I'm following you, Mr. Wynn. Can you be a little more specific?"

"Was there anything unusual about Miss Averdantis's appearance or any-thing that struck you as odd or different?"

"Oh, yes! I get you. Sure, sure– her hair. Yeah, her hair."

"What about her hair, Doctor?"

"Well, you know she didn't really have much. What there was of it was kinda patchy, you know?"

"Can you describe it in more detail?"

"Well, I don't know. I've never seen anything quite like it before– except on people who had radiation poisoning. It was odd. She didn't have any other kind of signs or symptoms of radiation poisoning, so at first I didn't know what to make of it. She had these small patches of hair, here and there, you know? But, mostly she was totally and completely hairless. Like I said, I never saw anything like it before– and I've been at this game for a long time, my friend."

"Where were these so-called patches of hair?"

"She had a patch right here, behind her ear. She had a little bit of her left eyebrow and some longer hairs growing in her left armpit. That really surprised me. We didn't see that until we got the body downtown and did a thorough once-over look-see. It's very rare to see any armpit hair on women these days, you know, let alone armpit hair in just one of the body's two armpits. That seemed unusual to me."

"To what did you attribute the odd hair patterns?"

"Well, we thought at first that it could be either a natural phenomenon or an unnatural phenomenon. So we ran some tests and did an analysis. These tests led us nowhere, so we shifted our focus. You know, science can sometimes take you only so far. Sometimes you have to shift to other disciplines."

"What discipline did you shift to?"

"Pure guesswork."

"What was the result of the guesswork?"

"We determined that it was the work of a crazed psychopath."

"And that's your opinion, based on decades of experience in your field and countless cases on which you worked?"

"It is."

"And what clinched it for you?"

19

"We were able to determine that the hair was removed forcibly." There was a disturbed murmuring in the courtroom.

"In other words, someone pulled her hairs out?"

"Yes."

"Was it done before she was dead?"

"Yes. It was done over a long period of time– weeks, maybe."

"Like torture?"

"Yeah, you could say that."

"Could you determine who did this?"

"No, unfortunately, we could not– not beyond a reasonable doubt, that is. I must say that whoever it was, he approached the task with great patience and determination."

"She died because she had no hair? Is that possible?"

"It's not only possible, but it has happened. We have seen it. We have received documented cases of it from all over the world. It is called *glaber mortem* and it affects not only humans, but also almost every species of mammal and bird on earth. We have a documented case of a giraffe dying of *glaber mortem* after being shaved from head to toe by an African tribe in preparation for one of their fertility festivals."

"So, what you're saying is that if you shave a person from head to toe, they might die?"

"It's more complicated in the case of homo sapiens, but yes."

"Why is it more complicated? What's the difference between animals and humans?"

"If you don't know that, then perhaps we should keep an eye on you, my friend. Ha ha! That's just a little hirsute humor, as we say. Don't look so serious. No, really, there is a world of difference. Somehow there is a sexual component when it's done to a human being. That's not too surprising really."

"Why's that, Doctor?"

"Well, it's very likely that there's a sexual component to just about everything that involves humans. You should know that. Anyway, there are those deviant characters that volunteer to have all their hair removed. That sort of practice is usually hooked into some kind of fetishistic ceremonial rite. It's all linked into the bygone days when fur was a protection against the elements and the enemy. The removal of the covering is an act of submission and a gesture of trust– and, by extension, love. This excites the libido and facilitates the sexual act."

"Sounds like you guys have it all worked out."

"Mostly, but we still don't know why the giraffe doesn't feel the same way about being hairless. We also don't know why some people die prematurely when they are devoid of hair, but that seems to be the trend."

"You mean that they die suddenly and unexpectedly?"

"No, no. I'm talking about long-term life expectancy. People who remove all their hair have a life expectancy two to three years shorter than others. We're not certain of the causes. It could be that the lifestyles of people who remove all their hair differs in other ways from the more traditional, hirsute lifestyle. It could be that they don't eat as well or that they get less sleep or that they expose themselves to more diseases than others. The jury's still out on the causes."

"So, it is possible that Evelyn Averdantis died as a result of having lost all her hair?"

"She may have suffered some sort of shock from the removal of hair. She's no giraffe, obviously, but mammals are mammals, if you know what I mean."

"Could the hair removal have accelerated Miss Averdantis's death by electrocution?"

"Hard to say. It is conceivable that the plucking of the hairs over a long period of time led to a chronic state of anxiety that destroyed the body's defenses. That made her more susceptible to the electric current and contributed to her death. I've seen cases where people were subjected to high levels of stress for extended periods. Those people manifested all kinds of symptoms and diseases. There was one guy whose eyes swelled up until one of them popped. Ptschew!" Guardian demonstrated the act of exploding with the fingers of his right hand. "You never saw anything like it. And it was all due to the stress he had on his job."

21

"What was his job?"

"He was an usher at the Grand Theatre, I think. Maybe it was the DeLuxe on 5th Avenue. That's not the point. The point is that prolonged stress can cause havoc on the human body– and not just the eyeballs, mind you. I recall a woman who was stuck in a marriage where her husband beat her and called her names. She managed that all right, but when she took a lover and he did the same to her, she couldn't handle the stress and she developed these splotches on her skin and lost control of her bowels. Eventually, she lost her mind and jumped out of her bedroom window. Poor husband stood there and watched it all and couldn't save her. I'm telling you, stress can do a lot of damage. There was a murder case a few years ago where a child was charged with killing its mother. If I recall the circumstances correctly, she collapsed and died in the cereal aisle of a Bohack's supermarket. Her child was grabbing every box of sugary cereals and screaming and crying when she'd snatch it from the kid's hands. The poor woman was so stressed out that her blood pressure caused her to suffer a stroke."

"They charged the child with murder? How could it have even known what it was doing?"

"Well, this child was twenty-four years old at the time, so it's reasonable to have held him responsible for his conduct. And, it just so happens that it wasn't the first time this particular person caused lethal doses of stress, resulting in death. There was a pattern of willful malice."

"Would you say there was a pattern of willful malice in this case, Dr. Guardian?"

"Most definitely. Willful malice of the most heinous sort."

"Was there any evidence pointing to a specific culprit?"

"Only the psychological profile, which I am not qualified to present here."

"Of course. Thank you, Doctor. No more questions."

"Mr. Bright, your witness."

"Yes, thank you, Your Honor." Bright walked up to the stand, looking down, pressing his hands together with the thumbs under the chin and the tips of the index fingers touching his nose, in a very pensive manner. Finally, he looked up at the witness. "Dr. Guardian, were you able to definitively determine the cause of death as electrocution?"

"I did say electrocution."

"Yes, but you indicated that you had that cause in mind when you started work on the deceased. Was it definitely electrocution?"

"Now, before I answer that question, let me say that determining the cause of death in *any* case can be a long and elusive process. Many tests are performed. Measurements are taken and analyzed. Spectrographic results are compared. Known and trusted scientific theorems are challenged. New theories are proffered, then discarded– often during the course of one lunch hour and a cocktail or two. Materiel is procured and paperwork is processed. The stomach growls, the forehead perspires and gets wiped. Wives gripe, children cry, dogs sigh and everyone grows tired and old. Bags form under the eyes, then the eyesight fails. Next, you lose your coordination and can't cut a straight line into a perfectly good cadaver anymore. What do you have in the end? Answers? Sometimes yes and sometimes no. Do the bad guys get away? I'd say yes, but that's not why I'm here." He shifted in his seat, propping himself up. "You asked me a question, Mr. Bright, for which I've been chasing the answer down for decades. Often, we aren't given nearly enough time to go through what must be done in order to *discover* the truth. Yes, Mr. Bright, I said *discover* the truth. That's right. You don't *find* the truth. You wouldn't know where to start looking for it in the first place. No, you grope around, staggering through the darkness until– *foom*!– you fall into its lair, where it sits laughing at you with those impenetrable Oriental eyes, seeing right through your diplomas and your starched lab coat and past your pocket protector– right straight through to your soul. *That's* what being a medical examiner is all about, Mr. Bright."

"So, you were not able to determine the cause of death?"

"Nope."

"Makes you want to tear your hair out sometimes, eh, Doc?"

"Ha! I see what you mean. No, Mr. Bright." He rubbed his head. "In my case, it's just male pattern baldness, I'm afraid. I came very close to buying a hairpiece. Nothing too fancy, mind you, just something to fill in the ever-widening gap up there. The wife nixed it. Her uncle had a really bad one, you know what I mean? He had the kind that looked like a plastic rug. Well, anyway, the wife nixed it."

"No more questions."

"You may step down, Doctor."

4. Detective Phil McKenna

"Your Honor, the State calls Detective Phil McKenna."

A middle-aged man, with a pronounced paunch, and dressed in an old, cheap brown suit took the stand.

"State your name and occupation, please."

"Phil McKenna. I am a plainclothes detective for the police department. I work in the homicide department."

"And, Detective McKenna, were you the investigating officer in this case?"

"I was."

"Tell the court how you became involved in the case."

"I was on duty the day that Evelyn Averdantis's body was found. My partner, Mel Rodriguez, and I took the call at headquarters at 10:15. We responded to 714 19th Street and proceeded to the eighth floor apartment. Patrolmen Gucci and Booker were already on the scene and had secured the location to protect whatever evidence might be found there."

"Was the defendant, Mark Pitt, there when you got there?"

"No one other than the victim and officers Gucci and Booker were there."

"When did the coroner and crime lab crew get there?"

"About thirty minutes after Rodriguez and I got there. I called for them after I arrived."

"What happened then?"

"Rodriguez and I started knocking on doors and questioning the neighbors. That's when we found out about Mr. Pitt."

"Who had found the body?"

"We never found out."

"Who placed the initial call to the police?"

"It was placed anonymously."

24

"Did the call come into the police station directly or was it placed through the 911 service?"

"The call came into the local precinct directly."

"Who took that call?"

"Desk Sergeant Puffer took the call."

"What information was Sgt. Puffer able to give you about the caller?"

"Not much. He wasn't sure if it was a man or a woman who called. The connection was poor and the voice may have been disguised. He said he even thought it may have been a crank caller, because the voice was strange and because the caller declined to give his or her name and phone number."

"So, this was basically an anonymous tip?"

"Correct."

"And yet you followed it up anyway?"

"We have to check these things out. Nine out of ten times– well, maybe eight out of ten times it turns out to be nothing. This time we hit the jackpot." McKenna paused and shifted uncomfortably. "Sorry, that may have been a poor choice of words."

"That's quite all right, Detective. When you got to the apartment and saw the victim, what were your thoughts?"

"My thoughts? Let's see…"

"Objection, Your Honor." Bright rose to his feet. "No one cares what Detective McKenna's thoughts were or if indeed he even had any."

"Now, I object to that cheap shot, Your Honor! Mr. Bright may have no respect for law enforcement in this City, but it doesn't give him the right to insult the good detective, who is just here in his role as a public servant, trying to do his best."

"Both of you are sustained. Proceed, Mr. Wynn."

"Let's put it this way, Detective McKenna, had you ever seen a scene such as the one you beheld that day in the apartment at 714 19th Street?"

"Sure I have. I've been a cop for nineteen years now, so I've…"

"You've seen young, bald women in bathtubs before?"

"Huh? Oh, that! Well, can't say that I have seen exactly *that* before. I've seen bald men in bathtubs." He started ticking off on his fingers the things he'd seen in his long career. "I've seen young women in bathtubs– dead, I mean. I've seen just a pile of body parts in a bathtub. I've seen a baby's head in a toilet bowl. I've seen two dead bodies, locked together in a life or death struggle where both of them died. They strangled each other with their bare hands. That's unusual– to have both perpetrators dead. I've seen a dead body hung in a closet like an old suit. I've seen bodies stuffed into refrigerators. One was stuffed into the cabinet under a bathroom sink. I once saw a dead body hanged on a Hunter ceiling fan. The body was twirling around like some kinda ice skater, you know, pirouetting, until we shut the fan off. We found a body stuffed into a dump truck's tire that was on the truck. The driver had noticed that the tire was rotating funny, but didn't call us until the smell got really bad. A lot of times it's the smell that gets people to notice a dead body and call us. That's what's so unusual about this case."

"How's that?"

"Well, usually when it's not the stench of a rotting corpse that gets people to notice, it's because either the body is in plain sight– like on a street corner or washed up on Bulton Beach– or an acquaintance knows the person who's deceased."

"So, what you're saying is that because Evelyn Averdantis's body was not in plain sight, someone who knew her must've called in the report."

"Yes, either that or the person who killed her phoned in the report."

"Ah, I see. Sergeant McKenna, when you questioned the defendant, Mark Pitt, did he admit to making that call to the station house?"

"No, we couldn't make him admit it. And, believe me, we tried."

"Oh, I believe you, Sergeant. I know how hard you boys work down there in homicide. When you couldn't get him to fess up to making that call, did you call in a voice expert?"

"What for?"

"To compare his voice to the one that was heard on that call."

"Well, there wasn't no recording done of that call. They don't have recording equipment at the local precincts."

26

"Of course. I forgot. How long was it before you were able to talk to the defendant?"

"We didn't get to talk to him until three or four hours later."

"How did you catch up with the fugitive?"

Bright perked up. "Your Honor, my client was not a fugitive. He had no involvement or knowledge of this tragedy before Detective McKenna notified him and was not 'on the lam', despite what Mr. Wynn would like us to believe."

"Sustained."

"Okay, technically he wasn't a fugitive."

"He wasn't a fugitive– technically or otherwise. Your Honor, is it possible to get Mr. Wynn to drop that word from his questioning?"

"Mr. Wynn, counsel for the defense has a valid point. You will cease referring to the defendant as a fugitive."

"Thank you, Your Honor."

"Proceed, Mr. Wynn."

"Detective McKenna, what was the defendant's reaction to the so-called news that his girlfriend was dead?"

"He *acted* upset."

"So, you weren't convinced that he really was upset?"

"We-e-e-e-ell, you know," he shifted his bulk in his chair and re-crossed his legs to put weight on his other hip, "I've been a cop in this town for a long, long time and you get to know. You get to be able to tell the truth from the lies."

"Do you believe that Mark Pitt was lying?"

"Whoa! Your Honor!"

"Sustained. Do not answer that question, Detective. Mr. Wynn, you know better than that."

"Of course I do. I'm sorry, Your Honor, I forgot myself in my fervent quest for the truth. Detective McKenna, did you subject Mark Pitt to a lie detector test?"

"Yes."

"Are you a State-certified lie detector administrator and evaluator?"

"Yes, I am."

"I have here the results from that test. Can you take a look and verify that this is, in fact, that test?"

McKenna took a look at the long scroll and nodded. "Yes this is Pitt's test result. You see my initials here." He pointed to an elaborate mark under the graph lines.

"Is it standard procedure that the detectives involved in investigating the crime also administer the lie detector test?"

"In this city it is."

"Very good. Now, to the question 'Did you kill Evelyn Averdantis because you hated her?', what did the defendant answer?"

"He answered 'no'."

"And what did you make of that answer?"

"We knew right then that it was not a crime of passion. He killed her for some other reason– probably financial gain."

The defense attorney jumped up, almost tipping his chair over in the process. "Your Honor, what sort of question is *that* to ask on a lie detector!? And then to make that assumption!" Bright was livid. "You can't allow this, Your Honor! I demand to see this man's State certification."

McKenna reached into his back pocket and pulled out a tattered and folded paper. "Here you are, counsel." He held it forward to the incredulous attorney. Bright unfolded it and read it, then silently handed it back to the witness.

"Your Honor, I still say that the form of the questions asked of my client were inappropriate and unacceptable for a lie detector exam."

"Your Honor, what would my learned friend prefer that the police ask a murder suspect? Maybe Detective McKenna should have asked what Mr. Pitt had for breakfast, huh?" Wynn smirked as he shook his head in exaggerated disbelief.

"Actually, we did ask that. It was question eight or nine, I think."

"You see, Your Honor, my exalted foe can't even complain about that!"

"Gentlemen, let's stop the vitriol and sarcasm. Mr. Bright, your objection is overruled. Detective McKenna is State certified, as you yourself saw. It follows that his questions follow a certain strategy that is designed to distinguish the truth. You may proceed, Mr. Wynn."

"Thank you, Your Honor. Sergeant McKenna, just for the record, did you design the strategy you use in these lie-detector questionnaires?"

"Me? No, they were designed by psychologists, working with local and federal law-enforcement agencies. All we do is pick from a menu of questions based on different approaches that match up to different sets of circumstances. The one we used for Mark Pitt is just one of those targeted approaches. Some of them are more direct than others. His happened to be more direct."

"Was there an advantage to using a more direct strategy?"

"Well, for one thing, it greatly reduces the risk that the perpetrator– or in this case, the subject– will be able to avoid answering for his motive for the crime. Remember, we have to establish the motive for the crime. In this case, there was a murder. We've found that it's very difficult to get somebody convicted if the jury isn't told of some sort of motive for the crime. For some reason, if the jury isn't convinced that there was some reason for it, they don't want to believe that the perpetrator would have committed the crime. So we give 'em the motive, using a very elaborate and clever series of finely crafted questions that lead the subject down the slippery slope to self-incrimination. It's amazingly effective and all *very* scientific."

"Would you say it's completely foolproof?"

"Nothing is *completely* fool-proof, but this is about as close as you're gonna get. We've put a lot of bad men behind bars– or worse– all thanks to this program. And we've had very few fatalities, though one or two perpetrators ended up as vegetables."

"So, now that we can all be satisfied that this is not some hare-brained scheme that you have concocted," he shot a significant look at Bright, "let's get back to the particulars. What result did you come up with for question twenty, for example?"

"Question twenty. Let's see. Ah! Question twenty asked Mr. Pitt if he felt bad that he had not killed other people in his past."

"And what was Mr. Pitt's response?"

"He said no."

"And what did you infer from that, Detective McKenna?"

"Well, that answer really set off alarm bells with us. We started looking into the subject's past and looking at missing persons reports to see if we could determine who else he had killed."

"Did you find any other..."

"Your Honor, this is unconscionable! Who, in their right mind, would come away from that answer with an assumption that the person had killed other people? Are you going to let this continue?"

"Yes. Sit down, Mr. Bright. You may proceed, Mr. Wynn."

"As I was saying, did you find any other victims in Mr. Pitt's vile wake?"

"We're still checking leads. There are a *lot* of missing persons and it's very hard to connect them to someone who they may never have met. We're doing our best."

"I'm sure you are, Detective. And I know you are short-handed in the department. It's a mighty big city and there's a lot to do."

"Your Honor, if Mr. Wynn doesn't stop patting Sergeant McKenna on the back, we'll lose him to disability for a shoulder injury."

"Sit down, Mr. Bright."

"We'll ignore the sarcastic comment from the defense. Let's move on to question thirty-one."

McKenna flipped the pages over. "Question thirty-one asked the subject if he truly believed he would get away with murdering Evelyn Averdanis."

"Averdantis."

"I know, but that's how the name is spelled here."

"Anyway, what was the answer?"

Bright rose to his feet again. "Please, Your Honor. This is not right. This is just not fair. The question is unfair!"

"Mr. Bright, how can a question be unfair? The defendant signed the release, allowing the examination. Surely, he must have expected to be asked about his role in his girlfriend's death. What reasonable complaint could you possibly have about the question?"

"Your Honor, I hardly need to tell you that the form of the question is unfair. It is predicated on the assumption that the subject– in this case, Mark Pitt– is, in fact, guilty of murder." He waited for a reaction from the judge. "Your Honor, that's the whole purpose of this trial– to determine whether or not Mark Pitt is or is not guilty of murder! Don't you see?"

"Hmm. What are you saying, exactly? Is this just another ploy of yours to give the jury your slanted viewpoint, Mr. Bright?"

"Your Honor, the presumption of innocence is part of the foundation of our justice system. The defendant must be proved guilty in order to be convicted."

"I thought that's what we were doing here."

Bright stared at Judge Tuilgy for a long time, then he let out his breath in one long sigh. "Of course, Your Honor. Thank you, Your Honor." He sat back down, staring at the judge the entire time.

"Excellent! You may continue, Mr. Wynn."

"Thank you for sorting that out, Your Honor. Detective McKenna, what was Mark Pitt's answer to the question of whether he believed he would get away with Evelyn Averdantis's murder?"

"He answered that kinda strangely. He said, 'how could I?' We didn't know what to make of that answer."

"Why's that?"

"Well, mainly because there's really no evidence that we could find that would in any way link him to the actual crime."

"And what do you attribute that to?"

"It's obvious that the defendant was able to either destroy all the key evidence in this case, or he has concealed it somehow. So, it struck us as either ironic or maybe disenginous..."

"Disingenuous?"

"Right. I could never pronounce that word. If I was this guy, I'd be pretty confident that I *would* get away with it. I would've answered that, yes, I believed I would get away with it. He didn't. That still bewilders me."

"Do you think it was some kind of ploy or trick on his part?"

"Must be. I don't know what else to think."

"Let's move on to question number forty-one."

"Uh, forty-one is– let's see– 'Do you feel bad, having killed your girl-friend?' His answer to that one didn't surprise us at all."

Bright could be seen with his hand over his eyebrows, shaking his head.

"And what was his answer?"

"He said he felt terrible about her death. They almost always say that, because they know if they don't show remorse, they'll probably get the chair."

"Actually, they haven't used the chair in this state in more than twenty years."

"The gas chamber, then. The gas chamber, the guillotine– whatever. The point is they will say anything to avoid it. I've had cold-hearted killers break down and sob when we asked them if they felt bad about what they've done. Can you believe that?"

"What do you tell them?"

"I tell 'em don't waste their tears. They shoulda thought about how sorry they were going to be before they committed the murders. Then I usually tell 'em how hot they'll get when we fry them with a few hundred thousand volts. That *really* gets them sobbing. Ha ha. I tell 'em all sorts of stuff. Not all of it is true. I tell them their testicles will swell up and pop– just like two kernels of popcorn. I tell 'em their eyes will get so hot that they'll melt and drip right out of their sockets. Ha ha. I tell them they'd better keep their mouth shut or they'll bite their tongue off and it'll fall into their lap. Ha ha!"

"But, we don't use the electric chair anymore."

"I know. I just like having fun with them. Don't take it so seriously, Wynn. They're just murderers. Anyway, I make 'em feel better about things."

"How do you do that?"

"Well, by telling them all that horrible stuff is going to happen, and then it doesn't. See?"

"Of course. Let's talk about the interrogation."

"Okay."

"According to the transcript, Mr. Pitt denies any wrong-doing and asserts his innocence in the death of his girlfriend."

"That's right. We couldn't crack him."

"Did he offer any explanation as to how she died?"

"Not really. He said she was feeling a bit under the weather a day or two before she died. He told us she had been suffering from a headache the previous night, which prevented him from having what we in the department call 'carnal relations' with her."

"Did you ask him if she had taken any medication for it?"

"We did."

"And what was his response?"

"He said she took some aspirin."

"Did you obtain samples of aspirin from the apartment or from the deceased girl's pocketbook?"

"No, we did not."

"Why didn't you?"

"We couldn't find any."

"Did you ask the coroner to check during his autopsy? And did the autopsy show any traces of aspirin in the deceased girl's body?"

33

"We did. No, it did not."

"What conclusion did you draw from that?"

"We had to conclude that the defendant was lying."

"Did you ask the defendant where he was the last morning of Evelyn Averdantis's life?"

"Yes."

"What was his response?"

McKenna read in a dead monotone from his notebook. "We asked him, 'where were you this morning?' and his reply was, 'I don't know. I guess I was on the subway. I went to Beach Point Park to take some photos, you know, by the lake there. I was there. Or maybe I was on my way there. I don't know. I might have been on the subway on the way there or maybe I was there already. I don't know. What time do you think?' At which point I said to him, 'I don't know. You tell me.' To which he replied, 'well, I was either on the subway or at the park. Or, maybe I was getting a frank from the guy at the entrance.'"

"And what did you deduce from that answer?"

"It was obvious to all the officers present that this fellow couldn't get his story straight."

"Did you check with the guy who sells hot dogs at the entrance to Beach Point Park to see if he recalls ever seeing Mark Pitt?"

"We did check around. There are several hot dog vendors at Beach Point. None of them remember seeing the defendant."

"Hmmm. Looks bad. Did…"

"Your Honor! 'Hmmm, looks bad' is a completely inappropriate interjection. Mr. Wynn should know better than that."

"Of course, you are right, Mr. Bright. I simply forgot myself as I got caught up in the moment. Overwhelming guilt pervading the atmosphere made me slip up."

"Judge, are you going to let that one go?"

"Certainly not, Mr. Bright. Mr Wynn, please refrain from such flagrant displays of amateurishness."

"I am sorry, Your Honor. It is beneath me."

"Proceed with your questions– *questions*, mind you!"

"Thank you. So, Detective McKenna, did you question anyone else in an effort to confirm or debunk the defendant's so-called alibi?"

"We questioned the token booth clerks at both the Bradley Street Station and Rous Street Station of the Number 14 line."

"And?"

"Neither one recalls seeing the defendant."

"Anyone else?"

"We questioned people who were hanging out in Beach Point Park and no one recalled seeing the defendant, nor did they have any idea what we were talking about. We walked up and down several streets and looked for anything which would exonerate the defendant."

"And did you find anything– any little thing, no matter how tiny and insignificant– that would point away from Mark Pitt's guilt."

"Nothing at all. And I'll have you know that we spent a lot of time in this effort– especially since he had no prior record for his crimes."

Bright was up again. "Your Honor, my client has no prior record because he has never committed any crimes!"

"That makes sense. You seem upset by that."

"Of course I am, Your Honor. This– this brilliant representative of Highbridge's Finest just stated that he has no record for his prior crimes– as if he had committed some!"

"Well, Mr. Bright, it's fair to say that he *might* have committed some, for which he has not been arrested and therefore has no criminal record."

Bright stood frozen and dumbstruck. Finally, after a few seconds, he turned to look at Pitt, then looked back at Judge Tuilgy before waving his hands in front of him and sitting down without uttering another word.

"You may continue, Mr. Wynn. Mr. Bright seems to have resolved his objection within his own mind."

"Thank you, Your Honor. Detective, since we obviously have some Doubting Thomases in our midst, is it fair to say that your department did all that it could to find something to exonerate Mark Pitt?"

"Yes, we busted our– humps to get that guy off the hook. Too bad, huh?"

"Were you able to figure out what he used to kill poor Miss Averdantis?"

"Unfortunately, no. Hell, we can't even figure out *what* killed her, let alone how he managed to do it without leaving a trace. The coroner liked electrocution, but there were no wet appliances and no blown fuses. It was a very frustrating investigation. It was especially demoralizing because we've had so damn many cases lately where we can't figure out how the person died or who might have killed them– I mean how the suspect killed them. Of course we know *who* did it."

"Of course."

"It's a tough job, Mr. Wynn."

"And believe me, Detective McKenna, we– all of us– appreciate the work you do. No more questions, Your Honor."

"Your witness, Mr. Bright."

"Thank you, Your Honor. Sergeant McKenna, how many people were in Beach Point Park the day of the murder?"

"I can't answer that question. There's no way of knowing."

"How many days elapsed between the death of Evelyn Averdantis and when you and your men went to Beach Point Park to interview the vendors there?"

"Let's see." He counted on his fingers as he looked into space. "Um, ten days."

"Do you find anything extraordinary in the appearance of the defendant, Sergeant?"

"Like what?"

"Exactly my point. So, since you can think of nothing on your own which is extraordinary about my client, do you really expect that a bunch of people having a good time in a large city park would recall seeing him ten days prior?"

"I know it was a long shot, but we tried everything we could to clear Mr. Pitt."

"What would you need to clear him of, Detective? What's your reason for thinking he did anything that he'd need to be exonerated for?"

"I don't understand. He's our prime suspect in this case, that's what."

"Why do you think he committed a crime?"

"He had the means to do it and he had the motive and he had the opportunity."

"You said he had the means to do it. What's 'it'?"

"What do you mean?"

"What's 'it'? 'He had the means to do *it*'."

"Murder Evelyn Averdantis! That's what 'it' is."

"How do you know she was murdered?"

"Well, how else could she have died?"

"I don't know, Sergeant. Isn't that a question *you* should be able to answer before you accuse anyone of murder?"

"Ha. You obviously don't know how the police work. It's not that simple, Mr. Bright. I was like you when I started out, but I soon learned that the ugly truth is that even when a crime hasn't been committed, a crime has been committed."

"What does that mean?"

"Funny, you asking *me* that. You supposedly studied law. There's a statute against most things– either explicitly or by inference. You practically can't pass gas without breaking some damn law. You look skeptical, but I'm telling you the truth. Look in the court records if you don't believe me. My partner testified last May in a trial that basically boiled down to whether or not this guy was guilty of passing gas. He was. So, he was convicted and now he's serving a twenty-month stretch in Allensville."

"That's all well and good, but my client is on trial for murder– not passing gas. And, if he's convicted, he will not be serving a mere twenty-month stretch. This is a very serious charge. Are you aware of that?"

"Of course I am. What do you think? You think we just trump up some charge and try to make it stick by fabricating evidence and testifying against the defendant? We didn't just decide on a whim that Mark Pitt was guilty of this thing. We, um, we get together and put our heads together and we hash it all out and, um, you know, we approach this thing from every angle and apply professional tactics– I mean methods– and this is what we came up with. You think I look forward to sending people to the chair?"

"We don't use the chair anymore."

"It's an ugly business and it's with a heavy heart that I sit here and send a young man, who might have turned out all right under different circum-stances, to be grilled by so many volts of electricity that it takes cables as thick as your wrist to deliver it. Do you think this was all a lark?"

"Do you *really* think Evelyn Averdantis was murdered?"

"Well, she's dead isn't she? At least she looked plenty dead to me. And she didn't wake up when we poked her and jostled her. And she sure as hell didn't wake up when Doc Guardian took her apart."

"Yeah, but how can you be sure she was murdered?"

"Oh, come on, Bright. She was a young woman. Young women don't just drop dead all on their own. They need help, and who better to help than her so-called boyfriend, eh? I'm sorry, Bright. I know you want to get your cli-ent off scot-free. It'd be a real feather in your cap. But, unfortunately, Pitt's guilty and you're going to have to just deal with it."

"So, in other words, because the coroner couldn't determine the cause of death, you concluded that she was murdered. Is that correct?"

"Yeah, that's what I said."

"And you found no evidence that would support Dr. Guardian's pet theory that she was electrocuted?"

"Not exactly."

"No blown fuses or short-circuited appliances, correct?"

"Correct."

"Did Dr. Guardian report any signs of poisoning?"

"No."

"Did you find anything in the apartment that could have been used as a poison without leaving an obvious trace for Dr. Guardian to find?"

"No."

"Did your investigation turn up anything in Mark Pitt's past that would lead you to believe he had obtained some sort of specialized knowledge about poisons?"

"No, not exactly."

"What do you mean by 'not exactly'?"

"Well, I don't know. I guess I mean no, we didn't– not specifically."

"Anything in Mark Pitt's past that would lead you to believe he received some special knowledge that could be used in killing someone without leaving a trace of the evil deed?"

"You mean other than the body? Well, he took anatomy classes in college. He got high grades, too. So, I suppose it would be possible for him to use that knowledge to kill someone."

"You mean instead of him using that knowledge to improve his understanding of the structure and form of the human body in order to depict it more accurately in drawings and paintings?"

"Yeah, sure. You know, I sense some sarcasm in that question, Mr. Bright. I'm just doing my job– and I've done a pretty solid job for the City for many years now. After a while, you get so you can smell a rat, you know?"

"Is Mark Pitt a rat, Sergeant McKenna? If so, how is it he's on trial just like us humans deserve?"

"I can't answer that. I'm just a cop."

"You must also be a– what do they call them– a taxonomist, too."

"If I was, I'd have stuffed and mounted Mark Pitt a long time ago! That's for sure."

"Taxonomists don't stuff animals, Sergeant."

"Well, whatever they do– mummify them or whatever! You're getting on my last nerve, Bright."

"Getting back to your team's investigation for a moment– were you able to dig up any witnesses who could testify that they saw Mark Pitt in or around the apartment during the time period that Dr. Guardian said was a likely time of death?"

"Not really, no."

"What about Miss Laniny?"

"The neighbor upstairs?"

"Yes. She seems to be the sort of neighbor who knows the comings and goings of the fellow tenants."

"She said she was locked in her apartment, as she put it," he flipped the notebook's pages, "because of the beast in the hallway, lurking outside her door."

"Were you able to question this character she calls the beast?"

"Nope."

"Why not?"

"Well, just as she says, the guy hides in the darkness whenever you try to approach. And it wouldn't come down when we called out. He just stayed out of sight and didn't make a sound, so we couldn't interview him."

"You didn't go up the stairs?"

"No, we didn't. It was dark up there."

"You didn't use a flashlight or something?"

"No, we didn't. It's kinda hard to explain. Look, it was *very* dark up there."

"I don't understand."

"I didn't think you would."

"Are you going to try to interview this guy– this so-called beast?"

"We did."

"You *did* interview him?"

"No, we *tried*. We couldn't."

"I don't get it."

Wynn stood up. "Your Honor, can we move on at this point? It's obvious that the witness is uncomfortable talking about this and he *did* say they tried to interview the beast."

"Your Honor, I don't understand why the police can't just walk up a dark stairway to interview someone who might have something very important to say regarding this case."

"Mr. Bright, the Detective made it clear that they did make a good faith effort to interview this potential witness, but could not do so. I don't find that to be unusual in any way. Please drop this line of questioning and move on."

"But…" Bright took a deep breath. "All right. Let's see. I guess I have no other questions at this time."

"Very well. You may step down, Sergeant."

From the Highbridge Morning Star:

> After the opening arguments yesterday, the jury heard the first two witnesses in the trial of alleged murderer and artist, Mark Pitt, accused of killing his live-in girlfriend, Evelyn Averdantis, at their loft in Lingstrome Flats. In the first full day of the trial, prosecuting attorney Ambrose Wynn, husband of chanteuse Lynn Maguire, called the State's Medical Examiner and the lead Detective to testify. The Coroner, while reluctant to absolutely pinpoint the cause of death, indicated strongly that Pitt most assuredly could have committed the crime. Detective Phil McKenna confirmed that Pitt cannot account for his whereabouts at the time of death and also revealed that Pitt made several incriminating statements to police during the thorough and painstaking investigation.
>
> Judge Tuilgy certainly had his hands full during the proceedings. Several times during the opening arguments and also while examining the witnesses, the lead attorneys nearly came to blows over the aggressive legal tactics being employed by each other.
>
> Pitt faces life in prison, if convicted.

5. Trudy Titsworth

"Your Honor, the State calls Trudy Titsworth to the stand."

Trudy Titsworth made her way to the witness stand, where she was sworn in. She was dressed conservatively, in bland colors, and wore her hair stylishly short. Wynn removed his eyeglasses and strolled up to question her.

"Ms Titsworth, how are you acquainted with the deceased, Miss Averdantis?"

"I was her hairdresser."

"Where do you work?"

"I own Trudy's Tresses on Neptune Avenue."

"How long have you owned Trudy's Tresses?"

"Two years. I was a hairdresser years ago– that is until I got married. But I didn't have my own shop until two years ago."

"How long had you known Miss Averdantis?"

"A couple of years. She was a regular customer– from the time I opened the shop until– that is, you know, until, um…"

"Did she stop coming into Trudy's Tresses for haircuts?"

"Yes. She stopped coming in January of last year. I only saw her once since then. And then I read in the papers– oh, dear!" She buried her face in her hands.

Wynn offered his handkerchief. "Here you are, Ms Titsworth."

"Thank you. Thank you. This is just so awful."

"Yes, quite. Did Miss Averdantis decide to go to another hair cutter?"

"I thought so, at first. You know, you lose customers and get others. People move. But, then I bumped into her on the subway one day. Of course I didn't recognize her at first, you know, because when I look at someone, I see their hair first and she– well, you know."

"Why didn't you recognize her?"

"Because– because– oh!" Titsworth burst into tears again.

"Please Ms Titsworth, try to compose yourself."

"I'm so sorry, Mr. Wynn. I just can't help it. I'll try harder. Honest I will. Oh, my. Anyway, as I was trying to say. I couldn't recognize her at first, because she– Oh, heavens!" Titsworth's slight frame was shaking with sobs.

"Please Ms Titsworth. You must pull yourself together and tell us why you couldn't recognize her. *Please*, Ms Titsworth."

"I didn't recognize her, Mr. Wynn, because– because she was *bald*!" Titsworth broke into sobs again as the audience murmured.

"Ms Titsworth, did you ask her why she was bald?"

Titsworth swallowed hard. "I didn't know what to say. I'm sure you can imagine how I felt. I could hardly form my words I was so upset. She'd had such lovely hair– so wavy and healthy. Her hair had a natural sheen to it that no amount of dying or treating could get rid of. She was blessed to have such hair. Such a lovely color, so satisfying to cut and style. Now look at her. Oh, dear me!"

"Did Miss Averdantis recognize you that day on the subway?"

"Of course she did, Mr. Wynn. A woman doesn't forget who cuts her hair. It's a very, shall I say, intimate act. A woman sits motionless while another woman touches her hair and scalp and neck. The hair stylist touches the woman in a gentle but assertive manner. Her fingers brush past the woman's ears and jaw and she leans against the woman and can smell the perfume from her body and feel the heat rising from her and she…"

Wynn interrupted her. "Yes, Ms Titsworth, it's quite clear that Miss Averdantis must have recognized you right off. Did you talk about anything with her on that occasion? Did you ask why she hadn't been in to see you?"

"As I said, Mr. Wynn, I was flabbergasted. And I could plainly see why she hadn't come in to see me."

"Why was that, Ms Titsworth?"

"I cut hair. She had no hair. So, of course there was no reason to come to me. I could figure out *that* much without asking. I wanted to ask her what happened to her hair, but I thought better of it. I don't like to get involved in other people's relationships."

"To what relationship are you referring?"

"Why, to her relationship with him– that man there. That is, if you can call it a relationship."

"Why do you say that?"

"Well, I don't like to pry, but a hair stylist has a special relationship with her clients. As I said, you hear things. I heard things about them. About him and their so-called relationship."

"What did you hear about Mr. Pitt?"

"I object, Your Honor. Anything Ms Titsworth says about my client is hearsay. She was not acquainted with Mark Pitt."

"Overruled."

"Your Honor...!"

"You may answer the question put to you, Ms Titsworth."

"As I said, I don't like to pry, but I do recall her saying that he liked to do things– certain things, if you follow my meaning– and that she was forced to oblige him– or else."

"Or else what, Ms Titsworth?"

"Or else there'd be consequences."

"What sort of thing was Miss Averdantis forced to do for her so-called boyfriend?"

"Again, it was really none of my concern, mind you, but I seem to recall one instance where he wanted her to disrobe and sit motionless in a contorted position for an extended period while he had his way with her."

"Did Miss Averdantis describe this position to you?"

"Let's see. Well, I don't quite recall if she described it to me or not. I can say that I did come away with a very vivid impression of how vulgar and demeaning this position must have been. I can tell you that *I* would never consent to such treatment by any man."

"Would you classify this treatment as unnatural?"

"Your Honor, Ms Titsworth was not called as an expert in the naturalness of things."

"Your Honor, Mr. Bright is forgetting that the witness is an expert hair-dresser and, as such, she is constantly dealing with whether or not something looks or feels natural."

"I will allow it, Mr. Wynn."

"Ms Titsworth, was this treatment unnatural?"

"Yes."

"Thank you, Ms Titsworth. Your witness, Mr. Bright."

"Ms Titsworth, have you ever seen any of these images that I am holding before you?" Bright held up some 8x10s and leafed through them so that the witness could see each of them in turn.

"I have no recollection of seeing these images." She turned her head to the side and tilted it back.

"Your Honor, I hold in my hand several images of pictures that the defendant executed in oil paint. Ms Titsworth, isn't it possible that the female figure depicted in these oil paintings is, in fact, Miss Averdantis?"

"I have no idea. I'm not an art critic."

"Isn't it possible, Ms Titsworth, that the defendant 'had his way' with Miss Averdantis by sketching and painting her while she was posed in physically strenuous poses?"

"I don't know. I suppose it's possible. I don't know about such things."

"So, then, isn't it possible that this so-called treatment of Miss Averdantis by the defendant, which you attempted to paint with a very dark and sinister brush, calling it unnatural, was, in fact, simply an artist and model relationship?"

"I wouldn't know. Why are you asking me such questions?"

"Because you're on the witness stand, Ms Titsworth. Come now, Ms Titsworth, we are being a little disingenuous, aren't we? Are you married?"

"Am I married?"

"Are you married? That's a pretty simple question."

"No, I am not married."

"Have you ever been married?"

"I was married, once upon a time. Yes."

"What was your husband's name?"

"His name was Otto. Otto Bettnasser."

"And what did Otto do for a living?"

"He was the owner of the most important art gallery in the City– Bettnasser Gallery."

"So you must be familiar with the art scene and certainly understand something of the artist-model relationship, do you not?"

"I don't know. I suppose so. I wasn't very much involved in the art business like Otto was."

"As the owner of such an important art gallery, did your husband make a lot of money?"

"I really don't know."

"You don't know?"

"I didn't handle the finances. That was Otto's responsibility. He was good with figures."

"Are you saying you haven't any idea of how much money that gallery made for you?"

"That is what I am saying."

"Without naming a figure, would you say that the gallery made, let's say, a *lot* of money?"

"I just don't know."

"You and your husband lived in a thirty-nine room, multi-million dollar mansion off of M Street. How could you not know that the gallery made a lot of money?"

"I don't know. I suppose I never thought about it. When you put it that way, I guess…"

"Well, now that all that's gone and you cut hair for a living, and you live in a studio apartment, you must have an inkling of the amount of money that can be made at a highly successful art gallery."

"Is that a question?"

"No. What happened to that mansion?"

"It was auctioned after Otto was– after Otto left me."

"Where is Otto, now, Ms Titsworth?"

"He is buried in Evergreen Cemetery."

"Oh? I thought you said he left you. Did he leave you?" Titsworth didn't respond. "Otto *didn't* leave you, did he?" She sat, tight-lipped. "Did he leave you, Ms Titsworth?"

"He was run over by a Number 39 bus as he was crossing the street."

"So he *didn't* leave you." Bright was trying to gauge her expression. "Or, maybe he *did* leave you? Maybe the Number 39 bus that killed your husband killed him *as* he was leaving you. Is that it, Ms Titsworth? Was he leaving you that stormy night, nearly three years ago? He was, wasn't he? Who was he leaving you *for*, Ms Titsworth?"

"I don't wish to answer your stupid questions. They're just stupid, that's all– stupid. And I don't wish to answer them." She tilted her chin up and to the right and began to hum *I've Got Rhythm* quietly to herself.

"Ms Titsworth? Ms Titsworth, who was Otto Bettnasser dumping you for? Maybe I should rephrase that. For whom was Otto Bettnasser dumping you? Was it one of the young men from his stable of young artists, Ms Titsworth? You can hum until your hair goes white, but we *will* get at the truth."

"What an awful thing to say to a woman!" She began to sob once more.

"Your Honor, Mr. Bright is badgering the witness!"

"Your Honor, the witness has decided not to answer my questions. I have to badger her."

"Ms Titsworth, you must cease your humming and sobbing and answer the questions put to you. You took an oath." Titsworth stopped, composed herself, looked sadly at Judge Tuilgy and nodded silently.

"Thank you, Your Honor. Ms Titsworth, do you have self-esteem issues?"

"I object, Your Honor. What does Ms Titsworth's self-esteem have to do with anything?"

"Perhaps nothing, Mr. Wynn, but since I am intrigued by this line of questioning, I will allow it. Proceed, Mr. Bright."

"What about it, Ms Titsworth?"

"I, um, suppose my self-esteem is no different from anyone else's."

"Where did you go to school, Ms Titsworth?"

"St. Mary's School. Why do you ask?"

"Isn't it true that, when you attended St. Mary's School, the other children used to taunt you?"

"I don't know. I guess they kidded me a bit."

"Kidded you a bit? Isn't it true that your parents filed a report with the school administration because of this so-called kidding? The report claimed that the other students tormented you, that they called you 'Titsworthless' and would ask you 'what are your tits worth?' when they'd see you in the hallways and on the playground?" Bright picked up a file from the defense table. "Ms Titsworth, I have in my hand copies of the school report on the matter. Your parents allege that you came home crying every day and that you refused to go back to school and that you wanted them to kill you."

"So?"

"So?! You think it's normal to want your parents to kill you?"

"I never wanted my parents to kill me! How can you say such a thing? You are an awful man to even *think* such a thing. My parents were gods. No one could have wished for better parents than mine. I didn't want them to kill me, I wanted them to *let* me die."

"Ah, I'm sorry. I'm just going by what's in the report here. I certainly didn't mean to malign your dear mother and father. Are you still close to them?"

"Am I still close to them?"

"Yes. Are you?"

"Am I still close to them? Um, I don't really know if I was ever close to them. You can't be close to a god. I don't think they liked me all that much. I think I was probably a disappointment to them. I was never as brilliant and accomplished as my older brother, Teddy. I was not as beautiful and statuesque as Tilly, my little sister. I was just the scrawny, whiny middle child."

"So, what about your self-esteem?"

"Just for argument's sake, I guess you *could* say that I have slightly lower-than-average self-esteem."

"By the way, what *are* your tits worth?"

Titsworth's jaw dropped.

Wynn jumped up, swinging his arms to get the judge's attention. "Your Honor, this is– aaghh! I don't even have the vocabulary for it! You can't let this go on, Your Honor! You must put a stop to this lurid attack by this– this so-called public defender."

Bright picked up another file folder from the table and waved it above his head. "Your Honor, I don't ask this question just to titillate. This question has a direct bearing on the credibility of this witness."

"Proceed, Mr. Bright."

"Thank you, Your Honor. Ms Titsworth, according to the hospital records, it says here that your tits are worth quite a large sum– more than $7,000. Isn't that a fact?"

"Yes."

"I'm sorry, can you speak up? I doubt anyone could hear you."

"Yes!"

"Who paid for that hospital bill?"

"I did."

"Now, according to your tax records, you were not employed at the time that this hospital bill came due. Where did you get the money to pay this bill, Ms Titsworth?"

"I got it from my husband."

"Did he know what you needed it for?"

"No. I didn't tell him."

"You just asked him and he just handed you the $7,000?"

"No. It was more complicated than that. I never did tell him what the money was really for. I told him I needed the money for an automobile."

"You couldn't tell him it was to enlarge your chest, but you *could* tell him it was for a car?"

"He was fine with that. I didn't think I could tell him the real reason. I thought he would disapprove. I could always buy things of value– material goods or property. He was fine with that kind of purchase. He never wanted me to spend money on myself, though."

"Did he ever tell you why?"

"No, but I found out, eventually. He thought it was a waste."

"He thought your spending money on yourself was a waste?"

"He never said those words exactly. He would say that I was good enough or sometimes he would say I was satisfactory."

"Satisfactory?"

"That's romantic, huh?"

"Did your husband– was your husband happy with you– the way you were, I mean?"

"No, he wasn't. And he didn't want me to change because he would never be happy with me, no matter what I did. I'd suspected the reason for years."

"Was there was another woman?"

"Another? Yes. Not another woman, though."

"Are you telling us, Ms Titsworth, that the late Otto Bettnasser, the owner of the biggest art gallery in the City, great philanthropist and trusted mentor to an entire community of artists and art collectors, was a so-called homosexual?"

"Believe it or not, I am." There was an audible gasp from the courtroom. "So you see, although I didn't know it at the time, Otto didn't care about my naturally flat chest because he had no use for breasts– no interest in them. And by extension, he didn't care about me. Not one lick."

"Not one?"

"Huh?"

"Never mind. Look, I know this is very difficult for you, Ms Titsworth, but I do have more questions I need to ask you."

"I'll be all right, Mr. Bright. I've learned to deal with it emotionally. My psychiatrist has helped me process much of this emotional turmoil and I have put Otto where he belongs."

"Where is that, Ms Titsworth?"

"I told you– Evergreen Cemetery."

"Oh, I thought you meant, you know, psychologically. Getting back to the matter at hand, when did you first realize that Otto was a homosexual?"

"It wasn't for a long time that I knew for certain. I had my suspicions. He was always very attentive to young male artists. He never showed a female artist in the gallery."

"Are there many female artists out there?"

"I assume so. Anyway, he didn't ever show any."

"Aside from his preference for showing male artists, were there signs? Behavioral quirks or figures of speech can give someone away. Was there anything like that?"

"Shortly after we met, I went to his office and he was with a young male artist. Otto was in front of this boy, naked and on his knees in the middle of the room. I was shocked and dismayed, so I asked him what was going on."

"What did he say?"

"He said he was suggesting poses for the young artist to use in his next painting."

"What did you do?"

"I apologized and excused myself."

"You believed him?"

"Why, yes. I had no reason not to. Now, reflecting back on it, I realize that he must have been suggesting more that just poses."

"Were there other instances?"

"There was the time that I came home earlier than I had expected to and discovered Otto and a young artist, both entirely naked, entwined in an embrace on the oriental rug in the parlor."

"What were they doing, Ms Titsworth?"

"Well, I thought at first that they were fighting. When I became alarmed and cried out in shock and fear, my husband jumped up and stammered that he could explain everything."

"What did he offer as an explanation for this lewd display?"

"I'll never know. I'm afraid I didn't give him a chance to explain. You see, I was so sure that they were wrestling that I cut him off and said that no explanation would suffice and that I would not tolerate any kind of violence in my home. I eventually came to realize that they were not, in fact, wrestling and that submission would not have been the *end* of the encounter, as it is in a Greco-Roman match. It seems so obvious now, but at the time I had no reason to think anything else."

"Aside from these two incidents, was there anything in his behavior that could have led you to believe he was a homosexual?"

"Maybe I shouldn't say this, but, when we made love– I can see the shock in your face, Mr. Bright. Yes, he did make love to me– in a way. When we did make love, he would lean over my shoulder at the moment of supreme pleasure and call out my name just before he collapsed onto my back. On more than one occasion I could have sworn he called out the name 'Rudy' instead of 'Trudy'. I thought at the time that his speech was impaired by his convulsions, but he might really have been saying 'Rudy', which was the first name of one of the artists he was showing at the gallery at the time."

"Did he continue to have sexual relations with you during these times when he was carrying on with these young proteges?"

"Yes. Otto had a voracious sexual appetite. He only stopped having relations with me the night he found out about my breast enhancement surgery."

"Tell the court how he found out about it. Didn't he see the difference?"

"He never looked at me. We were in bed and in the customary position and he reached around me to grab my chest and he grabbed more than he had expected to grab."

"How did he react?"

"He was horrified. He became instantly disinterested and never showed any interest in me again."

"Is that why you never had children?"

"No, we could never have had children."

"How's that? Are you barren?"

"How can I say this? People cannot have children in the way that Otto made love to me. And he never did it any other way."

"I think I see. When did Otto Bettnasser meet the defendant, Mr. Pitt?"

"More than two and a half years ago, I think. It was only a couple of months before he gave him that big exhibition. When Otto took a shine to an artist, it didn't take long before they started reaping the rewards. It was that way with Mark Pitt, too."

"Did your husband fall in love with the defendant?"

"I object, Your Honor! He's talking about two men."

"What are you objecting to, Mr. Wynn?"

"Well, to the idea of two men, you know, falling in love."

"I share your repugnance at the thought, Mr. Wynn, but the objection is overruled. Proceed, Mr. Bright."

"Did he fall in love, Ms Titsworth?"

"I don't know. He was certainly infatuated with him. He was so loopy for Mark Pitt that he would call him all the time and write him stupid love notes." Titsworth rolled her eyes in disgust.

"I have one of those notes here. Would you be so kind as to read to the court from this love note?"

"If I must." Titsworth took her reading glasses from her purse and opened the letter. "It's dated April 10. Do you really want me to read this? It's kind of tawdry."

"Go ahead, Ms Titsworth."

Titsworth shrugged her shoulders and began to read aloud.

> "My Dearest Markie, now that *Prima Vera* is burgeoning everywhere, my thoughts and dreams have inevitably turned to your beautiful mind and body. I know that I have not yet convinced you of the merits of my special kind of lovemaking..."

She dropped her hands to her thighs and looked up at Bright and then at Judge Tuilgy. "Are you sure you want me to read this here?"

"Yes. Please continue."

Titsworth sighed and picked up the letter again. "Well, you asked for it. This is all quite embarrassing, Mr. Bright."

"We appreciate that. Please continue, Ms Titsworth."

"Let's see, where was I?

> ...my special kind of lovemaking, but if you would give me a chance to work my magic tongue up and down..."

She dropped the letter again and removed her glasses. "Listen, Mr. Bright, I really find myself very, very uncomfortable reading this sort of thing. Couldn't you just enter it in the record or something, without my having to read it?"

55

"Yes, I must protest, Your Honor! Mr. Bright is putting poor Ms Titsworth in an unnecessarily awkward position. I'm not even certain that she should be the one to read this filth."

"I'm sure there's a precedent for it. I will allow it. Please proceed, Mr. Bright. I want to hear more."

"Certainly. Thank you, Your Honor. Ms Titsworth, I really feel terrible, forcing you to read this document. Unfortunately, we have no choice in the matter– especially since a man's life is on the line."

"Very well.

> ...a chance to work my magic tongue
> up and..."

"Excuse me, Ms Titsworth, but did your husband have a magic tongue, as he boasts in the letter?"

"I wouldn't know. He never used it on me."

"Yes, of course. Not one lick. Proceed."

> "...a chance to work my magic tongue
> up and down your– your..."

Titsworth threw the letter out of the witness box and into the middle of the courtroom. "I can't read this thing and you can't make me!" She crossed her arms tightly across her chest.

"All right, Ms Titsworth. We probably don't need to know about this stuff anyway." Bright picked up the letter and slipped it in his breast pocket. "We'll move on. About the letters, did Mark Pitt ever reciprocate these attentions?"

She dabbed her forehead with a handkerchief as she answered him. "No, I don't think so. I think Mark Pitt was the first artist to ever reject Otto's attentions."

"Did this quell your husband's ardor at all?"

"On the contrary, it drove him wild with desire to have someone, whom he wanted, reject him like that. He became fixated and obsessed. He dreamed up romantic fantasies of him and Mark Pitt sunbathing on tropical islands and skiing in Switzerland."

"Given the chance, do you think your husband would have carried through on these fantasies?"

"Maybe some of them. Some definitely not."

"Why do you say definitely not?"

"Otto couldn't ski."

"No more questions, Your Honor."

"Mr. Wynn, do you wish to follow up with this witness?"

"Yes, just a couple of questions, Your Honor. Ms Titsworth, would the world have opened up for Mr. Pitt if he had allowed your husband to have his way with him?"

"I'm sorry, I'm not sure what you mean?"

"Would Mr. Pitt have had the world on a silver platter? Would he have been able to write his own ticket, so to speak? Would he 'have it made', in the vernacular?"

"In the art world? I suppose it wouldn't have hurt his chances any."

"Is it possible that Ms Averdantis– merely by existing– was somehow preventing Mr. Pitt from advancing himself in the art world?"

"I suppose it's possible."

"Did you ever hear either your husband or Miss Averdantis speak about this issue."

"My husband never spoke about business with me. I don't think he knew Evelyn. Poor Evelyn always seemed supportive of Mark Pitt when she spoke of him to me. She was under his spell, I guess– just like my husband was. And now they're both dead."

"No more questions, Your Honor."

"Mr. Bright?"

"No more questions."

6. Larry Cezanne

"Your Honor, the State calls Lawrence Cezanne to the stand."

A pale-skinned youngish man of medium build made his way to the stand. His shoulders drooped as he walked, pigeon-toed, across the courtroom. Once he had taken the oath, he sat in the chair and pushed his metal-framed glasses up on his nose.

"Mr. Cezanne, what is your occupation?"

"Um, I'm a painter."

"What kind of painter are you, Mr. Cezanne?"

"Um, I'm an art painter. I'm a, um, I'm an artist-type painter. I, uh, paint paintings, you know? Like my name, you know?"

"I'm sorry?"

"Like my name. An artist– like my name, you know what I mean?"

"And what sort of work do you do?"

"I do, um, tonal paintings, you know, of city scenes. My favorite artists were the post-impressionists, you know? Anyway, I play with value relationships and, um, you know, brushstroke, so that I get the look. You know, the gallery look."

"Ah, yes. Well, Mr. Cezanne..."

"Um, it's pronounced 'say-zonn' not 'suh-zan'."

"Say-zonn. Okay. All right. Well, Mr. Cezanne, you say you are an artist. Are you acquainted with the defendant, Mark Pitt?"

"Um, I am."

"And how long have you known Mr. Pitt?"

"I, um, I've known him since, um, grad school. It's been about, uh, six or seven years, I guess. Since grad school I've known, uh, Mark. No, longer than that. He, um, went to my high school, but I didn't know him then. So, I guess it's been, um, six or seven years. About that, anyways. Six, maybe seven years, about. Maybe closer to seven, I guess. I don't know. Seven– give or take."

"How did you meet Mr. Pitt?"

"Well, um, as I said, I've known him since high school, off and on."

"Forgetting about high school, how did you meet him six or seven years ago?"

"Um, we met at an opening– an opening, um, at a gallery about five years ago. I guess I've known him five years– not seven."

"Can you describe the circumstances of your meeting?"

"It was, um, an opening, you know?"

"Did you recognize each other from high school? Did someone introduce you?"

"No, I, um, well, in a way we did. I mean they did. Sorry."

"Which? You recognized each other?"

"Um, no."

"So, someone introduced you?"

"No, not really."

"What, then?"

"Well, we got there early 'cause we wanted to make sure we got our, um, you know, our share of the wine and stuff."

"Mr. Cezanne, who is 'we'?"

"Um, me and my girlfriend. My girlfriend and me, I mean."

"Go on."

"So, um, we get there and it was this gallery that's, um, closed now. They used to show all this, um, bad art– not *bad* art, but, um, like this so-called bad art that was bad, you know, on purpose. So, they had these installations with all these tape recorders and these spinning little men and this like beeping-buzzing sound and, um, this screaming that was playing over and over again. It was really sort of like war, you know, like killing and dying and, um, what do you call it– suffering, you know? And so after a few glasses of wine this whole scene is really starting to freak me out, so I decided to step outside to take a smoke and, um, get my head clear. You know, just to calm down, because the screaming is getting me nervous– not like, um, I don't know, just nervous, you see what I mean? So, I'm standing out there in the cold and I bum a cigarette from this guy and he's, um, talking to me and he's talking about his friend."

"Was that Mr. Pitt?"

"No."

"What about meeting Mr. Pitt?"

"Um, I'm getting to that. So, this guy is telling me he showed up with a friend and, um, he tells me he's giving his friend some space, you know? 'Cause his friend is makin' time with some chick who got a really hot ass. Can I say that, Judge? I'm sorry."

"That's fine, Mr. Cezanne. Please proceed."

"Okay, so, um– where was I?"

"A chick with a hot ass."

"Oh, yeah. So, um, he's giving his friend a chance to, um, make her, you know? And he's telling me that this chick is so hot they had to open the windows or everybody'd pass out from heat stroke. And this guy's laughing his ass off. Sorry, I said ass again. Anyway, I still was woozy from all that crap in the gallery and, um, I didn't really care about him or his friend and that chick with the hot ass. All I wanted was to just be left alone, you know, before I, you know, threw up or something. So, I decided to go back inside and, um, you know, to get my girlfriend and get out of there and go somewhere else or go home or whatever, 'cause my head's a mess. Um, so I go back in and in the little sorta side gallery they had there where these horrible noises are blasting through the speakers. And there's my, um, girlfriend standing there laughing with this guy…"

"Was this man the defendant, Mark Pitt?"

"Yeah, and he's got his arm around her waist and his hand is resting on her freakin' ass!" Cezanne shifted in his seat.

"The chick with the hot ass?"

"Um, yeah. It was my girlfriend, um, that the guy was talkin' about when he said there was a chick with the hot ass and the windows, you know?"

"*Did* she indeed have that nice a rear end, Mr. Cezanne?"

"I object, your honor."

"Sustained."

"Um, yeah, she did."

Bright popped up out of his seat. "Your honor, he answered the question."

"Mr. Cezanne, when a question has been objected to, you mustn't answer it unless you are instructed to do so."

"Sorry, Judge."

"What did you do after you saw this blatant violation of your girlfriend's posterior, Mr. Cezanne?"

"Well, what would *any* man do? I, um, froze. I stood there like an, um, like an– I don't know what. Then he, um, leans in real close and, um, he whispers something in her ear and I can see his hand squeezing her ass."

"Her hot ass."

"Yeah."

"What did she do?"

"She, um, her eyes got wide, then she kinda looked at him, like she's sizing him up or something. Then she, um, just smiles at him, crooked like a smirk or something, and puts her arms around him and gives him this, um, big kiss."

"What did the defendant do?"

"Um, he put his other hand on her ass. I mean on her other ass, you know, um, not her other ass, I mean the other half of her ass. You know, the way the ass has two halfs."

"And what was your girlfriend's name, Mr. Cezanne?"

"Um, her name?"

"Yes. Tell the court what your girlfriend's name was."

"Her name was Evelyn Averdantis."

There was a collective gasp from the attendees.

"Mr. Cezanne, what did you do after you saw them kiss?"

"What do you mean?"

"Well, for instance, did you challenge this predatory viper to a fight? Did you…"

"I object!"

"Sustained."

"My apologies. Did you challenge *Mister* Mark Pitt to a fight?"

"Um, no, not really."

"Why not? Were you afraid?"

"Um, I don't know."

"Did Mark Pitt exude a vicious and dangerous nature that struck fear in your heart?"

"Well, um, I'm not sure."

"Were you convinced that this so-called member of society would kill you where you stood if you tried to take any action or raise any protest against his vile treatment of your dear girlfriend?"

"I, uh, well, you see…"

"Did you already suspect him, Mr. Cezanne, of being a cold-blooded murderer?"

"Your Honor, Mr. Wynn is not only leading the witness, but is asking him if he suspected the defendant of committing a crime which had not yet even been committed!"

"I shall rephrase the question, Your Honor. Mr. Cezanne, did you suspect Mark Pitt of anything?"

"Like what?"

"Well, of any sort of unusual abilities, for instance."

"Um, I don't know. I, uh, never thought about it. I know he's bigger than me. Is that the kind of thing you mean?"

"No, but thank you for your forthrightness in that regard. No, I was thinking more in terms of unusual abilities– not his physique."

"Unusual abilities?"

"Yes, anything unusual– beyond what other people you have known can do. Or some characteristic that clearly falls outside of the realm of what most *normal* people in our society exhibit, perhaps? An unusual strength or a special power, for instance?"

"Objection, Your Honor. The witness is an artist. He is clearly not an expert on what is normal."

"Your Honor, I am not asking Mr. Cezanne to give expert testimony. I am simply asking him to sketch the character of a person he knows very well, and to bring to light any strange or extreme traits. That's all."

"Your Honor, Mr. Wynn has *not* established that the witness knows my client well. He has established only that my client kissed and groped Miss Averdantis at an art gallery and that he is, shall we say, a 'better man' than Mr. Cezanne."

"I object to Mr. Bright's assertion that a bigger man is a quote-unquote better man, Your Honor. It has been firmly established– and I myself have been told many a time– that size, in fact, does not matter and that…"

"Look, we're not interested in your expertise in the field of manhood. You've got a witness on the stand and you're leading him with these questions…"

"Gentlemen! Let's not have another squabble. We need to conduct a trial. You both know the rules. Mr. Wynn, please continue your examination."

Wynn looked like he had more to say to his counterpart, but he let out a deep sigh and nodded. "Yes, of course, Your Honor. Mr. Cezanne, getting back to the matter at hand, and forgetting for the moment about Mr. Pitt's unusual abilities, how well did you get to know the defendant?"

"Um, well, I guess. I, um, stayed friendly with them."

"Despite his nefarious seduction of your girl that night in the gallery?"

"Yeah, well, I can't really blame him a hundred percent for that. I mean it wasn't, um, working out all that well, um, between Evelyn and me, you know? I mean, I think she was kinda looking for another bed to, you know, jump into. She was..."

"Yes, but Mark Pitt played a pivotal role in bringing that about, didn't he?"

"Uh, sort of. I suppose you could think that, but really she was, you know– well, even that guy I was talking to outside the gallery that night said that she had a hot ass. Everybody who knew her said..."

"I suppose we've spent far too long on this particular subject, and really should get to the heart of the matter."

"Your Honor, the District Attorney just cut off his own witness's testimony. He should let the witness at least finish his sentence."

"Your Honor, I was just trying to cut some of the fat off the proceedings so that we can present the case to my friends in the jury box in the most efficient and considerate fashion. This may be a long, drawn out trial and I'm sure Mr. Bright is just as interested as I am to not let it get bogged down in endless anecdotes."

"Overruled."

"Your Honor, can't we at least let Mr. Cezanne finish his sentence? It sounded rather interesting and I'm sure that the jury..."

"Your Honor, I doubt very much that Mr. Cezanne remembers at this point what he was going to say– if indeed he was going to say anything at all. And I feel that, regardless of how interested Mr. Bright is, we should probably move on at this point. Anyway, Mr. Bright will have a chance to ask him about it when he gets his chance to cross-examine him."

"Yes, yes, let's move on, gentlemen."

"Thank you, Your Honor. Mr. Cezanne, I apologize for the pointless interruptions. Let's move forward and get your testimony and send you back to your job, without further delay."

"Actually, I don't, um, have a job– you know– to get back to, that is. Not right now, at the moment, I mean."

"That's fine. That's fine. You stated, I believe, that you became friends with Mark Pitt, and that he cast his spell on you, too?"

"Well, um, I didn't say he cast a spell..."

"The exact wording is not the issue here. Sufficed to say that you came into his sphere of influence and fell under his spell. Did Mr. Pitt begin taking advantage of your good nature right away? Or did..."

"Your Honor, the witness has not yet testified that my client ever took advantage of *him*– just Ms Averdantis's willingness to offer her sizzling posterior and spread her legs for him."

Wynn didn't let the Judge reply. "You're right, my poor yet dauntless friend. I will rephrase my question. When did Mr. Pitt start taking advantage of your good nature?"

"Um, did he?"

"Yes he did."

"Your Honor, something must be done! The witness is asking the questions and Mr. Wynn answering them!"

"Mr. Wynn, you are not to answer questions from your witnesses. Do you understand?"

"Yes, of course, Your Honor. I believe there was some confusion there."

Bright smirked and rolled his eyes. "So it seems."

"Mr. Bright, please refrain from snide little asides."

"Sorry, Your Honor. I'm afraid I got caught up in Mr. Wynn's confusion there for a moment."

"Mr. Wynn, can you pose proper questions for the witness?"

"Yes, of course, Your honor. I believe I did, but Mr. Cezanne gave an unexpected answer."

"I believe Mr. Cezanne has been taking his cue from you. Please proceed."

"Yes, Your Honor. Okay, now. Mr. Cezanne– may I call you Larry? I feel as if we have become friends."

"Oh, Christ!" Bright moaned and threw his head back and looked at the ceiling.

"Mr. Bright! You promised me!"

"Sorry, Your Honor. I did promise you." Bright sat up straight.

"Your Honor, I'm finding it very difficult to proceed with my friend, Larry, while the defense keeps bouncing up and down like a trained poodle, barking at every question I pose."

"Never mind. Resume your examination."

"Larry, what became of your relationship with the defendant?"

"Um, we became friends."

"Did you see him socially?"

"Yes, um, he was friends with some of my friends, you know, being an artist you run into the same people at, um, openings. So, we, um, sorta became friends, you know?"

"You held no grudge about how he acted at that gallery that night, mauling your girlfriend?"

"Nope."

"Why not? If it was me, I'd have torn that devil's testicles from his body and danced the Frug on them."

"Yeah, well, I didn't do that. I'm not, you know, a good dancer, really. I don't know the Frug. As a matter of fact, um, I met a girl that night after the opening. So, it all turned out okay, you know? She's, uh, very sympathetic, very, you know, nurturing."

"Tell us about meeting her."

"Well, there's not much to tell. I, um, was walking with Evelyn and my friend, Giorgio, who had come with us that night and, um, we were going to the subway and I wasn't feeling well, you know, with everything that was going on that night and all the wine I had at the gallery. So I was bent over the curb and, um, throwing up and Evelyn was rolling her eyes and telling Giorgio she wanted to go back to the gallery. I think she wanted, you know, to go back and make out some more with Mark or something. And this group of people comes up from the subway station and I'm emptying my stomach onto the sidewalk and one of the women puts her hand on my back and is telling me stuff to make me feel better. Turns out she wants to be a

66

nurse and she doesn't care that I'm, like, vomiting in the street– as a matter of fact, she thinks it's just great. It gave her an opportunity to, you know, practice her nursing skills, I guess, in a real life, um, situation. I coulda been taking a dump and I don't think it would've fazed her one bit, you know? She woulda just whipped out a bedpan or something."

"Your Honor, this line of questioning has no bearing on the case and is quite revolting."

"Sustained."

"Why did Ms Averdantis want to get back to the gallery?"

"Um, probably to stick her tongue down Mark Pitt's throat. Why else? The show stunk, so it wasn't, you know, for the aesthetic experience. It didn't take her long to, um, get together with him."

"Speaking of which, is it your belief that Mr. Pitt– how can I put this?– injected some sort of supernatural elixir directly into Evelyn Averdantis's system when he tongue-kissed her?"

"An elixir? I don't know about that. It seems kind of far-fetched…"

"Isn't it possible that Mark Pitt has a chemical property in his saliva that enslaves the souls of…"

"Your Honor, this is not a science fiction movie. This is the real world and this is an American courtroom. There are no magic elixirs in people's spit that enslave the souls of unsuspecting women."

Wynn pointed at the defense lawyer. "How do you know, Bright? There are more things in heaven and earth, Mr. Bright, than are dreamt of in your philosophy."

"Please, gentlemen, let's skip past the theories about black magic and the John Barrymore imitations and get back to the facts of the case."

"Certainly, Your Honor. Getting back to your relationship with the defendant, Mr. Ce– I'm sorry, Larry– did you ever visit him at his apartment?"

"If you can call it an apartment. They lived in a, um, sort of loft. It was an old brush factory, I think. I lived in an apartment. They had a lot of space, big windows, high ceilings, but it was pretty rough, you know? They didn't always have heat or, like, hot water. The landlord was a jerk. They had a crazy lady who lived upstairs who was always asking about a beast or something."

"Did you visit the apartment– or the loft, I mean?"

"Yeah, plenty of times. They had these art parties there sometimes. I went to some of those. They'd, um, have these people over and there'd be poetry and some guy playing the guitar, or something. I didn't like it."

"Why didn't you like it?"

"I, um, thought they were all a bunch of phonies. They looked like they thought they were all in some kind of, um, movie or something– like a happening, you know? Everybody trying to out-*unusual* each other, you know? I didn't like the scene. I guess that makes me unusual."

"Was there black magic at these so-called art parties?"

"Some, yeah. I guess. What do you mean?"

"Black magic, witches, warlocks, evil rites, sacrifices– that sort of thing."

"Um, I don't remember anything like that. Maybe some sacrifices. I can't remember."

"Did that stuff start after you'd leave the party?"

"It must have, 'cause, um, I sure don't remember seeing it."

"Did the defendant preside over this collection of Satan's servants?"

"Did he preside? Um, I don't know what you mean."

"Did he hold court over these phonies, freaks and miscreants– like a prince ruling over his minions?"

"Oh, I get you. Yeah, sure. He did that. He ruled over them. Yeah, that's right, he presided."

"Did your friendship with Mr. Pitt finally end?"

"Yes."

"When did it end?"

"After he killed Evelyn."

"Objection!"

"Sustained."

"Larry, did your relationship with the defendant end after Miss Averdantis died?"

"Yes."

"What do you think of the defendant's artwork, Larry?"

"What do you mean? Do I like it?"

"What's your professional assessment of his work?"

"I wouldn't do the kinda thing he's doing. I mean, I don't know if I'd have the guts, you know, to do that sort of imagery. You know, he's doing some pretty far-out stuff there – you know, pussies and stuff. I don't know, I guess it's pretty good. I mean, nobody's doing that kinda thing nowadays– at least not doing it well, anyway."

"Do you think what he's doing is crazy?"

"Your Honor, Mr. Cezanne is not qualified."

"Sustained."

"Is the *art* he's doing crazy?"

"Um, sure. I mean, it's too much, you know what I mean?" Cezanne paused. "On the other hand, it's selling, you know, for some big bucks, too. So, you know, you gotta wonder who's crazy. Maybe I am. I've got twenty-five or thirty tasteful little views of Highbridge, um, just sitting in my painting racks at this moment, you know? I can't even sell them for five hundred bucks."

"Did you believe that Mark Pitt killed Evelyn Averdantis? Is that why your relationship ended?"

"Um, no, not really. It was just that, you know, when you're, um, arrested and carted off to jail and tried for murder, your social circle kinda changes. I haven't seen him in a long time. Not that, um, I don't like the guy, but, you know, I don't get by the detention center too often."

"Thank you, Larry. Your Honor, I have no more questions."

"Your witness, Mr. Bright."

69

Bright approached the stand, tapping a pencil against the palm of his left hand. "Mr. Cezanne, you stated that you didn't hold a grudge against my client. Isn't it true that you tried to hire another artist to murder Mark Pitt just seven months ago?"

"No, that's not true. Why would you say that?"

"Isn't it true, Mr. Cezanne that you yourself planted a bomb in Mark Pitt's tabouret, back on October tenth of last year?"

"No way."

"And that the only reason it failed to go off is that it was jammed by a Grumbacher palette knife that had fallen into the mechanism– a palette knife that had your fingerprints and *only* your fingerprints on it?"

"No! You got it all wrong."

"And isn't it true that you bought an identical palette knife two days later at Lloyd's Art and Sign Supplies on Robinson Avenue?"

"No! Well, um, actually, that *is* true. I did buy a new palette knife. But, that was, um, because mine was stolen. People are always stealing stuff out of my studio."

"Isn't it true that, on October thirteenth of last year– a mere three days after your assassination attempt failed– you rented a car from Avis and tried to run Mark Pitt down as he crossed 19th Street? Instead you missed him and crashed the car into the side of a westbound Number 5 bus. Isn't *that* true?"

Cezanne squirmed a bit in his chair, avoiding the accusatory stare of the attorney. "I don't recall any cars. I don't own a car. I can't recall."

"You don't recall attempting to kill Mark Pitt or you don't recall crashing the rental car?"

"No, it was a long time ago."

"Didn't you just recount– in great detail, I might add– the story of how my client stole not just the heart, but also the hot ass– as you so quaintly put it– of Evelyn Averdantis away from you? That happened even longer ago than your assassination attempts." Bright stared at Cezanne for a moment, looking for a reaction. "Nothing to say, Mr. Cezanne? So, do you concede that it is true, but that you no longer recall?"

"Yeah, sure. No, um, wait. I don't concede that. You're twisting my meaning. I feel confused and my elbow hurts." Cezanne grimaced and rubbed his right elbow.

Wynn rose to his feet and waved a regal hand. "Your Honor, my esteemed colleague keeps referring to the unfortunate attempts– I mean *events*– as quote-unquote assassination attempts. It has not been proved that they were anything more than mere coincidences. They could have happened to anyone."

"Mere coincidences!? Your Honor, Mr. Wynn is deluded if he..."

"Gentlemen, stop sniping. Objection is overruled."

"Thank you, Your Honor. Mr. Cezanne, now that you had a moment to rest your elbow, has your mind cleared up enough to answer questions again?"

"Um, I don't know. It depends on the question, I guess."

"I see. Well, let's try this one, just to test it out. Do you recall telling the agent at the counter at Avis– a Mr. Abner Abernathy– that you wanted to rent a car– and I quote– 'big enough to take out a creep'?"

"Uh, let's see. I mighta said it. It sounds like something I might say. I'm not sure." Cezanne shook his head and pounded his left ear with the palm of his hand, like he was trying to dislodge something that was stuck in there. "My ear is ringing."

"Maybe if you'd stop whacking your head it would stop ringing."

"No, it was ringing, you know, before I did that." He shook his head again, then he reached down and rubbed his leg. "Ooh, I've got a cramp."

"What's next? Is your left lung going to collapse?"

"That's not funny. I'm like suffering, you know?"

Wynn rose to his majestically full height. "Your Honor, this savagery must end. My witness can't take much more of this pressure."

"Relax, Mr. Wynn. I haven't lost a witness yet. Continue, Mr. Bright."

"Thank you, Your Honor. Have you been seeing a psychiatrist, Cezanne?"

He stopped rubbing his leg. "Huh? Oh, yeah. Dr. Weiner."

"Was it your idea?"

"The psychiatrist? Uh, no, it wasn't exactly my idea."

"Whose idea was it?"

"I don't know."

"Wasn't it ordered by the court?"

"Sure. Whatever you say."

"Do you have a problem with your eyes, now?"

"No, why?"

"Because you keep rolling them. I thought maybe they were spasming or something. Your Honor, can you instruct the witness to stop rolling his eyes and answer the questions put to him?"

"I can instruct him to answer the questions, but he can do whatever he likes with his eyes. Mr. Cezanne, I realize you are an artist and in the care of a psychiatrist, but you must answer the questions put to you by Mr. Bright. Do you understand me?"

"Okay, I'll answer his dumb questions. Don't know what good it'll do you. He's just confusing things."

"Good. Here's another dumb question for you. Do you know a man who goes by the name of H.B. Sweatclown?"

"Who?"

"H.B. Sweatclown. Do you know him?"

"Um, no, I never heard of him"

"I have here a photo that I'd like you to take a look at. Can you see it clearly? Is that a picture of you?"

"Who? Me?"

"Yes, is that a photo of you?"

"Yeah, I guess so."

"Do you recognize where it was taken?"

"Um, based on the painting on the wall behind me, it, looks like an opening I went to at Zone Doubt Gallery."

"When was this opening?"

"Um, I don't know. Maybe a year ago?"

"Who is that standing next to you with his arm around your shoulder?"

"It, um, looks like H.B."

"I thought you said you didn't know H.B. Sweatclown?"

"I didn't say that. Of course I know H.B. *Everybody* knows H.B. I didn't know his last name was Sweatclown."

"How could you possibly not know this guy's last name? He's a famous arts critic."

"I must've, um, forgotten it, I guess."

"Even if you didn't know his last name, how could you claim to not know somebody with the name 'H.B.'? I happen *not* to know anybody by the name of H.B., but if I did know someone named 'H.B.', but didn't know his last name, and someone asked me if I knew an H.B. *Whatever*, I wouldn't automatically answer no."

"Well, you're not me, are you? You're you."

"Thank heavens."

"Your Honor, what the heck is that? For all Mr. Bright knows, it may be great to be Lawrence Cezanne."

"I suppose it's remotely possible. Sustained."

"My apologies, Your Honor. I'm certain being Lawrence Cezanne is better than it seems at first glance."

"What do you know about being me?"

"Nothing much. I do know that I wouldn't stand by while some guy came along and grabbed my girlfriend's ass and not do anything. I wouldn't have stood there, glued to the floor like a waterbug in a roach motel while they sucked on each other's tongues."

"Aha! I *did* do something!" Cezanne's face became flushed and he pointed his finger at Bright. "I, um…" Cezanne looked blank and far away for a second, then the color drained back out of his face.

"You what, Mr. Cezanne? What did you do?"

"I, uh, I, uh…"

"What did you do, Mr. Cezanne!?"

"Your Honor, could you instruct my esteemed colleague not to yell in my witness's face?"

"Sit down, Mr. Wynn. This is finally getting interesting."

"Well, Mr. Cezanne? We're waiting for your answer. Even Judge Tuilgy is interested in what you have to say, now."

"What was the, um, question?"

"Your Honor, please instruct the witness."

"Mr. Cezanne, you have been asked a question and you must answer it or be held in contempt."

"I, um, think this guy already holds me in contempt."

"Stop the farce, Cezanne! What *did* you do?"

"I didn't do anything. I got drunk."

"That's not all, is it? What else did you do?"

"I threw up. I don't remember. Maybe I didn't do anything. I don't know."

"Your Honor, I move that we place this witness under arrest for contempt of court and throw him in the City Jail downtown. Maybe a night or two in the holding pen with the bums, rapists, freaks and throat-slashers will jog his memory– that is *if* he survives his cohabitation with the members of the Ripped Skulls Gang we have awaiting arraignment right now."

"You wouldn't do that, would you? I'm no criminal. Okay, okay! Um, I'll tell you. It's, uh, going to sound silly."

"Don't worry about how it's going to sound. You've sworn an oath to tell the truth. You must tell the court."

"Even I don't, uh, believe it, necessarily. But, I thought it was the only way I could, you know, get revenge."

"Revenge for Mark Pitt and Evelyn Averdantis making a fool out of you?"

"Kind of."

"How did you try to exact your revenge?"

"I, um, made a voodoo doll."

There was a nervous murmuring in the court when the words were spoken.

"A voodoo doll! Do you know what you're saying, man?"

"Yeah, I guess."

"Voodoo! Just the word gives me the chills. What possessed you to make a *voodoo* doll, for chrissakes?"

"Um, I didn't know what else to do. I mean, I'm not good at a lot of things, you know?"

"What did you hope to accomplish by making a voodoo doll?"

"I, um, figured if I can't have her then nobody would."

"Wait a second. You made a voodoo doll of *Evelyn*? I thought…"

"Yeah, well I had uh, you know, some of her hair. You have to use something that, um, possesses the spirit of the person– like fingernails, a picture, hair. I had some of her hair."

"You wanted to hurt *her*? Why?"

"She dumped me. I felt like a dick, you know? I'm sorry, can I say that? Well, that's how I felt, anyway– like a dick. A sad, limp…"

Judge Tuilgy interrupted him. "We get the picture, Mr. Cezanne."

"Yes, Judge. Sorry. It's just that, you know, I felt bad."

"Mr. Cezanne, when you made the doll and attempted to do mischief to Miss Averdantis, what did you try to do– what harm did you wish on her?"

"What do you mean?"

"Well, did you stick pins in the doll?"

"Sure."

"What part did you stick the pins into? What harm did you try to do to her specifically?"

"Oh, I get you. I stuck pins *everywhere!*"

"Everywhere?"

"Yeah, um, I didn't take any chances. I didn't miss a spot." Cezanne ticked off on his fingers as he listed the locations of the pins. "I stuck pins in her head– front and back and sides. I stuck them in her legs and arms and feet and back and eyes and ass and..."

"I think we got the idea. Did your psychoanalyst know about this hobby of yours?"

"Um, I don't think so. I didn't tell him. So, I don't think so."

"Why didn't you tell him about this doll?"

"I didn't think it was, you know, any of his business. And then I figured I might have to tell him about the one I made of him, and that would have gotten, um, awkward, you know?"

"Where'd you stick the pins for him?"

"Just his crotch."

"I have no more questions, Your Honor."

"Mr. Wynn?"

"Yes, just a question or two, Your Honor. Larry, as far as you know, did your voodoo do any real harm to Ms Averdantis?"

"Um, I doubt it."

"Why do you doubt it?"

"I read up on it afterward and you're supposed to cast some kinda spell or something. I didn't do any of that, so I don't think my doll had any magic."

"Thank you, Larry. No more questions, Your Honor."

"You may step down, Mr. Cezanne."

7. Millicent Averdantis

"Your Honor, the State calls Millicent Averdantis to the stand."

A tall woman in her middle years took the oath and the witness chair. She was well-dressed in very conservative clothing, and her hair and make-up were expertly and tastefully prepared. It was obvious that she took excellent care of her appearance— one of those women who was probably older than she appeared at first glance.

"Good morning, Mrs. Averdantis. I realize that this is very difficult for you. If you hit an emotional breaking point and can't go on, just put up your hand or something and we'll stop. Okay?"

"Thank you, Mr. Wynn, I will be fine. I may be a lovely woman, Mr. Wynn, but I am also a strong woman— like oak. I do not break so easily. I've outlasted three husbands, you know."

"Excellent. Well done. Now, let me start by asking you to paint for us a portrait of your daughter, so that we may understand better what happened to her."

"What happened to her? You make it sound almost as trivial as— as— skinning her knees. This is not some boo-boo that can be sprayed with Bactine and covered with a Band-Aid. My dear Evie is cold and dead. You can't spray *that* with Bactine. There isn't enough Bactine in the universe to bring her back from the dead."

"No, indeed."

"And you use the term, 'paint a portrait.' That would be something you should ask Mark Pitt to do for you. Lord knows he painted many such portraits of my dear Evie while she lived with him in that— that— smelly cave of his. I wouldn't be shocked if he did paint her while she was dying in that putrid bathtub. What that man subjected my dear little Evie to. Rat droppings in her underthings! Rat droppings! Can you imagine? Can *anyone* imagine? Oh, dear! The things he subjected her to! The awful tortures of posing endlessly for his hideous creations. Have you seen his so-called artwork, Mr. Wynn?"

"Yes, I have."

"At least that's what they call the stuff— artwork. Ha! I'm sorry, Mr. Wynn, but what they've decided to call artwork these days used to be called garbage and would have been hauled away to the ash dump out there where the airport is now. That's what that young man's output deserves, if you ask me. Do you know that he has actually exhibited his dreadful creations in public? And some of the abominations are images of my poor Evie, displayed in vulgar contortions, painted in lurid colors and slapdash brushstrokes. He made a mess of her life just as he did of those disastrous canvases– just to make a buck! Oh, it's so depressing. How he could have thought that he had any talent as an artist is beyond me. These young men these days think that all they need is a Bachelor of Fine Arts degree and the world will throw itself at their feet. They don't think they should have to pay their dues. They expect everybody else to help support them as they sit there coloring. The worst part is that that is *exactly* what happens! And to top it off, he's quite successful now! It boggles the mind."

"Did Mark Pitt expect to be supported?"

"Of course he did! He expected my poor Evie to support him during his lean years. He wanted her to pay half the rent. Can you imagine? And then she was expected to accommodate his vile appetites, too. Ugh! I shudder every time I think of him putting his grubby, filthy hands on her and kissing her and– oh, dear!"

"Did your daughter complain about him to you?"

"Did she complain?"

"Yes, did she complain? Did she tell you how abusive he was or how cruel he had been to her? Anything like that?"

"Why, no, she never did– not to me, anyway. She never was much of a complainer. She never had a bad word to say about him. Hmm. You would have thought with all that seething evil destroying her body and mind that she would have said something– confided in me. Perhaps he held some sort of spell over her that prevented her from revealing the horrifying truth? I don't know. I've heard of such things. In Haiti, I believe, they do that sort of thing all the time. He has at least one friend from the islands, probably from Haiti. Maybe he learned this dark power from him?"

"Mrs. Averdantis, do you know why your daughter, poor Evie, was missing most of her hair?"

"Some twisted fetish of his, I'm sure. He's a very twisted man…"

"Your Honor, the witness is not qualified to assess my client's twistedness." Mark Pitt leaned over, tapped Bright on the arm and whispered something to him. "Or lack of twistedness, Your Honor. In fact, he may prove to be not twisted at all." Mark Pitt rolled his eyes and shook his head. "I mean he *will* prove to be twisted– I mean *not* twisted. Sorry."

"Sustained. Mrs. Averdantis, we all understand how awful it is to lose a child, but you must refrain from referring to the defendant's psychological state, since you are not a certified psychologist."

"I do apologize, Your Honor. I will no longer mention his mental state."

"Proceed, Mr. Wynn."

"Mrs. Averdantis, did you visit your daughter at their apartment?"

"That awful dump? I saw it, yes. I would have visited her more if I could have laid my hands on one of those radiation suits they use down in New Mexico. I've never seen such squalor– except maybe in Jacob Riis's photographs of old tenements, or something. The filth! And it smelled something awful. He had his paints and turpentine. He sprayed things in there. It's no wonder poor little Evie lost all her beautiful hair. It probably fell out from blood poisoning. Maybe that's what killed her. Nothing could live in that place."

"Uh, Your Honor, I object."

"*You* object? Mr. Wynn, you cannot object to your own witness's testimony."

"But, Your Honor, she is making an assumption about the cause of death."

"Sorry, Mr. Wynn. If Mr. Bright has no objection, her testimony must stand. Do you object, Mr. Bright?"

"I do not object, Your Honor."

"Thank you, Mr. Bright. Please continue, Mr. Wynn."

"Mrs. Averdantis, in your visits to their apartment, did you notice any sort of extreme behavior from the defendant? Perhaps something inexplicably malevolent?"

"As far as I'm concerned, *everything* that man did was inexplicably malevolent. But, you're thinking maybe something out of the ordinary, I suppose? Well, let's see." She placed her index finger over her lower lip. "Inexplicably malevolent, eh? Hmm. Something he did in front of me? While I was present?"

"Yes, something cruel and awful that would serve as a portent of the sort of cruelty we are certain he perpetrated later against your poor Evie."

"Your Honor, Mr. Wynn may be the only person who is convinced of the cruelty of my client. Would it be possible for him to refrain from leading the witness and making wild assumptions about the supposed guilt of the defendant, poor Mr. Pitt?"

"Poor Mr. Pitt?! You've got it backwards, Mr. Bright! This woman's daughter is lying cold in her final resting place while your so-called client sits smugly in his chair, casting evil glances at every unsuspecting soul in this courtroom."

"Gentlemen, please refrain from sniping at each other. We have a trial to conduct and neither of you is helping matters with this sort of conduct. Sit back down, Mr. Bright. Mr. Wynn, you will ask questions of your witness without the liberal seasoning you have been employing. Do you understand me?"

"Yes, Your Honor. My profoundest apolo…"

"Save it, Mr. Wynn. Please proceed."

"Mrs. Averdantis, your poor little Evie was adopted by you and Mr. Averdantis when she was a very little child. Tell us about her."

"What is there to tell? She was a baby girl, just like any other. She cried and made messes, as I'm sure you are aware is the hallmark of children. But," she let out a big sigh, "she eventually grew out of making the messes and became a girl that was able to conduct herself properly in the presence of others. She didn't like certain foods. She broke her toys. She liked doing art, but we had to put our foot down when it became apparent that she couldn't do her art without making dreadful messes. We had given her warnings and even spanked her, but she persisted in dripping paint and getting glue everywhere, so we were left with no choice but to take the art supplies away from her and donate them to the church."

"How old was she when that happened?"

"Three or four. I can't recall if she had just turned four. Anyway, she was upset. She cried and cried. My husband and I were worried that she would never stop crying. Children can be so unreasonable, Mr. Wynn."

"She did stop crying, though?"

"Yes, she did. She lost some of that starch by then, too. She became quite cooperative after that. I've always felt that it is best if a parent never gives in to a child's wishes. That's the way my mother raised me and you can see how it turned out. I always strove to never give into the child's wishes. I believe that by not satisfying Evie's wishes, I gave her advantages over the other children."

"Did she have a happy childhood?"

"I'm not quite sure what to say. She was never a particularly demonstrative girl. She didn't have many friends growing up. She became more popular later on in high school– especially with boys. When she was young, she was not a girl that laughed much. Come to think of it, she didn't laugh much later on either. Maybe she was happy. I don't know. I don't laugh much. Maybe I'm not happy either. I don't know. What is a happy person, anyway? Is it someone who just sits there laughing his fool head off like one of those frightful dummies at the amusement pier? I'd like to think not. Is it someone who doesn't care how they look or act in society like some tribesman in the jungle, squatting in a loincloth and eating roasted monkeys for dinner?"

"Have you ever tried wearing just a loincloth, Mrs. Averdantis?"

The witness bolted even more upright than she already was. "Excuse me?"

Wynn turned a vivid red color– almost tending toward purple. "I'm sorry, uh, I just, um, was thinking, uh, thought, uh, that it must be, um, that it must be a difficult life, you know, with just a loincloth covering your– your modesty, so to speak."

"Oh. Oh, yes, of course. You must be right about that. I thought for a second– well, never mind what I thought. Where were we?"

"You were describing your poor daughter's happiness."

"Yes, of course– her happiness. She wasn't a very happy girl, despite having me as her mother. We gave her everything she could have wanted or needed. We spared no expense on her clothing and her hairdos. It was 'nothing but the best' for poor little Evie. She was taken around the world to exotic hotels and museums. She visited all five continents– except for Antarctica. There's no way that I would take a child to such a cold and uncultured place such as that. What would a person do there, anyway? Stand around in a blizzard, being pecked at by penguins? That's not for me, Mr. Wynn, and I won't let any daughter of mine be subjected to such inhospitable conditions." She paused to brush some imaginary imperfection off her skirt. "I think that may be what upset me the most about the conditions in

82

Mr. Pitt's lair. I hesitate to call it an apartment. She had to contend with so much there. Why, did you know that there was some sort of frightful beast that lived in the stairwell of that building? To this day, I fail to understand why she felt comfortable there. Mr. Wynn, she had rat droppings in her dainties!"

"Yes, so you said, Mrs. Averdantis. You stated that she became popular when she was in high school. I believe you attributed it to her popularity with boys?"

"Yes, that's true. I never understood why she was so popular with boys when she had such bad luck with the girls in her school. Much as it pains me to say this, I have found out that she– she 'put out', so to speak. She made herself available before marriage."

"How did you feel about that?"

"I was horrified, as any mother would be. I don't recall ever addressing the subject directly with her, but I'm certain that she knew how I felt about such shameful and demeaning behavior. She knew that I would disapprove of her having such fun– I mean allowing filthy boys to have fun with her– at her expense, I mean."

"So, what happened?"

"What happened? The inevitable happened. She got knocked up. That's what happened. That took some time and money to correct. Isn't it ironic that the daughter of a married woman, who for years couldn't get pregnant no matter how hard she tried, got pregnant, practically without lifting a finger?"

Someone in the courtroom muttered, "just her skirts," loud enough to be heard by all. This was followed by titters and chuckles.

"Order! Refrain from such comments or you will be ejected from the courtroom. Continue, Mr. Wynn."

"What about the father of this baby, Mrs. Averdantis?"

"What about him? I never found out who the father was. I'll be honest with you– and it pains me to say so– but I don't think *she* ever knew who the father was. As I said, she was a *very* popular girl. She was head of her class in that category. I shouldn't have been so surprised that she ended up with this third-rate mess-maker over there." She pointed dismissively toward the defense table. "*Him* an artist? Not by my estimation he isn't. We own artwork. We know what art *really* is, and it is certainly not that– that– oh, what's the use."

"Just one more question, Mrs. Averdantis. Do you believe that Mark Pitt murdered your daughter?"

"Yes, Mr. Wynn. I'm certain of it."

"Your witness, Mr. Bright."

"Thank you. Mrs. Averdantis, do you recognize the painting depicted in this photograph?" He handed her an 8x10 color photograph. Mrs. Averdantis took the photo in her hand and lost all the color from her face.

"Mrs. Averdantis?"

"Ye– yes." Her voice was tight and the photo shook visibly in her grasp. She noticed her own hand trembling and placed her right hand over her left to keep it steadier.

"Describe for us the circumstances under which that painting was executed."

"Um, what? I'm sorry, what did you say, Mr., um…"

"Bright. Mr. Bright. Let's take it one step at a time. Does the painting show a woman?"

"Yes."

"Is the woman kneeling, with her hands and head pressed to the floor."

"Yes."

"Is the woman's posterior raised up toward the viewer?"

"Yes." She didn't look at the photo before answering.

"Is the woman completely nude?"

"No."

"No?"

"No, she is wearing a diamond bracelet from Tiffany's."

"That's interesting. I didn't notice that."

"A woman notices these things, Mr. Bright."

"Except that wrist is not visible in the painting."

"Nevertheless, she is wearing it." There was a murmuring in the courtroom.

"Mrs. Averdantis, is that bracelet anything like the one you are wearing at this moment?"

There was a long hesitation. "Yes." The crowd emitted a loud, shocked gasp.

Wynn jumped up and approached the bench. "Your Honor, may I get a look at that photo, please?"

"I have another copy for Mr. Wynn right here. We didn't have time to get it framed. I hope that's okay."

Wynn took the photo and looked at it as his eyes widened and his jaw slowly dropped open.

Bright went back to the witness stand. "Mark Pitt is known as an artist that works from life. In other words, Mrs. Averdantis, he never uses photos and he paints what he sees. Do you know what my next question is?"

"Yes! Yes! I posed for this– this filth! Is that what you want to hear?"

"Only if it's true."

"Well, it *is* true!" She threw the photo out of the witness stand. When she saw that it landed face-up, she scrambled from the stand and pounced on it. Clutching the photo and remaining on her knees, she continued sobbing. "I'm sorry. Oh, dear! Yes, I posed for it. Lord help me, I *commissioned* the thing!"

"*You* approached *him* with the idea?"

"Oh, god! What a mess I've made of things. What a dreadful mess! Yes, I approached him with the idea."

"What, you just walked up to him and said that you wanted him to paint your rear portrait? Is that what you're saying?"

She looked up and stared at Bright with a harsh smile on her face. "Ha! You think it's all so easy, don't you? You lawyers have it all figured out. It's so simple for you." She rose to her feet, still clutching the photograph. "Well, I've got news for you, Mr. Bright…" She stared at him, then retreated to the witness stand without uttering another word.

"What? *What*?! You've sworn an oath, Mrs. Averdantis– the whole truth. Remember?"

"Ha! The whole truth. Isn't that a joke! I don't think any one of us in this room knows one tenth of the whole truth about anything– especially not our own lives." She sat back in her seat and spoke in a calm, almost resigned tone of voice. "Never mind, Mr. Bright. I can't recall what I was going to say, anyway."

"Ma'am, you must tell what you know. A man's life is at stake. Now, why did you commission that rather suggestive portrait of yourself?"

She signed and brushed more imaginary imperfections off her skirt, not realizing that her knees were filthy from the courtroom floor. "If you must know the truth, he needed the money– badly. They had just had a lot of expenses, including an exterminator for those rats I mentioned, and a new refrigerator. So I asked him if I bought a painting, would that help? He said yes. I told him that I hadn't had my portrait painted since I was a newlywed and that I wanted a current portrait done. He told me that he doesn't do formal, traditional portraits. I already knew that, of course. Anyone at all familiar with his work would know *that*. So, I told him he could do any kind of portrait he wanted of me."

"Did he suggest this particular pose?"

"Yes, he came up with that pose."

"Didn't that shock you, Mrs. Averdantis? I mean, did you expect that kind of thing?"

"Nothing he did or said shocked me. Then again, *everything* he did and said shocked me. I suppose this didn't surprise me too much."

"Why would it not surprise you– to be asked to pose in this manner by your daughter's boyfriend?"

"Because, Mr. Bright, Mark Pitt had already seen me many times in that position."

The courtroom, which had grown quite quiet, listening to this revelatory testimony, stirred anew with excitement. Judge Tuilgy had to quiet them down before the public defender could continue.

"I'm sorry, Mrs. Averdantis. Did you say he had seen you many times in that position?"

"I did. You see, Mark Pitt and I were lovers."

Judge Tuilgy had to employ his gavel many times before the courtroom began to calm down. Bright looked at Pitt, who just stared back expressionlessly. Wynn's mouth was hanging open and he suddenly looked very pale as he scanned the courtroom in a daze.

"As a matter of fact, since you are seeking the so-called whole truth, I will say that Mark Pitt and I were in bed when the subject was discussed."

"How long were you and the defendant having an affair?"

"At that time, it had been several months."

"I thought you despised him– as a person and as an artist?"

"I did. I still do, I think. I don't know. Does it matter what we despise, Mr. Bright? I love cigarettes, but I don't want to have sex with a pack of them– although I do stick them in my mouth and suck on them. But, that's not the same thing really. Mark Pitt has no filter tip. Maybe that's what sets him apart from all the other men I've known in my messed-up life. I recall now that I did despise him. Poor little Evie would talk about what a rat he was and how terribly he treated her. I hated him for that. I didn't like anyone being mean or hurtful to her– poor thing. She would call me up and cry on the phone, describing how he had insulted her or neglected her. Well, one day I asked her why she stayed with him. You know what she told me? She said he was great in bed. She said he treated her like a queen and satisfied her in every way."

"Did that make you more inclined to like him– hearing how well he treated her in their lovemaking?"

"No! I hated him even more after I heard that. I'd spent more than twenty years with a man who couldn't have satisfied a woman even if she had just been released from a two-year stretch in prison. Then I hear that this low-life, self-centered artist is giving my daughter multiple orgasms every night– and believe me, Evie could tell the difference between good and bad sex if anybody could. I was livid."

87

"Come now, Mrs. Averdantis. Aren't you being a little unfair to your husband?"

"How am I being unfair?"

"Well, saying that he couldn't satisfy a woman just released from prison is a bit harsh, don't you think?"

"No, it's the truth– the *whole* truth, Mr. Bright. I met my husband the first night I was released from prison. We met in Dehoolie's Bar. I was so desperate for a male companion, I would have let Jiggs the Chimp buy me a drink that night if he had sidled up to the bar. Instead of Jiggs, it was Morris Arthur Averdantis who walked in. By the end of the night I was wondering why I had been so desperate to get out of prison."

"But, you ended up marrying him anyway."

"He had money and influence. He was never interested in me at all, really."

"Sounds like a bad set-up for a marriage."

"Not in my case. He never asked about my background. I never told him. I'm pretty sure he wouldn't have married me if he knew I had killed my first husband."

"You killed your first husband?"

"Any reasonable woman would have done the same."

"You said you hated the defendant even more after finding out that he was able to satisfy your daughter sexually, but you ended up having an affair with him. I still don't understand. And I thought you told Mr. Wynn that Evelyn never had a bad word to say about him?"

"She didn't really complain all that much. It was the usual stuff, you know? Men neglect women in many ways that they are unaware of. They can't help it. I didn't want to bad-mouth him just for trivial stuff like that. You wouldn't understand it all. I'm not sure that I understand it very well. I hated him for being able to make her happy– even if it was just physically. Lord knows I could never make her happy about anything. No amount of money thrown at her made a dent in her chilliness toward me. No exotic vacation made her appreciate me any more. She wanted a brother or a sister. I wouldn't give her one."

"Why is that? You could have adopted again."

"Morris wouldn't have it. He thought I wasted too much time and money on Evie already. When Mark Pitt came into the picture I hatched a plan to get revenge on everybody at once."

"I don't understand. What was the plan?"

"Don't you see? By sleeping with Mark Pitt I would be getting back at Morris by cuckolding him, and with Evie by sleeping with Mark, and at Mark by destroying his relationship with poor little Evie."

"Did your plan work as you'd intended?"

"Yes and no. It had the unintended result of making poor little Evie happy because I got pregnant and gave her a baby brother. It made Mark happy because neither one of us ever let on that we were having an affair and the scoundrel had both mother and daughter as lovers."

"What about your husband?"

"It made him happy at first because I was happier and easier to be around. In the end, the news of my pregnancy killed him."

"Did he have a heart attack?"

"I don't know. I think he might have died of shame. I'm not sure. The medical examiner couldn't find the cause of death in that case either."

"Why didn't you tell your daughter about you and Mark Pitt?"

"I was more ashamed than anything else. The whole reason for revenge against her disappeared when Mark and I became lovers. I guess I didn't want to hurt her."

"How did you conceal the portrait from your daughter?"

"I rented Mark a small studio where he could paint it and we could make love."

"Mrs. Averdantis, you didn't kill your daughter, did you?"

"Heavens, no."

"Do you know how she died?"

"No."

"What about her hair loss? Did she ever talk to you about that?"

"Oh, dear– her hair. I was always rather envious of her hair. She never said anything to me about it. Mark made some comment about a birthday present when I saw strands of her hair laid out on his studio bench. I thought he was joking. I had no idea."

"You didn't wonder about it when you saw her?"

"We didn't see each other very often this past year. I thought it best to maintain a discreet distance. I'm sure you understand, Mr. Bright. After all, I was sleeping with her boyfriend."

"Speaking of which, what has happened to your relationship with the defendant?"

"We're still lovers. We've begun talking about marriage. A child needs a father, you know."

"So, you'll live together then, as a family?"

"Unless we decide to give up the baby for adoption. I'm not so sure about motherhood. The jury is still out, so to speak."

"Gotcha. Are you sorry that poor little Evie is dead?"

"She *was* my daughter, Mr. Bright."

"Yes, of course. No more questions, Your Honor."

"Mr. Wynn, do you wish to re-examine the witness?"

"No, Your Honor."

"You may step down, Mrs. Averdantis."

8. Yopju Rimjam

"Your Honor, the prosecution calls Mr. Rop– um, Mr. Yopju Rimjam."

A pudgy and balding man of medium height and swarthy complexion and wearing a dark blue suit came forth. He was sworn in, and took the stand. He took a handkerchief from his breast pocket and wiped the droplets of perspiration from his forehead.

"Mr. Rimjam, what is your current occupation?"

"I am an analyst for the Tripp Group downtown in the Billerica Building on the twenty-third floor, sir."

"And who was your previous employer?"

"I worked for thirteen and one half years for The Loris Company on the forty-first floor of the Maynard Tower on Highbridge Avenue, sir."

"And who was your boss during those thirteen and one half years?"

"My boss was Mr. Averdantis, sir." He wiped his forehead again.

"The recently deceased Mr. Morris A. Averdantis?"

"Yes, that is correct, sir."

"Did you get to know Mr. Averdantis outside of the confines of your professional duties?"

"Yes, I did, sir."

"Did you become involved in his private life?"

"Yes, I did, sir."

"Did you visit his home?"

"Yes, I did, sir."

"Did you see him interact with his wife and daughter?"

"Yes, I did, sir."

"Did you ever meet Mark Pitt, the defendant in this case?"

"No, sir, I did not."

"Did you ever hear any talk about Mark Pitt in the Averdantis family home?"

"Yes, I did, sir."

"What things were discussed about Mr. Pitt?"

"I object, Your Honor. That would be hearsay."

"Sustained."

"Mr. Rimjob, did Mr. Averdantis talk to you about the defendant?"

"Yes, a little bit, sir."

"Were you aware of when Mr. Averdantis's daughter, Evelyn, first became involved with the defendant?"

"Yes, I was, sir. Mr. Averdantis mentioned his daughter's relationship with me on more than one occasion. However, I must say that I tried not to pry, sir."

"Of course. Did the Averdantises express any reservations about this relationship?"

"Yes, unfortunately, they most certainly did, sir. However, I must say that Mr. and Mrs. Averdantis expressed reservations about *all* of their daughter's relationships."

"So, this was no exception?"

"No, sir, it was not."

"Were all of Evelyn's boyfriends losers like Mark Pitt?"

"Your Honor! That's not cricket. Mr. Wynn is insulting the defendant again."

"Sustained. Please rephrase the question, Mr. Wynn."

"Yes, Your Honor. Mr. Ripjam, were all of Miss Averdantis's boyfriends thought of by her parents as losers?"

"Yes, I am afraid so, sir. Although, I must say that I tried very, very hard to remain uninvolved in the family's concerns. I must concede that Mr. Averdantis and his wife were not impressed by any of the young layabouts that their daughter spent her time with."

"And did Mark Pitt fall into that category?"

"Yes, he did, sir."

"Did they fear for her life?"

"Objection, Your Honor. The witness is in no position to relate someone else's fears to the court."

"Sustained."

"What was your opinion of the matter?"

"I am sorry, sir, but I did not involve myself in Mr. and Mrs. Averdantis's daughter's affairs.

Wynn tapped his pencil on the table a few times and let out a sigh. "No more questions, Your Honor."

"Mr. Bright?"

"Thank you, Your Honor. Mr. Rimjam, how well did you know the Averdantis family?"

"I was a friend of Mr. Averdantis and I was, many times, a guest in the home of Mr. Averdantis and his lovely wife and their funny, little doggy, Averitt. He was a funny little fellow. He would always sit on the floor at my feet and take hold of my trouser cuff in his jaws, ha ha, and chew the material into a sort of wet pulp and eat it. Ha ha!"

"Aren't you leaving out someone?"

"Am I? Am I leaving out someone?" He wiped his forehead. "I do not understand what you mean, Mr. Bright. What do you mean? Do you mean Petie and Bertha, the parakeets? Yes, yes, they were there, too. I recall them fondly. They sang such lovely notes to us from their cage during our dinner and after dinner until they died. I do not mean that they died right after dinner, of course. They lived a long time for birds– many years. And then they died. They did not die after dinner. They died, I believe, in the wee hours of the morning."

"We're not so concerned about Petie and Bertha here in this particular trial, Mr. Rimjam."

"No, of course you are not. It's just that you asked about the home, so I thought that you wanted to know about everything."

"I find it curious that you said you were a guest in the home of your boss and then paid a glowing compliment to his wife, calling her 'lovely'. Then you entertained us with heartwarming tales of Petie and Averitt and Bertha."

"You find that curious, sir?" He wiped his forehead again.

"Yes, because there was one family member you did not mention at all."

"Oh! Oh, yes, of course. You mean Evelyn, don't you? Didn't I mention her? I– I– must have thought that it goes without saying that Evelyn was there. Of course she was there, sir. Ha ha." Rimjam wiped his forehead again. "She, too, was a lovely girl. Mr. & Mrs. Averdantis raised her very well. Very well indeed. She had her problems with the boys, as I said, but she was quite a nice girl, I suppose."

"Why do you think you forgot to mention her, Mr. Rimjam?"

"Ha ha!"

"I mean, you talked at length about the pets. It seems incredible that you would have forgotten Evelyn. Wasn't she your favorite?"

"My favorite? What does that mean, sir? I liked that entire family, as I said. I cared about them very deeply– as if they were my own dear family."

"Tell us the truth, wasn't she your favorite Averdantis?"

"I'm sorry, sir. I don't know why you would say such a thing. Sure, I liked her very much, yes. Was she my favorite? That I am not so sure of, sir."

"Didn't you make more money off of her than off of Petie and Bertha and Averitt? In fact, didn't you make more money off of Evelyn Averdantis and her friends one year than you did from your salary at the Loris Company?"

Rimjam wiped his forehead. "Make money off Evelyn? What does that mean?"

"Isn't it true that your visits to the Averdantis home were not confined to wholesome family dinners and polite conversations over aperitifs?"

"Yes, certainly. I recall now that I played games with the family. I remember that we played cards many times, and on more than one occasion we played Monopoly. Though I must confess that I played quite poorly indeed, sir. Ha ha."

"Come now. I'm not talking about Monopoly or Chutes and Ladders, Mr. Rimjam."

"Charades? I am sorry, Mr. Bright. I am not– I don't know what game you are asking me about." Rimjam swallowed hard and adjusted his collar.

"I'm not talking about games, Rimjam. You're talking about games. Let's drop *this* charade, Rimjam. Isn't it true that you developed a special relationship with the very person that you forgot to mention a moment ago?"

"It is not true." Rimjam shifted in his seat and wiped his forehead. "I never touched her."

"No? Isn't it true, Mr. Rimjam, that you introduced Evelyn Averdantis to pot smoking before she was thirteen years old?"

"That is not true, sir. She was smoking pot when I first met her."

"Would you say you are a very precise and organized person, Mr. Rimjam?"

"I try to be neat in my work."

"Neat? I have here in my hand a book of receipts for things you sold, gave away or lent out to people that you knew."

"Oh, my goodness gracious."

"What?"

"Never mind, sir."

Bright leafed through one of those generic receipt pads that are sold in the office supply sections of any five and dime store. "We have, in our possession, no fewer than twelve books just like this one. In this one, you have no fewer than forty receipts for the sale of marijuana to friends and co-workers. Fourteen of them are made out to Evelyn Averdantis. Do you see the date of this receipt, Mr. Rimjam?" Bright handed him the book. "What is the date on that receipt? How many years ago was that receipt made out?"

"Eleven years ago, plus two months and a day."

"How old was Evelyn Averdantis at the time?"

"I don't know, sir."

"She was thirteen years old."

"Well, I did not know that."

"Did you think she was fourteen or what? Come on, Mr. Rimjam. You knew she was a young girl. In fact, you knew her age."

"Well, I don't know if I did know how old she was at the time, sir. How could I know if no one told me how old she was?"

Bright picked something out of a folder on the defense table. "What is this, Mr. Rimjam?" He handed it to the witness.

"Let me see. This looks like a birthday card. Yes, it says 'Happy Birthday', so it is a birthday card, sir." Rimjam tried to hand it back to the lawyer, but Bright had turned his back.

"What else does it say?"

He looked at the card again. "It says, 'when the world seems dumb and life's hum-drum, I'll be here 'cause you're so dear.' And there's a funny little cartoon of a puppy dog and some hearts floating around him."

"Who is the card made out to?"

Rimjam opened the card and looked inside. "My Dearest Little Evelyn."

"And how is it signed?"

"It says, 'Since I couldn't get you a Yoppy card, I got you a puppy card instead. Happy thirteenth birthday. Your devoted Yoppy'."

"Do I need to ask you who 'Yoppy' is, Mr. Rimjam?"

"No, it is me, sir."

"Is the year written on the card the same as on the receipt?"

He glanced at the card once more. "The same year, sir."

"So, when you said that you didn't know when you sold Evelyn Averdantis her marijuana that she was but thirteen years old, you were not telling the truth, were you?"

"I did not remember that when you asked me, sir. Now it makes sense, yes."

"Do you remember how old she was when you stopped accepting money from her for her drug supply?"

"I am not sure– I'm, uh, not..."

"Come, come, Mr. Rimjam. Did you really think you could sit in that witness chair and avoid being questioned about how you took advantage of that girl? The receipt books we looked at had exactly sixty-one entries for the sale of marijuana to Evelyn Averdantis. The entries for the sales of marijuana stop at some point for her, but continue for the several other clients you supplied. All of those clients were *male* clients, Mr. Rimjam, with the exception of Denise Mukowski, who we found out is morbidly obese. Did you stop supplying Evelyn with marijuana?"

"I must have, sir, if the entries with her name do not continue." He wiped his upper lip and forehead with his handkerchief. "I must have stopped supplying the marijuana to her then."

"We thought so, too, until we obtained this." Bright pulled a large ledger book from the pile on the defense table.

"Where did you...?"

"What was that? What did you say? Where did we find this? Hidden in the hole in the basement wall in your house– right where you left it. Here, Mr. Rimjam, let me swap that card for this ledger." He handed Rimjam the large book. "Turn to the marked page. What do you see?"

"I see entries, sir."

"What does 'E.A.' stand for in that log?"

"I don't recall. It was a long time ago. It might be anything, sir. It might be Earl Anthony, the famous bowling champion, for all I know. He has bowled many a perfect game, you know. It might very well have been him."

"Are you saying that you supplied marijuana to Earl Anthony in exchange for sexual favors, Mr. Rimjam?"

"No, sir, I am not saying that."

"Well, in your ledger book– written in your hand, correct?"

"That is correct, sir. That is my handwriting."

"All the items in the other receipt book are also accounted for here. Do you see that? Names and dates are all the same. There are some additional notations here in this book in the last column. Is that correct?"

"Yes, sir."

"In your ledger book, each of those lines that refer to E.A. have listed for them a cash amount for quantities of marijuana. Correct?"

"Yes, sir, that is correct."

"But where Evelyn's entries leave off in the receipt book, they continue here and begin to show 'services rendered' in exchange for certain quantities of marijuana and other drugs. Isn't that correct?"

"Yes."

"And doesn't it also have listed your cost for the drugs and also a notation for other expenses you incurred?"

"Yes, there are those notations. Yes." Rimjam blotted his forehead and upper lip again.

"These meticulous notations in the column on the far right include miscellaneous expenses– such things as motel fees and the cost of condoms. Isn't that correct?"

"Yes it is, sir."

"You're not prepared to tell us you were getting sexual favors from the Averdantis's parakeets, are you?"

"I object, Your Honor. Mr. Bright is attempting to belittle the witness."

"Overruled."

"I only ask that question, Mr. Rimjam, because you remembered the parakeets so well and forgot the young girl you were screwing in a motel. Did your relationship with Evelyn continue past the point when this ledger book leaves off?"

"Yes, on and off until she met Mark Pitt. She must have told him about us."

"Why did it end there?"

"He threatened to turn me in."

"Did he?"

"No, I told him he had no evidence. So, instead, he threatened my life and drove his knee into my testicles. I decided to walk away from the whole thing then and there except I could not walk for several hours after his knee damaged my testicles. I didn't relish the thought of getting another knee driven into my testicles."

"What about Larry Cezanne? Did Evelyn tell him about you?"

"Yes."

"And he didn't do anything or say anything?"

"No. I think she thought he would, but he did not, sir."

"Why'd you keep the ledger book and the receipt book?"

"I was planning to blackmail the family. I'm still planning to blackmail some of the others who are listed in the book."

"Did you kill Evelyn Averdantis?"

"No, sir."

"No more questions, Your Honor."

"Mr. Wynn, do you wish to ask Mr. Rimjam any more questions?"

"Yes, thank you, Your Honor. Mr. Rimjam, you said that Mark Pitt threatened your life. Do you consider that normal behavior for a civilized man?"

"Yes, sir, I do."

"You do?"

"Yes, Mr. Wynn."

"You consider that normal?"

"Yes."

"Do you think a man like that is capable of murder?"

"I did not want to find out. That is why I ceased and desisted my dealings with Evelyn."

"So, you did think him capable of murder or you wouldn't have made that decision, correct?"

"Yes, that is true, sir."

"No more questions, your honor."

"You may step down, Mr. Ripjam."

From the Highbridge Morning Star:

> The trial of Mark Pitt, accused of murdering his twenty-seven year old live-in girlfriend, Evelyn Averdantis, is entering its third day. Yesterday, lead prosecutor, Ambrose Wynn, husband of famed songstress, Lynn Maguire, elicited testimony from four character witnesses, including the late Miss Averdantis's mother, whose heart-rending testimony held the court in thrall for more than an hour. This trial is vying for the distinction as the Trial of the Century, with surprise revelations and emotional outbursts, and stories of voodoo, bald women, trophy wives, illicit affairs, commissioned paintings and East Indian drug dealers.
>
> One after another, the witnesses recounted their experience of the deceased, painting a poignant portrait of a girl who had much to live for before falling in with the wrong crowd and taking some fatal missteps along the way to her eventual demise. It is not yet clear how the defendant fits into this twisted tale of users and the discarded, but the prosecution seems to be gradually zeroing in on Pitt as the ultimate user and discarder of his former girlfriend.
>
> Today's testimony promises to be just as riveting as the rest of the trial has been, with famed arts critic and guru, H.B. Sweatclown, expected to take the stand. Wynn is also expected to call the first in an impressive team of psychologists, who will attempt to give the jury some insight into the inner workings of the mind of an artist and killer.
>
> Pitt faces life in prison, if convicted.

9. H.B. Sweatclown

A man, accompanied by a seeing-eye dog, walked across the courtroom and took the witness stand. After being sworn in, he sat down, his dog next to him at his left side. The dog sighed loudly and put his head down, making himself comfortable.

"You are Mr. H.B. Sweatclown, residing at 30 W Street?"

"Correct."

"We appreciate you coming into court to offer your testimony, Mr. Sweatclown. If at any point during the proceedings you find yourself growing fatigued, let me know and we can stop."

"I'm blind, Mr. Wynn, not weak. I was a Marine before I became what I am today."

"And what are you today, Mr. Sweatclown?"

"I am a writer and a guru."

"Is that how you earn your keep?"

"You could say that. The universe provides."

"Did the universe provide your seeing-eye dog?"

"Yes, it did. The universe provided you, too."

"Me? I'm not sure I follow you." There was silence. "Well, anyway, before you became a guru, what did you do?"

"I was an arts critic for *Highbrow Highbridge Magazine*. I also wrote theatre reviews for the *Highbridge Beacon* before it folded."

"So, it would be safe to say that you are well-versed in the arts?"

"Correct."

"Were you also an artist?"

"I tried painting at one point before I went into the service. I wrote several novels and a book of memoirs after I got out. I acted in several high school productions. I sang backup vocals and played tambourine for the Cracktones on their first two albums. But, no, I would not call myself an artist."

"I think you must be selling yourself short, given all that you have accomplished in the arts."

"Accomplishment is not creativity. I have known people who have done very little and accomplished almost nothing, but they are artists because they created something– something original– something unique. I tried for many years to create something. I was frustrated."

"But your books were bestsellers. The Cracktones had a string of hits over a three-year span. You sold all your paintings."

"I sold my paintings *after* I became famous. The books that I signed were worth more because they had my signature. My paintings became valuable for the same reason. Listen, Mr. Wynn, you'll have to take my word for it. This whole question has been at the very core of my existence for a long, long time. It's what has preoccupied me my entire adult life. It's what led to," he gestured toward his face, "this."

Wynn shifted uncomfortably, not certain how to react. "Yes, well– um…"

"It's all right, Mr. Wynn. Very few people understand. I know it upsets people. It upset my sister, Regina. She was against it from the start, and now she won't even talk to me. I'm hoping that someday she'll find a way, but I know that she may never come around. It's a toll that I'm paying on the road to self-discovery."

"Mr. Sweatclown, you've been in the arts, as a participant and as a spectator, for many years. I imagine you've gotten to know the so-called artistic mind pretty well. Is that a fair assessment?"

"I know artists. I know what hurts them, what chokes them and what nourishes them."

"You've written many reviews of art exhibits and many profiles of artists in your capacity as an arts critic. Isn't that true?"

"Hundreds of reviews and maybe– oh– eighty or ninety artist profiles."

"So, you can look at an artist and– oh, I'm sorry, Mr. Sweatclown, I misspoke."

"Ha! Please, I'm used to that. Let me tell you something that you may or may not believe, but I'll tell you anyway. Before I was H.B. Sweatclown, when I was just Hank Beauchamp, I was *truly* blind. Oh, I could distinguish photons– just like every creature that is born with functioning eyes can do. I didn't know what I was seeing, though. The whole reason I now have these gigantic sightless eyes on either side of my head is because I *knew* I was missing something. I knew there was more in the universe that I couldn't distinguish with my limited sight. The men and women who performed my operation promised that, afterward, I'd be able to see more and clearer than any other human being ever had. They were right."

"But– but, you're stone blind!"

"My eyes are sightless, but I am not blind. The doctors up in that mountain village were horrified. They were sure they would succeed in transforming my sight. When it became obvious to them that they had failed, they re-funded all my money. It's true that I couldn't see a blasted thing when I left their facility, and I was pissed off at them, but the High Priest who took me under his wing during the long healing process really *did* bestow the gift of extraordinary sight upon me."

"How did he do that?"

"Well, it wasn't through surgery. I don't think this is the time or place to go into great detail about it, but it was through his teaching and guidance, the judicious use of hallucinogenic drugs and a special ceremony. As part of the ceremony, I started out painted black and the paint was removed– washed away. I became reborn– in a sense, coming out of the blackness. That's how I got the name Sweatclown. It's a bastardization of *svart klon*, which roughly means 'black clone' in Norwegian. In a very real sense, I am not the same person who went there to get his eyes augmented. I am his clone. The effect was immediate and so startling that I gave away the money they refunded to me after the operation. I felt satisfied by the whole experience."

"What has the effect been on your life an career since then?"

"For one thing, I've become a far better arts critic."

"But, you can't really see the paintings, can you?"

"On the contrary, I couldn't really see the paintings before this whole expe-rience. I saw only my closely-held beliefs. Now? I see everything with a clarity that would scare you. You'd be surprised how much of a painting exists in the unseen."

"I'm afraid that I am not any kind of expert on art. I know what I like, I guess. But, do you know those things by Picasso with the three noses? That's definitely not for me. I like a nice scene with some water or trees, you know? You probably wouldn't look twice at something like that." There was a silence. "Oh. I'm sorry. I did it again. I apologize, Mr. Sweatclown. I'm just not used to…"

"It's fine, Mr. Wynn. Don't give it a second thought. I can *see* how you would make that mistake. Ha ha!"

"Ha ha! You are a good sport, Mr. Sweatclown, I must say. Now, getting to the matter at hand, how familiar were you with defendant?"

"Mark Pitt? We've met. I reviewed his show at Otto Bettnasser's gallery. I haven't seen Mark in a long time, of course."

"In your extensive experience with the arts and with your newly acquired mystical skills as a so-called guru, have you been able to determine anything in Mark Pitt's artwork or personality which could prove conclusively that he is *not* a psychotic madman?"

"Your Honor, I object to the form of the question."

"Overruled."

"Mr. Wynn, what is a psychotic madman?"

"Why, someone who would destroy a fine young woman, for instance."

"I see. Then I cannot say with any authority that Mark Pitt is not a psychotic madman. I know very few men who are not psychotic madmen. Most men, given the opportunity, would destroy– and in fact *do* destroy– fine young women. In that vein, I seem to recall from my days at the newspaper that you, Mr. Wynn, had a secretary named Virginia Bender who, by your definition, fell into the clutches of a psychotic madman."

"I am not on trial here, Mr. Sweatclown."

"I'm not on trial here either, Mr. Wynn. I've destroyed my share of fine young women– and I've been destroyed by them, too. Sometimes they were the same woman." He paused to wearily rub one of his great, sightless eyes. "I will say this, Mr. Wynn, Mark Pitt is quite an artist. He has that something that exists in the unseen in his works. Sure, his paintings are just sort of slapdash, careless-looking, hodgepodges that, at first glance, seem to have been left in an early, unfinished state. But they grow on you. The longer you stay with them, the more the quirky irregularities bother you.

105

They burrow into your being like some sort of tick. And just like a tick, they take something from you and they grow on you. He leaves just enough space in those raw and unfinished regions for the viewer to step into. It's not a pleasant sensation for most people, but those that experience it come away with a deeper understanding of themselves."

"Did you always see this in his work?"

"His work wasn't always that way. It changed not long after I had a talk with him."

"When was that?"

"That was about two years ago."

"What did you tell him to do?"

"Oh, I don't tell artists what to do. I saw his work at a group show downtown. I talked with him in general terms about his situation and his goals. He invited me to his studio."

"Did you go?"

"Yes, about a week later."

"What were your impressions?"

"Funny thing. The one thing that struck me was the irony."

"What irony?"

"Well, here he was, in the old brush factory on 19th Street and he was using the crappiest brushes. He was fighting his canvases with these unresponsive, uncooperative student-grade brushes. I told him he had to do better than that or he'd never get the paintings he yearned for, regardless of how talented he was or how hard he worked or how *long* he worked on them."

"What did he say to that?"

"He told me he didn't have the money to invest in better brushes. I told him to think creatively and he'd find a way."

"Did he?"

"He must have, because not long after that, I came across his work in another show and it was– well, it was a quantum leap. You could tell the work was by the same person, but it was as if he catapulted forward ten years in his development and expression. Frankly, I'd never seen anything like it– a change so rapid."

"Was it as if he'd made a pact with the Devil?"

"Objection, Your Honor. That term is quaint and too vague for use in a court of law. Unless Mr. Wynn can produce the Devil to confirm what a pact with him would consist of, I think it's inappropriate for the witness to speculate."

"Sustained."

"Mr. Sweatclown, the Devil aside, do you really think that a new set of brushes could make *that* much of a difference? Given that standard, all I would need to be a great crooner, for instance, would be a better microphone. Believe me, there isn't a microphone that's been invented that could make me into the next, oh, Jerry Vale, for instance."

"I think a more apt analogy might be comparing brushes to vocal chords. All I'm saying is that he went from a promising and talented painter who was doing *okay* paintings to a talented painter who was doing *great* paintings– almost overnight."

"Did you ask him about it?"

"Well, yes, we did talk about it when I saw him at the opening at Bettnasser's. He said he had spent a lot of money he didn't have and tried a bunch of different brands and different grades of brushes with no appreciable effect. I told him that *something* must've worked for him, because the paintings I was looking at certainly demonstrated a vast improvement. He told me that I was right when I told him to be creative. He said he found an alternative to commercially manufactured bristle and sable brushes. I asked him what that might be and he said it was a trade secret. I told him that I was glad for him and then we got interrupted by two friends of his and that was it."

"He never told you what that mysterious alternative was?"

"I didn't ask again."

"You didn't? I would think you'd be curious about what kind of brush could make such an enormous difference."

"I guess I just didn't get the chance to ask."

"Do you think Mark Pitt killed Evelyn Averdantis?"

"I'm not even certain she's completely dead."

"Her body's in the ground."

"I don't doubt it."

"I don't understand."

"I know."

"No more questions."

"Mr. Bright?"

"Thank you, Your Honor. Mr. Sweatclown, have you ever heard of something called the Cult of Pavitra Bala?"

"I can't say that I have."

"Do you know a man named Yogi Moran Rapur?"

"The name doesn't ring a bell."

"Did you ever meet Evelyn Averdantis?"

"Yes, I did– a couple of times."

"Is that right?"

"Is that a question?"

"Mr. Sweatclown, isn't it true that you met Evelyn Averdantis half a dozen times?"

"I suppose it could be true. I, uh, can't really recall how many times I met her. Might have been six times. I don't recall."

"What was your relationship with her, Mr. Sweatclown?"

"My relationship with her? She was a nice girl– earnest, soft-spoken, pretty."

"That's not what I would call a relationship so much as an assessment of her."

"You're right. That's what it is."

"How did you know if she was pretty? Beauty is in the eye of the beholder, as they say, and your eyes are sightless, aren't they?"

"Yes, they are. I'm not going to argue with you about Evelyn's beauty, Mr. Bright. I know she was pretty."

"When I asked you what your relationship with her was, you extolled her charms. That wasn't really an answer to that question, was it?"

"I'm not sure what you want. She was Mark Pitt's girlfriend. Before that, she was Lawrence Cezanne's girlfriend."

"And before that?"

"What do you mean?"

"Wasn't she Dick Bloom's girlfriend?"

"Yes, briefly she was. Unofficially, of course. He was married at the time."

"Who was Dick Bloom, Mr. Sweatclown?"

"Dick Bloom. Ol' Dickie Bloom. Ha! Who was Dick Bloom?" His seeing-eye dog made a low grunting noise and shifted at Sweatclown's feet. "Ol' Dickie and I were friends, you know."

"Did you know him long?"

"I grew up with him. I don't remember *not* knowing him. We were East End kids– before it all became developed. I lived on Nostrand Drive and he lived around the corner on Boe. They call that neighborhood Nostrand, now. Nostrand, Finklea, Maurice– it was all East End back in those days. Now it's like the damned suburbs or something. Back when we were growing up there were shanties and dirt roads and the old elevated line on Thirty-Seventh Avenue. It's all gone now. So is he, poor Ol' Dickie."

"Were you two close?"

"You could say that. We were inseparable. We practically lived together."

"You liked each other that much?"

"No, we *hated* each other that much."

109

"I don't understand."

"We were rivals. We fought against each other constantly. Neither one of us would give an inch. In everything we tried to best the other. Ha! He was one tough son of a bitch, I tell you. We competed in sports, school, insults, games, girls, jobs, cars, prestige, insults– everything."

"Do you realize that you listed 'insults' twice?"

"Did I? That's funny. No, I didn't realize it."

"Mr. Sweatclown, since you mentioned insults, let's talk about them."

"If you'd like. I'm not sure what this has to do with this case, but I'm game."

"Back when you were just plain old Henry Beauchamp, you were married, is that correct?"

"Yes."

"The woman you married had been employed by Dick Bloom, is that correct?"

"Yes, that's right. She was his secretary."

"Describe how you met her."

"Oh, it was just an afternoon, like any other. I went to Dickie's office because I had gotten some free tickets to the James vs. Riggins rematch at the Arena– you know, because I worked at the paper. Anyway, I walk in and I saw her perched on the desk and I just stopped dead in my tracks."

"She was attractive?"

"Yes, great figure– beautiful and plenty of sex appeal. So, anyway, not only did Dickie and I go to the fights, but he also brought along this bombshell secretary of his. He had been making it with her and so she came along. It was a great night, of course, with the main event ending in a knockout in the thirteenth round, but it was a great night for other reasons, as well. We all had a ball and got drunk afterwards at Pierre's Lounge– used to be in the Hudson Hotel lobby, remember? I made sure that ol' Dickie-boy had more than his share of highballs that night, you know what I mean? So, when Pierre's closed up, Dickie was three sheets to the wind. Veronica and I took him home and put him to bed. After that, I took Veronica home and put *her* to bed. We went those two rounds the fighters didn't get to, if you catch my drift. And, yes, it was another knockout. The rest is history."

"History, huh? How did Dick Bloom feel about you and Veronica?"

"Ha! He hated it. I think he was thinking of marrying her himself. I don't know that for sure. He never said that, but I put two and two together later on. He was definitely serious about her, though. Problem is, I beat him to the punch."

"Did it cause a falling out between you two?"

"Nah. It was all part of how we got along. Our relationship was one big, long falling out. He wouldn't hold a grudge about something like that." Sweatclown waved his hand, dismissively.

"Given the nature of your relationship with Dick Bloom, would you even be able to tell if he were holding a grudge against you?"

"Hmm. I suppose not, come to think of it. Well, I just assumed he took it in stride, like everything else."

"Would *you* have taken that in stride, Mr. Sweatclown?"

He smiled, though there wasn't any mirth in those great, staring eyes. "Maybe, maybe not. In any case, we'll never really know. Ol' Dickie-boy's not here to say one way or another, is he?"

"No, he's not. And that's another thing I wanted to ask you about."

"Oh?"

"Are you familiar with how Mr. Bloom met his end?"

"It was some sort of accident, wasn't it?"

"Not quite. He was mauled to death. The police believe it was a canine at-tack." Sweatclown's seeing-eye dog grunted and shifted at his owner's feet. "Yes, his throat was torn out and his jugular vein severed, leading to his death."

"That's horrible. Nobody saw who did it?"

"No, no one *saw* who did it."

"Must've been just a random sort of attack."

111

"Why would you assume that?"

"I don't know. Why would anyone want to take a dog to an office building after hours on a Friday, when everyone's gone home, just to commit a vicious murder of a man who has no enemies? No, it must have been a coincidence."

"It's not so cut and dry as all that. How many office buildings in midtown have feral dogs roaming their thirty-ninth floor?"

"I wouldn't know."

"You seem to know an awful lot about it, Mr. Sweatclown. But, there are problems to your theory. How did the dog get up there, for instance?"

"Took the elevator?"

"This crazed killer dog pressed the button for the elevator and then pressed the button for the thirty-ninth floor?"

"Sure."

"And then he killed Bloom, pressed the button for the elevator, got in, pressed the button for the lobby and left the building."

"Sure, why not? Dogs are remarkable creatures."

"How did the dog manage the revolving doors in the lobby?"

"Hmm." Sweatclown's slight smile got stale on his face as he cocked his head slightly down and to his left.

"I'm sorry, I didn't hear your answer, Mr. Sweatclown. How did the dog manage the revolving door?"

"That is hard to envision, isn't it?"

"What happened to your marriage to Veronica, Mr. Sweatclown?"

"My marriage? Oh, yes. We're divorced."

"On what grounds?"

"Infidelity. She was unfaithful."

"Oh, I'm sorry."

"That's all right. I've already dealt with all the emotional rigmarole. I've gotten past all that."

"Was this something unforeseen?"

"The affair? You could say that. I wouldn't have married her if I knew she'd have an affair."

"Isn't that in fact exactly what *you* did– with her?"

"How do you– oh, I see. You mean that the whole reason we got together in the first place was that she played around on Ol' Dickie. Is that it?"

"Yes, that's it."

"You're right, of course. I should have seen it coming. And maybe I did, Mr. Bright, but I didn't see with *whom* she would cheat on me."

"That's what really bothered you about it, wasn't it? You might have forgiven her cheating with anyone else, but never with that one person. Is that right? And how long did this affair last, Mr. Sweatclown? Was it a few days?" Bright waited for an answer while Sweatclown dropped his head, his great sightless eyes staring blindly at his hands fumbling in his lap. "Was it a few months? Huh, Mr. Sweatclown?"

"Two years." It was barely audible.

"Two years– my, my! And how many times did you see Dick Bloom in that period?"

"Twenty or thirty? I don't know. More maybe."

"And you couldn't see what was happening? Were they able to conceal it *that* well that a man with such experience as you couldn't see the signs?"

Sweatclown reared his head back and fixed his sightless gaze up at the courtroom lights. "I'll never forget the day they told me. Dickie was invited for dinner. My birthday had been a couple days before that. I thought Veronica and I were having him over as a late birthday celebration for me." Sweatclown chuckled a couple times before continuing. "I should've known better. Veronica cooked this chicken with rosemary dish that I didn't like. She said Dick liked it. She made zucchini, which I won't eat. She said he liked that, too. I told her she shouldn't bend over backwards for him– it's just Good Ol' Dickie. He'll eat anything we serve him. Then she said some-

113

thing that perplexed me. She said, 'yeah, but will *you* eat anything we serve *you*?' Then she laughed and kissed me. I didn't know what to make of that crack, but I had been living with that sort of cryptic remark for a long time at that point, so I didn't dwell on it. It all became clear to me when Dickie showed up and we had wine and sat down to dinner."

"How did they break it to you?"

"Well, Dickie shows up, alone as usual, and he whips out a bottle of five-hundred dollar champagne and says, 'we're going to celebrate freedom and liberation tonight!' So I asked him what he was talking about. I could hear Veronica laughing in the kitchen, and he says, 'you'll see, Hank. Finally, you'll see.' And I told him to stop acting like a fool. All that did was get *both* of them laughing."

"Did you say anything at that point?"

"I didn't know what to think, so I certainly didn't know what to say. I think I was hoping they had cooked up some nice surprise for me. I just kept my mouth shut. So, after some chit-chat, we sit down for dinner. I was sitting at one end of the table and Dickie's at the opposite end and Veronica in between. They reached across the table to each other and held hands and Ol' Dickie proposes a toast. I knew the reason for their odd behavior would come out now, so I raise my glass and he toasts Veronica being pregnant!"

"Did you know?"

"No! That's when it got *really* weird for me. Honestly, I was so disoriented by that toast that I doubted whether or not I was awake. It was like I was a spectator watching a play or a movie. I felt like congratulating her, but then it dawned on me that somehow I wasn't a participant." Sweatclown's color had heightened and his forehead glistened with perspiration. And something was dripping from one of his gigantic sightless eyes.

"You, um, have, uh," Bright choked down an urge to retch. "You– there's some– something's dripping from your eye, Sweatclown."

"Oh, I'm sorry. That happens when I get emotional sometimes. Which eye is it?"

Bright gagged. "It's, uh, the left eye."

Sweatclown used a handkerchief to wipe his cheek and eye.

"Your Honor, I object. It's obvious that this line of questioning, while thoroughly riveting, is causing Mr. Sweatclown great distress and causing that vile substance to leak from his eye. Hasn't my esteemed nemesis, Mr. Bright, heard enough?"

"Believe me, Your Honor, if I had known Mr. Sweatclown's eye would start, um– *that*, I'm not sure I would have pursued this line of questioning. However, I *must* continue. It is imperative and crucial to the defense of my client."

"You may proceed, Mr. Bright."

"Thank you, Your Honor. Look, Mr. Sweatclown, I'm sorry if this is difficult for you, but we must press on. I hope you understand."

"Of course. I understand. Where was I? Oh, yes. So, I'm sitting there watching this scenario play out in front of me and they start to laugh."

"It was a joke?"

"No, they were laughing *at* me! *I* was the joke. Suddenly, all the hundreds of little signs and signals came rushing back to me and they all fell into place. It all made sense. I'd seen all the signs, but somehow was blind to the truth. Needless to say, it was an uncomfortable evening for me. The thing that bothered me was that I couldn't see it coming. I felt I *should* have."

"What happened to your relationship with Dick Bloom?"

"We talked occasionally after that. Mostly, it was the price I had to pay to be able to sort things out with Veronica and get things in order during the divorce process."

"You didn't hold a grudge?"

"No, not really. I was okay with the whole thing pretty soon after the smoke cleared and the divorce was final."

"It wasn't long after the divorce was finalized that you went abroad to get your operation. What prompted you to submit to such an operation?"

"I'd heard stories of miraculous breakthroughs in vision– both physical and what they call 'super-physical'. I thought I could avoid the type of traumatic emotional event that befell me that fateful night if I had enhanced perception."

"How did you hear about the radical operation?"

"Oh, I'd heard rumors and stories."

"From whom?"

"You mean who told me these stories?"

"Yes."

"The particular person?"

"Yes. Who told you?"

"Dickie told me."

"Dick Bloom told you?"

"Yes. He told me. He mentioned it several times while I was at their apartment. He talked about it when we were at the lawyers' office. He showed me an article about it from some radical medical journal published in Germany. Yeah, Dickie told me all about it. He told me he was thinking of undergoing the operation himself. When I heard that, I was sure it was right for me."

"Did he have the procedure?"

"No. Turns out he wasn't really interested in it for himself."

"But, you just said…"

"Don't you understand? He said that to me just to get *me* to have it done. Don't you see? He wanted to do this to me." Sweatclown gestured to his face with his right hand.

"You think he…"

"Ha! You're pretty naïve, Mr. Bright. Yeah, Ol' Dickie wanted this for me. He knew what would happen. He set me up. I wouldn't have put it past him to have paid the doctors to botch the job."

"But, the doctors gave you your money back."

"Oh, I don't really believe he paid them. I *do* believe that he knew the operation would leave me like this, though."

"Your eye is dripping again." Bright was thankful that Sweatclown couldn't see him turn away in horror and disgust.

"Thanks." Sweatclown continued, while wiping his cheek and eye. "Oh, I don't mind anymore."

"Well you can't just let it drip, for chrissakes!"

"No, not that. I mean about being left blind. I've found a way to cope with it."

"What way is that, Mr. Sweatclown?"

"Oh, just some techniques I learned. And Fido, here, has helped me more that you could possibly imagine." He reached down and patted the dog. "Haven't you, boy? Yeah, you sure did, didn'tcha? Yeah."

"So, getting back to Evelyn Averdantis."

"Who?"

"The woman that my client is being wrongly accused of murdering."

"Objection, Your Honor!"

"Sustained. Mr. Bright, please refrain from expressing your beliefs."

"Certainly, Your Honor. It was a slip of the tongue. So, Mr. Sweatclown, you said that Evelyn Averdantis was Dick Bloom's girlfriend?"

"Yes. He was screwing her on the side. He complained that she was too thin. He liked them with a little more meat on them, you know what I mean? We're of that generation. Women used to be more voluptuous. When I was younger, you knew damn well when a woman was sitting on your face. None of these Audrey Hepburn, Holly Golightly types."

"Yeah, well, do you know of any reason why Bloom would have wanted to kill Evelyn Averdantis?"

"Come to think of it, I do recall hearing something about Evelyn wanting Ol' Dickie to break it off with Veronica and make an honest woman of her."

"Are you saying she was pregnant by Dick Bloom?"

"That's what I heard."

"Where would you have heard such a thing?"

"Why, from The Dickmeister himself. He was really worried about it. Of course, as it turned out, breaking up with Veronica was the least of his problems."

"What does his relationship have to do with his unfortunate demise? The two events were separated by a couple of years, weren't they?"

"He was screwing Evelyn right up to the bitter end– just the day before she died, as a matter of fact– right in his office on that fancy leather couch of his." Sweatclown's tone became strident.

"How do you know this, Mr. Sweatclown?"

"Know what?"

"These details about Bloom and Miss Averdantis? You make it sound almost as if you were there."

"I wasn't there, of course. And even if I *was* there, I couldn't have seen anything anyway. Could I?" Sweatclown was smiling.

"No, of course not. You wrote some very, very favorable things about the defendant, Mark Pitt. Do you really think that highly of his work?"

"Of course I do. He has transformed himself into an extraordinary painter. I only gave him his due."

"You didn't always feel that way about his work, though."

"Right. I said that he had gone through some kind of breakthrough. Before that, he was a run-of-the-mill ex-student, heading nowhere."

"His breakthrough as an artist coincided with his relationship with Miss Averdantis, did it not?"

"I suppose it did. Well, no, he had been with her for a while before he had his breakthrough."

"Was she devoted to Mark Pitt's efforts to become a great artist?"

"Yes, I believe she was."

"How devoted?"

"How devoted?"

"Yes, how devoted? What would she do for him in that regard?"

"I'm not sure I understand what you're asking."

"In your opinion, Mr. Sweatclown, do you think she would do *anything* to help Mark Pitt?"

"I don't know."

"Would she sleep with someone to help Mark Pitt, for instance?"

"I wouldn't know. I think that's a cruel thing to say about someone, and the poor thing isn't around to defend herself either."

"Or to confirm such a thing? You've never written anything complimentary about anyone just because someone– let's say– *bribed* you, have you?"

"That's a despicable thing, Mr. Bright. You realize, a person who did something like that would have no integrity."

"What would they have, Mr. Sweatclown?"

"I guess they'd have some spending cash for luxuries and diversions."

"Anything else?"

"Some dynamite sex, I suppose. If they were so inclined."

"Maybe some delicious revenge– against a lifelong rival, perhaps?"

"Sure, that might be the payoff for such an arrangement. I could imagine someone doing just such a thing as that."

"That might be a prime motivation, don't you think?"

Sweatclown smiled. "I didn't trade good reviews for sex, Mr. Bright. I wrote good reviews of Mark Pitt's work because it was good work."

"Still, how long do you think such an arrangement might last?"

"Speaking hypothetically, I would think an arrangement like that might last just a few months."

"I suppose trading sex for a good review is unlikely here. If there was such an arrangement, don't you think that the briber in this hypothetical arrangement would expect something more than just a favorable review in return for services rendered? I mean, there are several prominent arts critics in this city, and they don't all agree and they don't all solicit bribes, do they?"

"No, they don't."

"So, wouldn't it be reasonable to assume that, if Evelyn Averdantis was offering her most marketable asset..."

"I object, Your Honor! Mr. Bright is casting the unfortunate victim in this case in a terrible light in a most unchivalrous manner."

"Ha! Look who's talking about chivalry!"

"Mr. Bright, please conduct yourself in a manner befitting your profession. I am overruling Mr. Wynn's objection, but you hardly deserve it. Now, proceed."

"Sorry, Your Honor. You're right. I should refrain from calling into question the so-called character of my esteemed– and steamed– colleague."

"Yes, well, just skip the double-talk and please proceed with this lengthy and meandering cross-examination."

"Thank you, Your Honor. Mr. Sweatclown, see if you follow my line of thought with this question. Since there would be other avenues for Mark Pitt and Evelyn Averdantis to pursue to achieve a measure of success and fame with his art, why would she quote-unquote, 'give away the farm,' to one critic? That is, unless there was something else in the equation. That is if there was something that only this one critic could provide to ensure that success."

"I'd have to suppose you are right about that. It makes perfect sense."

"Do you practice yoga, Mr. Sweatclown?"

"No, I don't."

"I asked you earlier about a cult and its yogi, both of which you denied knowing."

"That's not one hundred percent correct."

"Would it make any difference to you if I were to say that you've been seen visiting 1770 Akeley Street on many occasions?"

"Why, pray tell, would that make a difference to me?"

"Oh, no particular reason– other than that is the North American headquarters of the Pavitra Bala Foundation."

"Is it?"

"The people who come and go there either participate in their yoga classes, which are offered three times a day, or they participate in the functions of the Pavitra Bala Foundation." Bright paused a moment. "You don't take yoga classes." Sweatclown yawned. "Are we keeping you up, Mr. Sweatclown?"

"Huh? Oh! No, I'm sorry. You were saying?"

"Do you know Rosie Petosky?"

"No. Am I supposed to?"

"She knows you."

"Does she? I'm sorry, I just don't recognize the name."

"She's a waitress."

"An out-of-work actress?"

"No, just a waitress. She works at the luncheonette on the corner of Akeley and Sixth. Does that ring a bell?"

"Should it?"

"Are you aware, Mr. Sweatclown, that you have been asking more questions of me than I have of you?"

"Have I?"

"You have." Bright picked up a sheet of paper from the piles on the defense table. "I have here a signed statement from Miss Petosky, the gist of which states that she has served you on numerous occasions in the luncheonette. Actually, it says 'humerous occasions', but that's a typo. It also states that you ate with and spoke with a Mr. Moran Rapur on those occasions. Miss Petosky is quite familiar with the Yogi." Bright paused, looking for a reaction, but it was hard to gauge emotion in those gigantic sightless eyes. "I think you are suffering from a strange disease. Do you want to know what it is?"

"No, but I bet you're going to tell me."

"You suffer from the odd misconception that because *you* can't see a damn thing, no one else can see you."

"Is that so?"

"You're still asking questions, Mr. Sweatclown."

"Is there a problem with that?"

"Why did you lie about knowing Yogi Moran Rapur?"

"I didn't. I just didn't recognize the name the way you'd pronounced it."

"Oh, come on!" Bright stopped and took a deep breath. "All right, we'll leave it at that. Why did you see him?"

"I needed information."

"About the Pavitra Bala cult?"

"About their practices. They have some very exotic beliefs, Mr. Bright. They're convinced that the hair of a pure woman has magical powers."

"Were you attempting to regain your sight?"

"I knew my sight was gone forever. No, I was attempting to help someone else."

"Was it Evelyn Averdantis?"

"Yes and no. It's hard to explain. She came to me for help, but not for herself."

"She wanted to help the defendant?"

"Yes. I– this is a little embarrassing."

"You have to say it."

"Well, I, um, I don't know what I look like exactly– I mean since the operation. I can feel my face and I know something has changed drastically, but I don't know what I look like anymore. I hear reactions and can sense people's reactions to my appearance. Needless to say, I hadn't had the pleasure

122

of the company of a woman since my so-called transformation." He took a deep breath and let it out as he continued. "So, when Miss Averdantis came to me for help, I figured I could, you know, get some, so to speak. She wouldn't accede to my demands without something extraordinary that she could take away from the deal. She didn't want the usual good reviews that most people would settle for. She wanted Mark to be a truly great artist. She had heard that I had some secret knowledge about painting and thought I could help Mark Pitt with this nugget of knowledge. I told her I did have this secret and would help him."

"And you initiated her into the Pavitra Bala cult?"

"No, you're getting ahead of me. I have no idea where she got that crazy idea. I had no special knowledge. Hell, that's the whole reason I flew overseas and got my operation in the first place. I wanted such knowledge myself! I was just talking out of my ass when I said I had that knowledge. To be frank, I would have said I could fly to Neptune if it would have gotten me into her pants. Strange thing is that the inspiration came to me when I was making love to her and I could feel and smell her hair. It came to me in a flash. I'd heard of the Pavitra Bala when I was recuperating in the mountains and I thought that her hair must possess that mystical quality they talk about. The first time I made love to her, while smelling her hair on my face, I had the most powerful, mind-blowing orgasm of my entire life. It wasn't perfume or shampoo, mind you. It was the smell of her hair."

"I thought you said it had to be the hair of a pure woman? Whatever she was in her life, Miss Averdantis was hardly a *pure* woman."

"The followers of this cult think of purity differently from the way we do. It has less to do with virginity and more to do with the purity of the soul. I believe Evelyn Averdantis must have had a pure soul. I think that's what was coming through. I think that's what affected me– as I'm sure it affected others."

"So, what did you tell her?"

"About what?"

"In return for her sexual favors."

"Oh, I gave her certain chants and ceremonies to perform and I told her that Mark Pitt would become a great painter by using her hair for his brushes."

"What? You are responsible for her hair loss?"

"I'm not responsible for her hair loss. I told her that Mark Pitt would become a great painter using her hair for his brushes. What she did with that information is her business– *was* her business, sorry. For the information I gave her, I received the best sex of my life– sessions that I will *never* forget– even if I get the worst case of Alzheimer's this world has ever seen. One thing about being blind is that you can't be distracted by a stupid facial expression or the clock on the wall– or someone's disgust of you, for that matter. And, if I may take a moment to pay Miss Averdantis a compliment, she was extraordinarily good in bed. Absolutely top-notch."

"Was that offered as expert testimony?"

Sweatclown smiled. "It's not hearsay."

"No more questions, Your Honor."

"Mr. Wynn, would care to question the witness any further?"

"No, Your Honor. I think we've heard too much already. I'm famished and all I can think about is digging into some spaghetti and meatballs at Lorenzo's."

"You may step down, Mr. Sweatclown."

Fido had already risen to go before his master had made a move to get up.

10. Dr. Arnold Bitsch

"Your Honor, the State calls Dr. Arnold Bitsch to the stand."

A well-groomed man in his early sixties, impeccably dressed in a three-piece suit, carefully made his way through the gate and across the courtroom floor to the witness stand, where he was sworn in.

"Dr. Bitsch..."

"Excuse me, Mr. Wynn, my name is European. It is pronounced 'beach', like where you and your child might build sandcastles– not 'bitch', like some dog with a litter of puppies fighting over her teats."

"Yes, of course. I stand corrected. Now then, you are a professor of psychology at St. Antoninus College in Belleville. Is that correct?"

"Yes."

"You are also the head of the art department at that College. Is that correct?"

"Yes."

"Dr. Bitsch, you have also written countless books related to the subject of art and human emotions. Is that correct?"

"Ha ha, I have not written countless books, as you put it. I have written nine books, to be precise. If a person cannot count to nine, then I would have to pity them, Mr. Wynn."

"Perhaps I was being a tad hyperbolic, Doctor."

"Can someone be a 'tad hyperbolic'?"

"I don't know. You're the expert, Doctor."

"I am not a Doctor of hyperbole, Mr. Wynn, though I employ it in my work, from time to time. I know everything there is to know about art and the human psyche. That is my area of expertise. Sure, I know a fine wine when I taste it, but I have little training in that realm. In my field I have much experience. I have successfully treated dozens of tortured artists and turned them into relatively productive members of society. Some people have thought what I have done is nothing less than miraculous. I don't know about that, but I do know that the rate of suicide in the artists I have treated is fairly low. And the rate of suicide in those that I have *successfully* treated is even

125

lower. I believe that speaks for itself. If you are asking if I am considered the foremost expert in my field, I would have to answer with a resounding 'yes, I am'!"

"I see. Yes, well, getting to the matter at hand, are you acquainted with the defendant, Mr. Mark Pitt?"

"Yes, he was a patient at a clinic I run."

"What is this clinic, Doctor?"

"It's called Masterpeace– with peace spelled with an 'ea' rather than 'ei'."

"You mean 'ie'?"

"Huh?"

"I before e– remember? Except after c?"

"Oh, yes, of course. Yes."

"So, what is this clinic all about?"

"It's just a little pet project of mine, down in Lingstrome Flats. We treat artists of various kinds– visual artists, actors, singers, poets, strippers. For a very small fee– because, you know, artists aren't made of money– we offer counseling services in an attempt to rehabilitate them and reintroduce them back into society."

"How can you make an honest man out of an artist, Doc?"

"It's a rather delicate process, you see, to untangle the web of associations that artists have made between their art and the multifarious aspects of their pathetic and damaged psyches. Artists operate under the delusion that the act of living and the experiences of the senses can and should be interpreted by them and regurgitated back at the viewer– or so-called patron of the arts– in exchange for accolades and financial gain."

"So, this is a delusion?"

"Indeed it is. Well, just think about it for a moment. If I sell you a piece of cake, you then have that cake and– despite the popular adage– you can eat it, too. But, what if I sell you my interpretation of a piece of cake?"

Wynn shrugged slightly.

"If I sell you my interpretation of a piece of cake, I can go buy a piece of cake and you starve. Do you follow?"

"Yeah, I think so."

"You seem unsure. That's completely understandable. You are a product of the convoluted society in which we live. You have been swayed by the uncertain mixed messages of the media, which are attached to the arts in an unhealthy relationship that serves neither party. The arts are hobbled and compromised by the media, and the media's message is obscured and polluted by the arts. This creates confusion and paranoia in the populace. No one is sure of anything. No belief system is above reproach. No child can be sure that his or her parents are living up to the standards of our society, because there is no reliable yardstick by which we can measure our populace. The numbers on the only yardstick we had, for a long time, have been obscured by graffiti."

"What does that mean, Doctor?"

"That means, my good man, that unless someone is precisely thirty-six inches long, we don't know much about them. You looked surprised, Mr. Wynn. Don't be. Look at it this way: What do we really know about anyone? What do we know about you, for instance? What makes you angry? What makes you embarrassed? What gives you sexual pleasure? What nauseates you? Did you know, Mr. Wynn, that for some people, what gives them sexual pleasure and what makes them throw up is one and the same thing? I don't make this stuff up. It takes all kinds, as they say. In my field of specialty, I've come across some fairly bizarre fetishes and practices in the art field. I've had subjects who could only achieve sexual gratification by sleeping with their models. I've had subjects who had no problems with their sexual performance *except* when they slept with their models. Hard to believe, right?– especially considering some of the models this poor soul I'm talking about had at his disposal. I've had painters who could only achieve orgasm– that's the technical term for it and we mustn't think of these words as dirty. Anyway, they only achieved orgasm when they penetrated themselves with Grumbacher oil pastels. Isn't that incredible? No other brand would do. So, it's certainly no surprise to me when you say that you do not know what I mean. Who would, given your circumstances?"

"I must admit, Doctor, that I never realized that there was so much to consider."

"Of course not, my good man. Don't feel bad. You, like nearly everyone in this courtroom– indeed in this entire City– are the product of an education system developed in the 19th Century, during a period of intense artistic and intellectual fervor and profound confusion. You may never have considered this before, Mr. Wynn, but your thoughts, beliefs, aesthetic taste, morality and your very character is programmed by the same forces that led famed artist Vincent Van Gogh to lop off his ear and send it in the post to his girl-friend. Think about it." He paused to let it sink in. "I can see that you are startled by that realization, and you *should* be. The 19th Century mindset gave birth to Freudian psychology. I can see that you recognize the name of Freud. Let me say something about Freud. Freud was a filthy pervert. That being said, he was also very clever fellow. How clever, we'll never know. The problem is that Mr. Freud lived in the past. As time marches on it tramples on the past and leaves it squashed and dusty– unrecognizable– like one of those gray discs on the sidewalk that used to be chewing gum. If you prefer, I will use the metaphor of time flowing like a river. Picture this: as time flows, it smoothes out and reduces the size of objects and leaves every-thing it touches wet. Many critics have written that Freud was all wet, but no one has been able to prove it. The main reason for that is that Freud no longer resembles himself– nor anyone else for that matter. It's not that he's smoothed out or some squashed gray disc on the sidewalk, but the fact is that time has transformed him and the river of time has moved him from his original position. Freud is a moving target. Do you see?"

"I…"

"Look, I know this is difficult material, and it's especially dense consider-ing that this is merely a murder trial and not some Masters-level college course. You are standing there, with your hands on your knees, peering into a river and looking for someone who is now seven hundred yards down-stream from where you're looking. Why are we talking about Freud, any-way? I don't see what he has to do with this case and the larger question of the intrinsic insanity of artists. Artists are tortured souls, and those that are not tortured souls have not yet been diagnosed with whatever is plaguing them. Look, let's not quibble. We really need to get to the truth in this case– as in all cases– so I'm requesting that we toss out all our preconceptions and examine what makes our poor, demented defendant, Mr. Pitt, tick, so to speak. It is very, very important to try to understand why it is that the art-ists' mindset is the way it is. Are you following me so far? I should add here that there are many so-called artists out there who do a painting and think that's all there is to it. And, in a sense, they are correct. And, to be fair, they sometimes are. You could think that way. Maybe you do. You could think, 'I did a painting'. But, those persons who think that way are not what we PhD-types call artists, per se. The 'ist' in artist is the key to this problem. You can make a meatloaf– well, I don't know if *you* can make a meatloaf, but let's say for argument's sake that you can– but being able to make a meatloaf doesn't automatically make you Julia Child. You're probably wondering what *does* make Julia Child Julia Child. I can't answer that, be-cause I don't watch television and I can't cook. I eat out all the time, ever since my wife left me, so I can't be Julia Child. Now, because I *can't* be

Julia Child, I *can't* tell you what makes her her. That's not the same as if I said to you that I *won't* be Julia Child. Then the result would be that I *won't* tell you what makes her her. I can see that you are beginning to see a pattern here. I see that little light going on over your head." Bitsch waggled his index finger at Wynn. "I'm certain, however, that it isn't the pound of butter she scoops into the pan or the brand of spatula she uses to lift a crepe that makes Julia Child tick. It may be all those things added together, but it isn't any *one* of them. Nor is it a particular soufflé. It isn't how much she weighs or how tall she is or where she hides her secrets."

"Secrets?"

"Yes, secrets."

"What secrets?"

"I don't know. And because I have no idea where she hides them, I can't find them. And I might not recognize them as such anyway. Even if I stumbled upon them on a dark and dreary night, piled up on the curb like so much rubbish out for collection, I might not know them." Dr. Bitsch paused and smiled. "I see you are bothered by my calling someone's secrets 'so much rubbish'. Ask yourself this: what isn't rubbish? Everything is rubbish– either it was at some point or it is right now or it will be tomorrow or the day after. We were talking about Van Gogh before. You know the name Van Gogh, correct? Of course you do. His ear became rubbish. It wasn't always rubbish. His paintings, which were rubbish when his ear was an ear, became valuable masterpieces after *he* became rubbish. The check that is used to pay for the Van Gogh masterpiece becomes rubbish. Now, I'm no expert on rubbish, mind you."

"Speaking of expertise, if I may interrupt you, Doctor, how did you prove the theorems about art and artists that you publish in your books?"

"What do you mean 'how'? You would best be served by asking *if* we proved them."

"Did you?"

"Why bother?"

"I thought you're supposed to prove your theories, otherwise they aren't worth anything."

"That's nonsense. I've been putzing around with statistics and surveys for more than thirty-five years and I can tell you, with the same assurance that the sun will rise in the east, that surveys and studies are designed to prove theories."

"So?"

"So? I'll tell you 'so'. Theories cost nothing and, ironically, they are the most interesting and thought-provoking component of all science. I'll tell you something about so-called research– you'll notice that they call it *re-search*– not search. Do you know why? Because the search was done in the theorizing, that's why. What's the point of searching again? That's the part that eats up all the time and money and all it does is pile data on top of the truth until you can't see the truth through the pile. It's as vulgar an act as vomiting all over a prime rib dinner. Maybe a better analogy would be to say that it's as vulgar an act as eating a prime rib dinner and then picking your teeth and flicking bits of beef onto your empty plate in order to prove that you just ate prime rib."

"But, how do you know something is the truth if you haven't proved it?"

"How do I know a prime rib dinner is truly that unless I eat it?"

"What? That's not the same thing, Doctor. You can't eat the truth."

"Who says you can't eat the truth? *I* eat the truth– for breakfast, lunch and dinner. There's nothing more delicious and nutritious than the truth, my friend. It's what keeps me spry. Maybe *you* can't eat the truth. Is that it? If you can't eat the truth, Mr. Wynn, it's because the truth is too hard for you to swallow. You need to open yourself up to the truth and let it in. Don't be scared, Mr. Wynn, it can't choke you. You know, a lot of people can't eat the truth. My ex-wife was one of those unfortunate people who could not eat the truth. She preferred to wallow in her muddy bog of falsehoods and self-deception. She wouldn't let the truth inside. And that's exactly why she's ended up with this guy she's married to now, living in her bogus world of comfort and security and ersatz love while the truth bays and howls at her from the woods just beyond her property line every night. Honestly, I don't understand how she…"

"Doctor, perhaps we should narrow our discourse to items of pertinence to this trial."

"Yes, of course. My apologies."

"No need to apologize. Now, let's see. Dr. Bitsch, you have treated hundreds of artists. Did you thoroughly evaluate those patients?"

"How do you mean, Mr. Wynn?"

"For instance, did you measure their propensity toward homosexuality and violence?"

"Yes, we assessed their tendency toward perversion. I came up with a chart that shows…"

"If I can interrupt you here for a moment. Can we set up the chart now?" An easel was brought forward and set up next to the witness stand, facing toward the jury. On the easel was placed a large full-color graph with lines meandering across from left to right.

"As I was saying, Mr. Wynn, I devised this chart, which I christened the Pervers-O-Meter, and is based on my theories about the high degree of perversion found among artists and actors."

"What does this chart illustrate?"

Bitsch pointed to the chart. "This black line here is what I call the Natural Function line. It represents what I consider to be the normal, healthy activities of an uncorrupted adult human being."

"What is that little gold star about half-way across the line, Doctor?"

"That star represents the subject who I thought embodied the ideal characteristics of that Natural Function line most closely."

"Who is that person, Doctor?"

"That's not important. Let's just call him Arnold, for now."

"What's that blue line that crosses it and swoops down at the right side?"

"That line represents the social functionality of artists and actors, etc."

"And that red line?"

"The red line that creeps up from left to right is the psycho-sexual quotient."

"So, explain to us what this chart shows, Doctor."

"Well, the purpose of the chart is to express in visual terms where the general population falls in regard to their level of perversion and dysfunctionality. Everyone, regardless of their degree of normalcy, falls somewhere on this chart. Most people fall into this cluster here," Bitsch pointed to a particularly dense cluster of tiny stars, slightly left of center. "The most exemplary members of our society can be found in this area here," he pointed to a light smattering of stars at the extreme lower left corner of the chart. "Depending on where a person is located on this chart, an expert can predict with reasonable accuracy and certainty, whether or not that person will commit heinous acts of indecency– or worse."

"What is that irregularly-shaped cluster, trailing off to the upper right?"

"That represents where the more artistically-inclined members of our community can be found. To be fair, it's not just artists and writers and actors in that cluster. You'll also find kleptomaniacs, arsonists, abortionists, communists and the like in that bunch."

"And, in your professional opinion, where does the defendant, Mark Pitt, fall on this chart?"

"Mark Pitt is represented on this chart by this black 'x', right here." He pointed to its location at the extreme upper right of the chart. There was a gasp from the courtroom attendees.

"So, what you're saying, Dr. Bitsch, is that Mark Pitt, sitting right there, expressionless and seemingly harmless, is an extremely demented and dangerous person?"

"Yes, that is what I'm saying."

"And this is based on your decades of study and experience with artists and performers?"

"That's correct."

"Thank you, Dr. Bitsch. No more questions, Your Honor."

"Mr. Bright, your witness."

"Thank you, Your Honor. Dr. Bitsch, how much time had you spent with the defendant when you saw him at Masterpeace Clinic?"

"I don't recall."

Bright lifted some stapled sheets of paper out of his briefcase. "These are your patient logs from December and January. It says here, Doctor, that you saw Mark Pitt twice, for a grand total of one hour and six minutes on January eighth and fourteenth last year. Is this correct?"

132

"I guess it is. If that's what the log says, it's probably true."

"Don't you think that a psychologist would need to spend more that sixty-six minutes with a person to be able to accurately assess how normal or dysfunctional they are?"

"Not necessarily. As a matter of fact, I've had many, many patients that I've been able to make snap diagnoses of. I think I know what you're thinking, Mr. Bright. You're thinking that you have to know a person for a certain minimum amount of time and that you need to ask them all sorts of standard psychologically pertinent questions and measure the patient's response against some agreed-upon standard response before you can consign them to the psycho pile."

"Well, isn't that true?"

"No, not in my experience."

"Tell us, Doctor, how do you diagnose a person as demented."

"It's not that easy, Mr. Bright. There are many ways to diagnose a demented person."

"Okay, then tell us specifically how you came to diagnose Mark Pitt."

"You have me at a disadvantage, Mr. Bright. I don't have the benefit of my notes."

"You knew you were going to testify against Mark Pitt and you didn't look over your notes? Why's that?"

"I'm not sure I have them handy."

"Do you have notes at all?"

"Certainly."

"Then, where are they?"

"Couldn't say. I'm a great thinker and saver of men. Filing isn't one of my strong suits."

"Are you sure you made notes? We couldn't find any notes– not for *any* of your so-called patients. When we went there we found that Masterpeace Clinic has nine three-drawer filing cabinets and two four-drawer cabinets, and not one of them contains any notes about any of your victims."

"Objection, Your Honor!"

"Sustained. Please refrain from cheap shots, Mr. Bright."

"Sorry, Your Honor. It was a Freudian slip. I meant to say clients– not victims. Doctor, there are financial records and calendars and patient appointment logs and endless questionnaires, filled out by your patients, but no notes by you– except in the margins of the questionnaires."

"Really?"

"We pulled some questionnaires that had been filled out by your clients, including the one filled out by Mark Pitt. Shall we take a look at it?" Bright flipped over the top page of the questionnaire. "Are these your notations in red pencil in the margins here?"

"Yes, they are."

"Okay, here is a sample of the type of answer that Mark Pitt gave to your questions. Let's see. To question number six, which is, 'Name a popular tyrant', Mark Pitt wrote 'Hitler'. You wrote in red pencil here in the margin next to the answer, 'sadistic tendencies'. Why did you write that?"

"Hitler was a sadist. Mark Pitt obviously revered him. That shows sadistic tendencies."

"How did you come to the conclusion that Mark Pitt revered Adolph Hitler?"

"That was the only answer he could think of for question number six."

"What other tyrant would he answer to that question?"

"There are hundreds of tyrants he could have answered. He could have answered any of those, but he didn't."

"If he had answered Stalin instead of Hitler, what would your notes have said?"

"Paranoid tendencies."

"How about Julius Caesar?"

"Overly-acquisitive."

"How about Mao?"

"Emotionally repressed."

"Napoleon?"

"Penile inadequacy syndrome."

"Attila the Hun?"

"Compulsive liar."

"Henry the Eighth?"

"Fear of commitment."

"Are there any tyrants that a person *could* name that would lead you to think they *didn't* have some psychological problem or syndrome?"

"No."

"What about question number thirteen? Lucky thirteen." Bright flipped the page. "Question thirteen is as follows: 'If you were visiting Africa and at the tribal feast the chief offered you his sixteen year-old daughter for the night, would you:
a) Feign a headache and decline the offer, risking certain death for insulting the chief
b) Decline the offer by claiming to be a homosexual and risk being offered the chief's fourteen year-old son, instead
c) Assassinate the chief, proclaim yourself the new chief and marry his daughter
d) Drink yourself into unconsciousness before the feast was over

Mark Pitt answered 'a', then crossed it out and answered 'c'."

"Yes."

"Your notes in the margin say that this indicates megalomaniacal tendencies, laced with sadistic and mysoginistic and pedophiliac leanings."

"That's correct."

"What would your notes have read if he had stuck with 'a'?"

"Cowardice and avoidance issues. Low libido, too."

"Doctor, are there *any* answers that your patients can provide for these questions that wouldn't result in such horrid diagnoses of abnormality?"

"I get the feeling that you don't grasp the whole picture, Mr. Bright. These are not horrid diagnoses of abnormality, as you phrased it. The normal state of man *is* abnormality."

"Are you saying that Mark Pitt is a perfectly normal person?"

"Yes, I am, but don't get the idea that he's not capable of rape, murder, torture, grand larceny, bestiality, blasphemy, homosexuality, treason, arson and pornography. He is."

"But by your definition, so are we all. Is that correct?"

"Certainly."

Bright scratched his forehead and took a deep breath. "Doctor, you say that you try to cure artists of aberrant behavior."

"Correct."

"Have you ever cured any artists?"

"Of course I have. I have cured– or helped cure– more than three hundred artists of what I call in my second book 'Psycho-Painter Syndrome', and helped them to readjust to life outside the mind-twisting influences of the studio."

"If that's true, tell us about one or two cases and how they worked out."

"I'm sorry, but I can't do that. It's a betrayal of the patient's privacy."

"You don't have to name any names, just tell us the circumstances."

"Okay. One young fellow that comes to mind had been suffering under the yoke of creativity for a good fifteen years, dating back to a defective upbringing. His parents were under the false impression that self-expression is a good thing and they encouraged the child– we'll call him 'Boris', which was, in fact, his name, but there's more than one Boris in this City, so I'm not worried about it. They encouraged him to paint, draw, write, sculpt and invent. That kind of upbringing inevitably results in the creation of a freak, if you will. When the child becomes an adult and the world is unwelcoming to his quirky, individualistic impulses, he descends into the spiral of frustration and depression. This frustration and depression is ameliorated only by the creative act. This leads to the cycle, which I identified and explained in my third book, and which I dubbed the 'depict or depress' addiction cycle. To someone like you, who is untrained in the practice of trying to save people from the edge of the psychological abyss, it may not sound like a serious malady, but let me assure you that it is. Without intervention, these cases ultimately lead to suicide."

"Oh, regarding suicide, Doctor, we gathered some statistics on that subject. Did you know that artists who were treated at your clinic have a much higher rate of suicide than either the general population or artists who have never set foot inside your clinic?"

"I told you it was serious."

"Did you hear what I just said?"

"Yes."

"Why is it that you think these artists think about killing themselves after you have cured them of their supposed dysfunctions?

"I don't know why a person would want to kill themselves once they were freed from the yoke of creativity. I have to believe that they were either always more suicidal or that they are so twisted in their habits and desires that once the avenue by which they played out their psychotic games has been removed, their malevolence festers within them until they can't stand it anymore. Then, ptsheww." He pantomimed shooting himself in the head. Anyway, my information shows quite the opposite. The arts communities have suffered suicide in epidemic proportions, and they always have."

"Where do you get this data, Doctor?"

"What data?"

"Regarding suicide rates in the arts communities."

"There is no data specific to suicide in the artist population."

"Then how can you make such a statement?"

"I'm an expert in this field, Mr. Bright. Remember, I've written nine books on the subject."

"Doctor, can you actually prove anything you say?"

"Doctor, can you prove? Ha! Proof. What is proof worth? Does proof feed the hungry? Does it clothe the naked? Can you sell some used proof and buy yourself some new proof? What does proof taste like? Does it smell? Proof! What the hell is it? And everybody's always asking me for it. How can a person prove anything that hasn't already happened? And what's the point of proving something that's already happened? That's kind of point-less, don't you think? Look, if I had to sit here and prove any of the stuff I've put in my nine books, I'd be at it till the day I die– and no one would be saved. Who's going to do my work if I don't? You? Your Brooks Broth-ers-suited counterpart over there?" He pointed to the prosecutor's table. "Let me tell you something about my approach to this work. I don't care about the past. I'm trying to salvage what's left of the future, and columns full of statistics are not going to help me do that. One of the things I talk about in my sixth book is that you can't accurately predict the future by looking at and tabulating the past. Just to give you a clearer picture of what I am talking about– it snowed on December 11th last year, correct?"

Bright rolled his eyes. "Yes."

"Look at the previous twenty seven December 11ths. It hadn't snowed on any of those days. What would you conclude from that? I conclude that it wouldn't snow on the next one, wouldn't you? Well, it did snow."

"That's a stupid analogy."

"Can you prove that it's a stupid analogy?"

"What?"

"Your Honor, I think we've heard enough esoterica at this point. Can Mr. Bright please elicit some relevant testimony from the Doctor? Or can we move on? I have witnesses lined up, just waiting for their chance to sink the defendant and put him behind bars forever."

"Mr. Bright, can you keep the testimony on track? Or shall we wrap this up?"

"Your Honor, if I may have just a few more moments?"

"Proceed, Mr. Bright, but please get to the point."

"Thank you, Your Honor. Dr. Bitsch, did the defendant make any statement in your presence that would indicate that he had any desire to harm or kill Evelyn Averdantis?"

"Not as such."

"Is that a no?"

"It's not a yes."

"I guess I'll have to settle for that."

"Yes, you will."

"No more questions– oh, wait a moment, Doctor. Is it true that the entire arts program at St. Antoninus is being phased out?"

"That's correct. I've been working for years to get the art department dismantled and the theater program terminated."

"But, you're the head of both departments. Why would you do that?"

"I finally succeeded in enlightening the Dean and the board members about the deleterious effects of the arts on the minds of young people. If you had any idea of how involvement in the arts has destroyed people, kept them from living productive, normal lives. If you could sense the dissatisfaction and disappointment that accompanies artistic accomplishment, it would break your heart. It's as bad as being born black in the South in 1830."

"How can you say that?"

"Think about it. These artists are slaves to their master, which, instead of the plantation owner, is this complex entity comprised of the artist's muse, whatever that is, and the addiction to adulation, greed, egotism and an insuppressible desire to communicate something."

"Sounds like you're describing yourself, Doctor."

The court erupted in laughter.

"Well, I never! Such impudence!"

Wynn catapulted from his chair. "That's enough, Mr. Bright! Your Honor, this is an outrage! Mr. Bright has crossed the line this time! I demand an apology on behalf of my witness! Dr. Bitsch is a distinguished man in his field. I *would* say that it falls beneath Mr. Bright to say such a thing, but I am no longer so certain that *anything* can fall beneath him."

"Mr. Bright, please confine yourself to asking questions of the witness."

"Yes, Your Honor. I have no more questions."

"Mr. Wynn, do you wish to reexamine the witness?"

"I don't know, Your Honor." He took a deep breath. "I'm so irate that I can't think of what to ask at this point. I guess I'll pass on reexamination."

"You may step down, Doctor."

Bitsch looked daggers at the defense table as he stepped away from the witness stand.

11. Mario Toponatica

"Your Honor, the State calls Mr. Mario Toponatica to the stand."

A swarthy man in a cheap-looking gray suit came forth, occupied the witness stand and took the oath. He was middle-aged and had remarkably dark eyebrows and, although he was clean-shaven, had a distinct five o'clock shadow. As he sat down, he passed his hand over his thinning hair, smoothing it down.

Wynn approached his witness. "Mr. Tapponatica, you are a high school teacher for The City?"

"Yes. I'm an English teacher at Sinclair High School."

"Have you always taught there?"

"No, before I was a high school English teacher, I taught arts and crafts at Barnum Junior High."

"When did you teach there?"

"I was there until about fifteen years ago."

"Were you there during the time the defendant attended seventh, eighth and ninth grades there?"

"Yes, I was."

"Are you acquainted with the defendant?"

"Yes, I am."

"Did you teach arts and crafts to Mark Pitt?"

"Ha! It would be fair to say that I didn't teach him anything."

"What do you mean by that, Mr. Tapponatica?"

"Toponatica. Please, call me Mr. T. That's what all the kids call me."

"Okay, Mr. T."

"What I meant when I said that is that Mark Pitt was basically unteachable–by me or anyone else."

"I object, Your Honor. The witness is not in any position to state whether or not another teacher could have taught the defendant. The fact that my client has a high school diploma, a Bachelor of Fine Arts degree and a Masters of Fine Arts degree I believe speaks to his accomplishments as a student."

"Overruled."

"Overruled?" Bright was incredulous.

"Do you have a problem with that, Mr. Bright?"

"I'm not sure I understand why my objection was overruled in this case."

"Proceed, Mr. Wynn."

"Mr. T, what makes you say that the defendant was unteachable?"

"Let's see if I can put it into words. I would say that he was different."

"Different?"

"Yes, different. He had a mind of his own and was very secretive. He paid no attention to his instructors. He was sullen and petulant. He never did his assignments properly. He'd sit there in class and ogle the girls– especially the pretty ones. He liked to stare at Lucy Miller a lot. Of course, she was especially pretty. She was blonde and she had started to develop a nice little chest by that time. She had this lavender top she liked to wear, and you could just barely make out her…"

"Aaah– I hate to interrupt you, Mr. T, but perhaps we should not spend too much time on Lucy what's-her-name and more time talking about the defendant. Agreed?"

"Oh, sure. So, I was saying that young Mr. Pitt would sit there ogling Lucy Miller, who sat one seat in front of him and two seats to the right– actually, to *his* left. She sat two seats to his right, if you look at them from the front of the classroom. Lucy didn't pay much attention to Mark. She was more interested in doing well in her classes than being popular with the boys. Now, as I am telling you this, I do recall seeing her hanging around with one boy in the schoolyard during lunch period and sometimes after school. His name was Derrick something-or-other. I didn't have him in any of my classes, but I asked some of my colleagues about him and those that did have him in their classes seemed to think fairly well of him. As for me, I wouldn't give you two cents for a kid like him. He was one of those greasy-looking, pimply kids who played sports and acted like a cocky little know-it-all. I never liked that kind of kid. I'd see them together from my class-

142

room window, him and Lucy. He'd touch her and she'd laugh. They'd sit and talk and he'd touch her."

"You mean he'd touch her in, um, inappropriate ways?"

"Well, I don't know. It looked inappropriate to me. It was mainly on her arm or something, but I could tell he wanted more. I'm sure he would have touched her all over if he had been given half a chance. I know his type. Anyway, I still wonder to this day if Lucy was laughing out of nervousness or if she really thought this Derrick guy was funny. I don't know. He didn't look so funny to me. I thought he looked like a brute. He's probably done time for assault or rape or something by now. I wouldn't be surprised if he's in jail right at this moment. He's probably knocked up some girl or other– hopefully not Lucy. I know he didn't ruin her before she graduated high school, anyway."

"How do you know that?"

"Because I taught at her high school, so I was able to keep an eye on her."

"That's remarkable."

"What is?"

"That you happened to be transferred to the same school at the same time that she graduated from Barnum."

"Oh. Yeah, well, that was not that remarkable– considering."

"Considering what?"

"Oh, nothing. Just an expression."

"Mr. T, can you give us more details about the grossly aberrant behavior of Mark Pitt when he was still just a miscreant-in-training?"

"Your Honor!"

"Yes, Mr. Bright?"

"That's more of Mr. Wynn's sly wit poking its head up again."

"Mr. Wynn, please refrain from characterizing the defendant in that manner. Let your witnesses assassinate Mr. Pitt's character for themselves. That's what they are called to the stand to do."

"Yes, Your Honor. I will do that. Mr. T, tell us more anecdotes that will shed some light on Mark Pitt's so-called character."

"Let's see what I can recall for you. I remember one time when we were doing an art project where I had the kids draw their favorite rock star, and he drew Beethoven."

"Yes?"

Toponatica stared at Wynn, at a loss for his meaning.

"What is the significance of him drawing Beethoven?"

"Ludvig van Beethoven is no rock star, for chrissakes! All the other kids were drawing people like Jim Morrison and Mick Jagger and Grace Slick, and he's drawing Beethoven. I told him that Beethoven is not a rock star and he said that James Brown isn't either and that I let Lucy Miller do James Brown and that wasn't fair. I said I didn't see what was wrong with James Brown and he said he's the Godfather of Soul– not a rock star, which was true, by the way. Then he said if James Brown is a rock star, then I'm Mario Lanza and then he laughed at me. And Lucy Miller laughed, too. That was the worst part." Toponatica paused for a moment and he looked at Wynn for a moment. "Well, maybe that's not the *best* illustration of his maladjustment. We'll let that one go. There was another time that I had the kids get together in groups and the assignment was to make a collage that was supposed to represent their neighborhood. So, some of the kids did these things with magazine pictures and advertisements and construction paper. Some of the collages came out really nice, actually. Anyway, Mark Pitt does this thing with broken glass and crushed beer cans and a picture of a dead rat and an ad from one of those teen magazines that showed some junkie strung out with a needle hanging from his arm. So, I told him that his piece was ugly and I gave him a low grade– I think I gave him a C or C-."

"What did Mr. Pitt do?"

"He said I didn't know what I was talking about. He told me that if I thought something was no good just because it was ugly, then I wasn't qualified to teach art."

"What did you say to that?"

"I told him that my qualifications were beside the point."

"Why'd you tell him that?"

"Well, because my degree is in European History. He was right. I wasn't qualified to teach arts and crafts."

"Then what happened?"

"I told him that if he made anymore wisecracks, I'd lower his grade to a D. Then he tells me he doesn't give a rat's ass– or a mouse's ass. That made me very mad, because the class broke up laughing. I thought that one was below the belt, but what really horrified me was when I looked over and saw Lucy Miller in her black turtleneck sweater, covering her mouth and laughing along with the others. He was an evil one, that Mark Pitt. It's not right, humiliating a hard-working teacher like that."

"What did you do?"

"I gave him a D on that project, as I'd promised."

"What did Mark Pitt do when you did that?"

"Nothing. He really *didn't* give a rat's ass. I'll be honest with you, I was the only one who gave a rat's ass about those kids. I wanted to instill a sense of honor and decency in those young minds, despite all the awful and destructive influences that were chipping away at their souls. Not too many of them were salvageable, I'm afraid. Lucy was a wonderful girl. I concentrated all my efforts on her. After that incident with Mark Pitt, I asked her to stay after class so that I could explain to her why that exchange wasn't funny."

"How did that work out?"

"I'm not sure that I achieved what I really wanted to achieve. I tried touching her– I mean *reaching* her, you know? I explained how I take a stand for them and how I attempt to guide them in the right direction. I told her how much of myself I give to the job. I told her how hard it was sometimes. I told her all about my lonely nights and desperate hours."

"How did she respond to your explanation?"

"I suppose it was all a bit too much for her to understand. It seemed to upset her and she squirmed out from under my arm and the conversation kind of died there."

"Why Lucy Miller?"

"Huh?"

"Why did you especially want to reach her?"

"Oh, um, well, I guess I, uh, just figured that she was the most, you know, promising. Do you know what I mean?"

"I'm not a teacher."

"No, of course not."

"Any other incidents with the defendant that you can recall?"

"I suspected him of vomiting all over my desk. I couldn't prove it, but he'd be the type to do it. "

"Someone vomited all over your desk?"

"Yeah. It was done after regular classes were over. The vomit was all dried in the morning. Pitt was in the building late the previous afternoon. He had the opportunity."

"What was he doing in the building late?"

"I'm not sure. I think he was working on painting sets for *Fiddler on the Roof.* I asked some of the other kids who had been working on the play with him, but nobody would fink on him. I even asked Lucy Miller, but she wouldn't admit knowing anything."

"Was she working on the play, too?"

"No, I just wanted– I thought she might know something. You know, no stone left unturned. Anyway, I told her she could trust me with any secrets she might have, but to no avail. You know we try to build trust with the students."

"Did you ask the defendant if he had vomited all over your desk?"

"No. He would have denied it."

"Anything else you can recall that might help this jury convict Mr. Pitt?"

Toponatica pondered for a moment before replying. "I can't recall anything else."

"Thank you, Mr. T. No more questions, Your Honor."

"Mr. Bright?"

"Thank you, Your Honor. Mr. Toponatica, when you transferred to Sinclair High School, did you ever have the defendant in any of your classes?"

"No."

"Other than the stories you told us a few moments ago, did you ever hear any stories or witness anything that the defendant did that would single him out as a problem student?"

"No, nothing specific that I can recall."

"One more thing, then, Mr. T. What grade did you finally give Mark Pitt in your arts and crafts class?"

"He got an A."

"After all the problems you had with him, you still gave him an A? And you remember his grade after all these years?"

"Sure. He was the best art student I ever had."

"No more questions, Your Honor."

12. Penny Dull

"Your Honor, The State calls Miss Penelope Dull."

A slightly plump, young woman with dyed red hair, wearing red and gray striped pants and a paisley blouse approached the witness stand and was sworn in. Wynn looked over some notes on the defense table, then slowly crossed the floor.

"Miss Dull, are you acquainted with the defendant, Mark Pitt?"

"You could say that. I was his girlfriend for three long years. My name is pronounced 'dool', like a duel to the death, by the way."

"Very well. Thank you for setting me straight. How did you meet the defendant?"

"He hit on me one evening when I went to an opening at Broad Strokes Gallery."

"Can you tell us about that evening?"

"Not much to tell. I had a friend named Betty who knew this woman whose girlfriend– they were, you know, like, dykes. I don't normally use that word, but that's what *they* called themselves. So, anyway, she had a crush on this chick and she wanted to see her, so we went to the opening. I mean, I didn't mind going, because they have wine and cheese and crackers and grapes at these things, so I thought, 'okay, why not?' I don't eat grapes, because they kinda disagree with me, so I try to stay away from them. I can drink wine, for some reason. Wine doesn't bother me the same way. I get a headache if I drink too much wine, but it's not like grapes. They usually have these gourmet crackers at these things. I like those. I like those cheese wheel things that have crushed nuts on the outside. So, anyway, she asked me along for– I don't know– moral support or something. With her, it's like everything is the end of the world, you know? And if she doesn't get what she wants– well, let's just put it this way: she has to get what she wants– or else. I reminded her that she was already going out with this woman. I think her name was Julie or Julia or Jane or something. She just laughed when I said that. What are you gonna do?" She shrugged. "I told her I didn't want to get involved if and when the fur starts flying. Because, you know, women can be really vicious. I don't know if you know that or not. She tried the same thing another time and that didn't end so well, let me tell you. I'm not sure she– well, that's another story for another time– maybe if we have a chance to get a cup of coffee sometime I can tell you that one. But, anyway, she wanted to go all out, so we had to get new outfits. Both of us had to get new outfits. You're probably thinking the same thing I did, right?

'Why do I have to buy a new outfit if I'm not the one making a play for this chick?' That's the way she does things. She can't do anything alone. I always have to go to the bathroom with her, because she has to have someone along to like hold her hand and stuff, you know? I don't know what she does at home, because you know she lives alone. Ha! Maybe she holds it in and just waits until she gets together with me or one of her other friends before she goes. Honest, I don't think I can remember one time when we were out when she went to the rest room alone. But, it's not just that. She made me go with her to Motor Vehicles when she took her written test. I had to sit there and wait for her. I already had my license. That's a good two and a half hours I'll never get back. I don't mind waiting on line, but I didn't have to be there at all. Try telling her that. She always has a million reasons for what she does. Anyway, so I said okay. I like these people, all right. I'm not that way, if you catch my drift, but they're cool people, so I figured I hadn't had a fun night for a while and I was overdue for some fun. I didn't make a ton of money at that time– actually, I still don't make squat, but at that time I made even less. I didn't pay much rent. I was living in a basement apartment, you know what I mean? It was a two-family house with a finished basement on East 32nd Street. An Italian family owned it and they lived right over my head. Alfredo and Rosa Spezzatura or Spazzatura– or whatever their names were. They were supposedly connected with the mob. Well, I don't know anything about that, but I do know that their fat-faced little brats ran around their apartment, day and night. It was like they never put the kids to bed. Thump, thump, thump. Thump, thump, thump. All day and late into the night. Then the crying. Waaaa! Waaaa! Then the chubby bastards would sneak downstairs sometimes and mess with my stuff. I hated that. Where'd they get the idea they could touch my stuff? It's my stuff, dammit! One time, I came home and they'd snuck in while I was at work and they made up this life-sized dummy. It was funny actually, when I think about it. They made this dummy that was supposed to be me, I guess. They dressed it up in my clothes. The brats even gave it a pair of my panties and they used my best bra and they made up the face with lipstick and my false eyelashes. I can't really blame them, though. They were just kids. It's their parents I blame. They never watched the kids during the day. The Mrs. worked at a bakery until noon, so she wasn't home. Her husband didn't seem to have a job. He was around during the day and would pop in and out. He drove an Imperial. He'd pull up at seven or eight each morning in his Imperial and there'd be some tart in the car next to him. Then they'd go in the house and it was his turn to thump, thump, thump, if you know what I mean. I'm sure you do. You've probably done the same thing, just judging from the way you look. So, while the Mrs. is making tarts at the bakery, he's making tarts in the spare bedroom at home, you catch my drift? I didn't say anything to his wife. The way I figured it, I didn't want to get involved, you know? I mean, if he really was in with the Mafia, I didn't want to end up with cement shoes and tossed into the bay just because I caused his marriage to break up. And I guess I made the right decision– so far, so good. I'm still here. As for the night I met Mark, I ended up buying a new top and this gypsy-style skirt with an elaborate pattern on the hem. I wore my best heels. And I wore my best bra– the one I mentioned that those brats had used on that dummy. So my friend and me walk to the subway– hey, I'm getting deja-vu right now like you wouldn't believe! Isn't that something? This is really weird. I could swear this all happened before. That's really strange. Anyway, so we walked to the number 5 train and I remember these guys– you know, these neighborhood guidos– they were hassling us and getting in front of us so we couldn't pass. Guys think they're so funny. Meanwhile, they're just dick heads, you know? Why do they think that kind of thing is funny? The short one grabbed Betty's vintage sunglasses and wouldn't give them back. They were playing keep-away with them and she was yelling at them to give them back and not break them. They were old lady's sunglasses, you know, like cat glasses, tapered and pointed. They were a kind of sick pink color with little rhine-stones in them– really cool. So one guy– the tallest of the bunch– holds the glasses behind his back and tells her she can't get them back unless she pays for them. So she says she's already paid for them once and isn't gonna pay for them again and if he doesn't give them back, she's gonna call the cops. She wasn't about to call the cops, but she figured it might scare them or something. So, this jerk says his way is a lot easier and quicker and won't involve any red tape. So she says, 'what do I have to do?' He says she has to kiss him or he'll throw them down the sewer. She just stood there, not saying a thing and turning red in the face. I've known her a long time and I can't remember the last time I saw her speechless. I thought she was angry, but she had a queer expression. She looked more embarrassed than anything else. She asked him one more time. Nothing doing. So what could she do? She paid nine dollars for them at the vintage store, so she puckers up and they kiss. But, they don't just kiss– mwaa– like that, you know? They lock lips and stay locked. He looked a little surprised at first, but then he gets into it, too. It was starting to get uncomfortable, you know? This guy's pals are as shocked as me. They whooped once or twice when they first kissed, but then it got weird and they shut up. So I asked if they'd rather get a room, you know, as a joke, but I don't think she even heard me. Finally, they stopped kissing and he gently handed over her sunglasses. And he's standing there with this big freakin' hard-on and this stupid look on his face. So the next thing she does is give this creep her freakin' phone number! I swear, I've never seen anything like this– and believe me, I've been around and I've seen some things, you know? You think *that's* something, but here's the kicker: they've been together ever since! Can you imagine? And I thought she was into girls. Well, needless to say, she didn't hook up with the dyke that night. She turned out to be a real loser anyway. She's got issues, you know? I don't think she can be in a real relationship. One of my other friends, who works the flea market on the weekends, says she's gone through women like– well, I probably shouldn't use the analogy here in court that she used. Anyway, Betty dodged a bullet. He gave her back her sunglasses, just like he promised. I suppose that's when she decided to give him her phone number. You know people seldom do what they promise, but he did. He's not really so bad looking either. He's kinda skinny and he's got big lips and like no chin, but he's okay, I guess. Anyway, she's happy with him. I thought that whole night was weird, you know? I mean, she meets this guy and ends up hooking up with him and I end up meeting him," she gestured toward the defendant, "all in the same night. That's a pretty wild coincidence, don'tcha think? I checked my horoscope for that day and it didn't say anything about meeting anyone. So, where was I? Oh, so we get on the number 5 train and we get to Turtle Street Junction and then we start to pull out and then we sit there– and sit there– and sit there. The idiots could have stayed in the station and let us go upstairs and transfer to the number 2 instead of waiting forever in the tunnel. We must have waited a half hour in that damn tunnel. And Betty is just sitting there, all weird on me because of Frankie– that's her new boyfriend's name– and I'm thinking I should've stayed home instead. I figured that by the time we get to the gallery, there won't be a single cracker or piece of cheese left. Then, to top it all off, there's a bum at the end of the car and he's stinking up the whole train and I'm sitting there about to barf. I know what you're thinking. You're thinking, 'why didn't she just get up and move to the next car?' Well, I'm sorry, but I don't walk between cars. I heard about some girl who went to my high school and she fell between cars on the El and I heard that she got mangled and cut to pieces and that chunks of her were falling down on the cars below. Now, I don't know if that's true or not, but I don't want to put it to the test. So, if it's a choice between the stench of a bum or being mangled by a subway train, I'll take the stinky bum every time. And I know the train wasn't moving, but it could have started up just when I was crossing from one car to the other and it could've lurched and I would've lost my balance. Well anyway, I survived 'Old Stinky'. It takes more than a stench to kill Penny Dull. Though, this particular bum really was horrible. If I was sitting any closer to him, I might not be here talking to you today."

"Yes, but could you tell us about your first encounter with Mr. Pitt?"

"I'm getting to that. I don't understand why they don't have some kind of laws about bathing. You know, they could have a sort of public nuisance law where they can throw you in the back of a police wagon and take you to a special facility– like a car wash, but for bums– you know, a bum wash. Anyway, I suppose you have to be able to measure exactly how stinky a bum is, and if they fall below a certain threshold, they go free. But if the dial registers in the red zone– zoop!– right in the wagon and straight to the bum wash for an industrial strength scrub-a-dub."

"What is this so-called dial?"

151

"I don't know– some kind of wand or something. You wave it at the bum and it registers on a dial and there's a red zone, you know, like in the movies or on your stereo. That kind of thing. And the wand has a long handle so you don't have to get too close. Seriously, the only thing I ever smelled that was worse than that bum was dead dog– at least I think it was a dog. *That* smell actually made me cry."

"Speaking of dead dogs, can you tell us about your first encounter with Mark Pitt?"

"Sure. So, as I was saying, Betty and I are on the train and we finally get downtown and neither of us knows where this stupid gallery is. I didn't have the faintest idea what the name of this place was, and I don't know if you know about art, but there are dozens of galleries down there. So, we start going into galleries and checking out the crowd. I told Betty to ask someone, but she's too shy in situations like that. I know what you're thinking, but that kissing marathon with Frankie was atypical of her, and he started it– she didn't. I finally asked this old guy who looked like he ran the place if he knew any galleries that were showing paintings that might appeal to lesbians. The dope thought *I* was a lesbian, 'cause he asks me why the artwork there didn't appeal to me. So I told him that sloppily-painted, pseudo-impressionistic paintings of bored-looking women sitting in cafés, sipping demitasses didn't interest me. He asks me what did interest me. All the time he's looking at me and Betty like a hungry alligator. He even had the same smile they have, you know what I mean? Of course you do– you had that same smile when you interviewed me in your office last week. So I told him *he* didn't interest me. And he said he could make it worth my while to be interested in him and that the same goes for my friend. I had to hand it to this guy, though. He had some nerve. He tells me he's the artist of that crap that was on the walls. He didn't use the word crap, of course. So I said maybe he shouldn't go around bragging about it. So he says he likes my spunk– or something like that. Then he asks me if I need work. He says he needs a good model. Well, I wasn't born yesterday– despite my youthful features– so I ask him straight out what the deal is. Just then, this woman walks up and puts her arm through his and presses up against him and wants to be introduced. Turns out this woman is his wife and he introduces me as an aspiring artist that he was just giving a few pointers to. She didn't swallow that load of B.S. So, we look around a minute or two more, then, just as we're leaving, he slips a business card in my hand and gives me a wink. What a loser– with a capital L!"

"Did you ever get to the gallery where you met Mark Pitt?"

"I'm getting to that part. So, Betty is still distracted and she's no help and I think she kind of gave up thinking about her dyke friend that she had the crush on. I figured we'd better keep moving so at least we're a moving target, so we walk into the next gallery up the street and it's got these real out-there, cutting edge sort of paintings by these young art stars, you know? Not only that, but they had these hors d'oeuvres on toothpicks– not just the usual cheese and grapes. They had these shrimp wrapped in bacon and little quiches and meatballs. They also had champagne instead of just wine. Very chic setup. Anyway, they've got paintings there that look like just what, you know, an artist might do before they really start painting the painting. The paint looks watery and all drippy. And there's this group of musicians in the corner and they're playing some sort of repetitive stuff– dah-duh-dah-duh-dah-duh-dah-duh. And I drank too much champagne and one of the musicians in the group is fat and has a big, red face and she looks sweaty and she's got this big red zit on her fat, white arm. And there's lots of people there and it's getting hot, so I try to find a rest room so I can vomit."

"It was a very nauseating evening."

"Huh? Oh yeah. Yeah, it was. So there is one bathroom, but somebody's in there, so I have to wait. While I'm waiting, I start to feel better, so I decide to skip the vomiting and grab Betty and get out of there. Problem is I can't find Betty. So, I go out into the gallery again and I see that fat, sweaty musician playing that dah-duh-dah crap on her base fiddle and, without warning, I toss my cookies. I tried to hold it in, but nothin' doin'. And some of it got on the wall and a little on the lower corner of a painting, too, but honestly, I don't think you could tell that someone threw up on it. It looked pukey to begin with. Anyway, I'm standing there looking at the chewed-up pieces of shrimp and bacon and quiche in champagne and I figured I wasn't making myself too popular, so I ducked my head down and charged for the exit. So there I am, standing out in the street and I've got vomit breath and that's all I could think about– my vomit breath and how I can get rid of it. I had a girlfriend who was bulimic. I used to work with her at Hudson Credit Union in their customer service department and it was this call center, you know? We sat at these desks all lined up in rows and took calls from customers and tried to help them. That was a horrible place to work. You know what they used to do? They were constantly hiring. You see their ads in the paper all the time and they'd constantly interview people. It turns out that there aren't even any openings for jobs, but they'd interview people and, when they'd find someone they thought was good, they hire them. Then what they do is have Simon, the manager walk them out into the department and introduce them to everybody as the new hire. While he's doing that, he points to someone and tells them to come to the office. That's when they got their walking papers. This happened two or three days a week! Can you beat that? I knew the drill and as soon as I saw someone being introduced around, I stuffed the stapler in my bag. And eventually, when my time came, I walked out with the stapler. I still have it. I don't use it all that much, but it's a nice souvenir. Anyway, the people who worked there always put on twenty or twenty-five pounds in the first year. But this one woman came in skinny and got even skinnier over her first few months, so I asked her what the trick was. She told me she stuck her Bic pen down her throat at 1:30 every day. The first thing I did was to try to remember if I had ever borrowed her pen for any reason. When I told her that I had no idea she did that, she said it was because she drank a glass of vodka afterward to clean her breath. So, there I am, standing on the corner, and I figure my best bet is to get some alcohol in my mouth as fast as possible, you know? I mean, the active ingredient in mouthwash is alcohol anyway. So I turn right to head uptown and these jerks are walking down the street and they yelled something at me– you know, the usual crap about my ass or thighs or something– and I'm thinking that if they got anywhere near my vomity mouth, they'd really have a shock. Now, I'm not too familiar with that neighborhood, but I figure there must be at least one bar and one liquor store for each and every good citizen of this City, and if I start walking, I'll find one. So, I'm going up Cord Street and there's that big bookstore on the corner of Eathan Avenue and there's a mob in there and spilling out onto the street. They must've had a big-time author there to sign his book or something. A little way past that bookstore is a discount liquor store. I can see the neon sign for it. So I have to walk around the mob to get to the liquor store and I stepped onto the subway grating and what happens? I break the heel of my shoe. That's what happens. Can you believe *that*? You know what's really funny? There's a shoe repair *right next door* to the bookstore! Of course, that doesn't make any difference because it was closed since it was like getting close to eight o'clock. But, I thought that was ironic. Anyway, I hobbled around the mob and step into the liquor store and bought one of those little bottles of vodka– not one of those tiny ones, but like a small, flat one, you know?"

"A pint."

"Yeah, probably. I knew you would know about that sort of thing. I'm not well-versed in buying liquor. I think I could count on one hand how many times I've been in a liquor store. I'm not a teetotaler or anything. I just mostly have guys buy me drinks, you know? Of course you do. I drink when we go out to clubs and bars, but I like mixed drinks. I don't know how they make them, but I know the names. I like fruity drinks like daiquiris. I like banana daiquiris, but I've never made one. I think you need a blender and I don't have one. Actually, I lied– I *do* have one, but it's busted. It doesn't have the glass part, because I dropped it and broke it. Now it just has the base, which still works, but you can't do anything with it. It just spins around. Anyway, I never really used it that much. It was a sort of impulse buy, because I wanted to make chocolate shakes one time, and that turned out to be a big mistake. I didn't even have the chocolate I needed, so I made these shakes that had chocolate ice cream and strawberries all mixed up together. Well, I shouldn't say it was a *big* mistake. They turned out pretty good in the end. They tasted good, anyway. I tried to make chicken salad one time and that came out horrible. I put in too much mayo and it made it kinda gloppy, you know? The bits of celery got pureed along with the rest, too. That really was a disaster. I don't think I ate the chicken salad. Too greasy. Instead of chicken with mayo in it, it was more like mayo with some chicken in it. The thing was, it didn't want to blend at first because it was too dry. Anyway, I dropped the thing and can't use it anymore. I guess I could buy a new glass part, but I just never bothered. I'm not sure I'd really use it enough to justify the expense. So I got the pint bottle and I took a swig right away– right there in the store before the guy even gave me my change. He musta thought I was a really hardcore alkie, you know? I could see he was worried about it, so I told him I needed it for mouthwash. Ha! You should've seen his face! Isn't that hysterical? Anyway, all the mouth-wash in the world wasn't going to fix my shoe. My grandfather was a shoe repairman, you know. He had a shop on Railroad Avenue back in the fifties. He had one of those places with the wooden booths and the machines. He could have fixed my shoe in a minute, but he's been dead for twenty years, so that wasn't an option. I asked the guy at the liquor store counter if he had any ideas– I mean, I *know* he had ideas, but I mean about my broken shoe. He said there was a shoe store that might be open, a couple of blocks up Cord Street, so I hobbled out of there and up the street. By the time I got to the corner I was walking on tip-toe, so I just kicked off the shoes and stuffed them in my bag and kept going. The guy was right, the shoe store *was* open, but they had all these expensive boutique shoes, you know? So I went to the salesman and told him what happened and he hesitated a minute and gave me the once over and said he might be able to help me. Now, you know and I know that men are always quick to say they can help you, but usually that means they can't do anything *for* you, but they want to do something *to* you. Well, maybe I was a little drunk from all that vodka mouthwash– I don't know– so I said okay. He tells me to follow him and he walks to the back of the store and through the curtain to the stock room and then all the way to the back, behind the shelves. This is where I figured he'll drop the bomb– you know, I'll give you these $100 shoes if you just do me. But, instead he asked me my size and looks through a stack of boxes and pulls out a pair of really nice black suede pumps with little rhinestones forming a swirling design that wraps around the back and he tells me to try them on. They fit great and they looked good over my striped socks, so I asked him what the catch is. He told me there was no catch, because the shoes were damaged or rejected or something. They were missing two stones in the design. He told me I could have them for free if I did some-thing for him. I told him he was slower than most guys would've been, which he just laughed at. Then he said that I have to go out with him. I told him I didn't know him and I wouldn't go out with him alone, but if I could bring a friend and he could bring a friend, I would do it. He stuck his hand out like he wanted to shake hands and said, 'deal!' I thought that was kinda cute, so I shook hands and gave him my phone number and started walking out of the store, but he called after me and asked what I was doing that night. So, I told him I was trying to go to a gallery opening and got side-tracked. He says that a friend of his is having an art opening that night, but he had to wait until nine o'clock to close up and then he could go. He said he thought I'd like his paintings. I didn't care about that. What do I care about paintings? So I went and called a friend of mine who lives in The Flats and she was going to go out to some club later, but I told her she had to do me this favor, then she could go to the club afterwards. She owed me a favor anyway, because I bailed her out of more than a few scrapes. She drinks too much and then she starts shootin' her mouth off and some people get upset, you know, which I can't blame them, and then somebody has to step in or else she'd really get what's coming to her. So, she agreed to meet at the shoe store at nine and we'd all go to the club– I mean the gallery– together. Look at me, I don't even know what I'm saying anymore. In the meantime, I'm carrying around this bottle of vodka– a pint bottle, which you pointed out– and I don't want to carry it around anymore, so I start getting rid of it in the most logical way I knew how."

"How was that?"

"I drank it, silly. I wasn't about to throw it out, since I paid good money for it, and I wasn't feeling charitable toward the bum population, since one of them almost made me pass out from nausea on the subway that evening. As you can imagine, by the time nine o'clock rolled around, I was feeling fine. I mean, I had had some food, but lost most of that in the gallery. Then I had gotten a Milky Way at the news stand while I was waiting to head back to the shoe store, but other than that, I was drinking on an empty stomach, so it went right to my pretty little head. Actually, my head is not so little. I wear a bigger hat size than Earl. I bet I wear a bigger hat size than you, too, from the looks of it. Earl is my current boyfriend. So my friend shows up five minutes late, but it didn't matter because the guy was still closing up. At like quarter after nine he finally comes out of the store and we head to the gallery. The whole way up there my head was spinning and I think I was making a fool of myself, because this guy is paying a lot more attention to my friend than to me and she looks like she's liking the attention a lot. I guess I'm a little competitive, because I was trying to insult her and make her look stupid, and the more I'm trying to make her look stupid, the more attention this guy's paying to her and the stupider *I* look. Finally, while we're at the gallery, I'm trying to show her my shoes and I'm lifting my foot, you know? The next thing I know I'm flat on my ass, right on the floor of the gallery and this boy comes over and asks me if I'm okay and I think he looks kinda cute. I don't think so anymore, but I was drunk then, I guess, so he looked okay to me. Anyway, that was my first impression. He looked tall, too, but I think that was because I was on the floor and he was way above me. So he helped me up and kinda brushed me off, you know? When he got to my ass, he paid a little too much attention to it, I thought. So I asked the guy from the shoe store if he was just going to stand there and let this guy feel me up. Well, he just turned to my friend and they both laughed and laughed. That made me mad and I felt like a real jerk standing there, so I just blurted out, 'why don't you two just run away together?' So they did! They just walked right out, leaving me standing there like a fool. I don't know why, but that made me really mad and then it made me sad. Then it dawns on me that the boy that helped me up is still brushing off the dust from my ass! So I turned and slugged him on his chest and yelled at him to quit touching my ass. Anyway, that's how we met."

"Who?"

"That's how I met Mark."

"I'm sorry, I think I missed something. Which one was Mark Pitt in your story?"

"The boy who was patting my ass!"

"Ah, yes! I'm sorry."

"If you knew Mark at all, you'd know it was just like him to steal the opportunity to pat a woman's ass like that."

"Yes, of course. As you say. But, tell me, how did you– you started going out with him after that encounter?"

"Sure. I couldn't help myself. I loved his cockiness. He goes for what he wants and takes it."

"Miss Dull, you say that Mr. Pitt 'goes for what he wants and takes it.' In your opinion, would you say that he is exceptional that way?"

"I guess so."

"Well, would you say that all your boyfriends have been that way? Or is he an exception to the norm?"

"I guess he's the norm."

"So, you'd say that he is different from most of your boyfriends?"

"Huh? No, he's a lot like my other boyfriends. They're all different. I guess I tend to attract that sort."

"But, wouldn't it be fair to say that Mark Pitt is perhaps just a bit *more* different from the rest of the pack?"

"Jeez, you make it sound like I'm a bitch in heat, with a pack of hounds sniffing my butt or something."

"I'm sorry about that. I eertainly didn't mean to cast aspersions on you. It was your boyfriends that I was maligning."

"Oh, okay. Well, that's sweet of you."

"How do you mean?"

"It's just that it's obvious that you think I'm too good for the run-of-the-mill kind of guy. I went out with a lawyer once. He was a lot younger than you, but that's okay. You obviously try to take care of yourself– you know, try to stay fit and all."

"I do. I try to get to the athletic club three or four days a week. I play some basketball with the fellas, and I play squash with one of the top defense attorneys in the City once a week."

"Yeah, I could see that. It seems to me that lawyers are very driven people. They expect a lot from themselves. They also expect a lot from their women."

"Well, we work very hard, you know. So, I guess we like to play just as hard when we can."

Bright rose to his feet. "Your Honor, can Mr. Wynn be instructed to steer this examination away from a detailed analysis of his leisure activities and back to the case being presented to the jury?"

"Mr. Wynn, please stick closely to the matter at hand."

"Yes, of course, Your Honor. I apologize. Miss Dull, how long did you and the defendant date each other?"

"It was a total of about three years– on and off."

"On and off?"

"Yeah, we sort of split up a couple of times and had our falling outs, you know."

"Tell us about one of your falling outs."

"I don't really know what to say about it. There was one time we were supposed to get together with these friends of his who were part of some sort of artist group that he belonged to. They used to get together and do artist things, you know, like smoke cigarettes and drink beer and talk about Rembrandt or Picasso or something. They used to meet once a week and they'd hire a model and do paintings or drawings. I think the group had been around a while– like fifty years or something. So, Tuesday night came along and off he'd go to this guy's loft and do his drawings and come home drunk and tired at about 11:30. So, one day he brings this guy home with him after the drawing session and he says that his girlfriend locked him out and he's been staying at the guy's loft where they hold their meetings, but that guy got tired of that arrangement. So, this guy was kicked out and Mark was suckered into giving him a place to sleep. Now, I ask you, where the hell was this guy going to sleep in our place? There wasn't enough room as it was, with all his crap everywhere and the easel and his tabouret and everything. I told him this, but he said the guy had no place to go. I said that I didn't care. He could sleep on the subway for all I cared. So this goes back and forth for twenty minutes and in the meantime this guy flops down on our couch and falls asleep! Just like that! Well, you know if he's gonna make use of our couch without even asking, he's bound to make use of anything and everything we had without asking. Well, Mark didn't want to hear that. He said the guy was tired because he hadn't had a good night's sleep since his girlfriend kicked him out. So I said, 'aww, that's too bad. Maybe he'd be more comfortable in our bed?' The he said I was being ridiculous. The poor guy was just having a run of bad luck and needed a place to crash for a night or two and I was being un-Christian. Un-Christian? I'm Jewish, for chrissakes! Of course I'm being un-Christian. Then he said that Christ was a Jew, and I told him that I didn't care if Christ was an atheist, this guy was not Jesus Christ and, if he was, he should sleep in the barn, since that's what he did in the New Testament. So Mark tells me I'm just trying to win the argument and I told him I'm not having a total stranger whose own girlfriend thought so poorly of him that she kicked him out and changed the locks. And he tells me I'm judging the guy and I don't know all the circumstances behind that. I told him I knew enough to make an intelligent decision, which he was incapable of making. He didn't appreciate *that* at all– especially since it was a cheap shot, I admit. I said that he didn't know thing one about this guy and I wanted him out of the house immediately. He told me he knew the guy was all right because he was a friend of the guy that rents that loft where they get together and draw. I told him it wasn't a very persuasive argument, because it sounded to me like that guy was a scumbag, too, and that old 'any friend of so-and-so's is a friend of mine' crap won't fly in my house. So he says he thought it was *our* house, and I reminded him that my name was on the lease– which it was, because he didn't have a regular job and I did. That's when he started calling me names, so I told him to take his new friend and find someplace to sleep together, because he wasn't going to be sleeping with me. So, he said, 'fine, be that way!' and he grabbed his cigarettes and stormed out. I had to call down the stairs to him to get back up the stairs because he forgot something. He forgot his friend, who was still sprawled out on our couch. He said he wasn't responsible for him and that I could do what I wanted with him. I told him I was calling the police and he said he didn't care what I did. That made me mad, so I didn't call the cops."

"You didn't call the police?"

"No, I made some tea instead and the whistling tea kettle woke him up– don't ask me why all our arguing and yelling didn't wake him up– and I had sex with him."

"What?!"

"I had sex with him. On the couch."

"He was a total stranger!"

"Yeah, I suppose. But, I was mad at Mark. He deserved it. He wasn't bad either."

"But, you– I mean, did you even know his name?"

"I think his name is Dean or Dane or something. Don't look so put out. Knowing somebody's name doesn't guarantee anything. How many people get divorced each year? All those people know each other's names, don't they? Did that save them from their misery? No, of course not."

"So you punished Mark Pitt by giving yourself to this so-called nameless man?"

"Yeah. Why? What would *you* have done?"

"What did the defendant do when he found out you'd slept with this man?"

"Oh, I don't think he ever found out– until now, that is. Ha ha!"

"How was that an effective punishment if he didn't know?"

"I don't know. Maybe it wasn't."

"Did you– did that occur– how can I put this? Were you predisposed to have sex with other men as a means by which you punish your boyfriends?"

"Huh? Am I getting you right? Are you asking if I sleep around to get even with my boyfriends?"

"Yes."

"What do you think I am? I almost never do that."

"I'm sorry, Miss Dull, but you must understand that we have to ask these kinds of questions to uncover the truth. Otherwise Mr. Pitt, as he waits on death row, would think he did not get a fair trial."

"I understand. I'm not really upset anyway. You can ask me anything you want– no matter how personal or private– and I'll answer."

"Thank you, Miss Dull. Now, regarding these blow-ups you and the defendant had…"

"I object, Your Honor. Mr. Wynn is characterizing these incidents as blow-ups all on his own. Miss Dull hasn't used that word."

"Sustained."

"All right, she didn't use that word, exactly, but if they're not blow-ups I don't know what they are, Your Honor. The defendant stormed out of the house! I believe that constitutes a blow-up."

"I agree. I have changed my mind. The objection is now overruled. You may proceed, Mr. Wynn."

"Thank you, Your Honor. Miss Dull, did the defendant ever strike you or threaten you in any way?"

"You bet! He was always threatening me."

"When he would threaten you, did you ever fear for your life?"

"Yes and no. He made a lot of racket and that could be pretty upsetting. On the other hand, he's not as big and powerful as you are, for instance, so it wasn't as impressive and scary as it could have been."

"I don't scare you, do I, Miss Dull?"

"Are you trying to?"

"Certainly not. It would be the farthest thing from my mind to scare you. With your so-called ex-boyfriend, though, you could never be sure he wouldn't try to hurt you, could you?"

"I suppose no one can really be one hundred percent sure of anything when it comes to someone's behavior."

"So you were constantly living with the possibility of death hovering over you in the guise of Mark Pitt, weren't you?"

"Huh? Oh, yeah, sure. Death was always hovering. Yes. You could see it in his eyes."

"It sounds like you were a very lucky woman– to have escaped the fate that awaited Miss Averdantis, I mean."

"Oh, yes. Very lucky."

"No more questions, Your Honor."

"Mr. Bright?"

"Thank you, Your Honor. Miss Dull, you testified that my client, Mark Pitt, represented some kind of deadly threat that hung over you all the time."

"Hovered over me."

"Yes, hovered over you. Now, just so that we all have a clearer picture of exactly what this threat was, can you tell us how you pictured this deadly threat was going to be carried out?"

"What do you mean?"

"This hovering threat of death…"

"Yes."

"What did you think was going to happen to you?"

"I don't know."

"Well, what was this threat you talked about?"

"Oh, I don't know. I didn't really talk about it."

"Would you like to talk about it?"

162

"Not really."

"But, you stated there was this threat. What was the threat?"

"I don't know what you mean."

"What was the threat?"

"You keep asking me the same question over and over again. I don't know what to tell you."

"All I want you to tell me is the truth, Miss Dull. What was the threat? That seems like a simple enough question."

"Not to me."

"Look, if I want to cook dinner for myself, there is a threat– however remote– of death by exploding oven or asphyxiation by gas, right?"

"Sure."

"If I live in a lousy neighborhood where there's a lot of drug addicts and crime, there is a threat of murder, right?'

"Yeah."

"So, what was the threat from living with Mark Pitt?"

"I don't know." She shrugged her shoulders.

"Who does? Mr. Wynn?"

"Your Honor, the witness cannot be expected to answer what I do or don't know."

"Sustained. Do not answer that last question, Miss Dull."

"Let me ask in another way. Did my client state at any time that he intended to kill you?"

"What do you mean, like did he say, 'I'm gonna kill you'?"

"Yes. Did he say that?"

"Let's see. No, not exactly."

"What did he say, then?"

"About killing me?"

"Yes."

"Not much."

"Miss Dull, you sat up here and talked and talked and talked about bums and erections and shoes and vomit and vodka– all manner of things, but when it comes time to say something of real substance against my client, all you can muster are responses like: 'I don't know' and 'Not exactly'. Now tell us, has Mark Pitt ever represented a real threat to your well-being?"

"When you put it that way, I'd have to say no, he did not. I sorta liked him, you know? The problem with him was that he was more interested in his artwork than anything else in his life– including me. He was good in bed, of course, or I wouldn't have stuck with him. He was especially good when he finished something, like a big painting, if he was happy with how it came out. He sorta disappeared while he was working on something, though. It was like he wasn't even there– mentally, I mean. Not like he was retarded, but I mean that he was physically present, but his mind was in his artwork. One of the reasons I liked to pose for him was that I could spend time with him. Otherwise, forget about it."

"So there was no threat of death, was there?"

"There was more of a threat that he would disappear into one of his paint-ings. I suppose it was worth it, though. I mean, he is a really good artist. At least, I think so. I liked his paintings, and I don't usually give a crap about art. I don't know what happened after we split up. Frankly, I don't even really know *why* we split up. That's not true. I walked out on him when he took up with her. There's no way in hell that I'm going to put up with a boyfriend who screws around on me. Well, I didn't walk out. I kicked him out."

"You are referring to Miss Averdantis, I assume. Hadn't you already kicked him out when he met Miss Averdantis?"

"Yeah, her. Probably I had. Who knows? It's all a blur. But, to be perfectly honest, I blame myself a little for him taking up with her."

"Why is that?"

"I think he took my infidelity kinda hard, you know? It made him uncomfortable. It probably hurt his pride. I didn't think he cared enough to notice, but he did."

"How did you know he found out?"

"He started doing paintings of me getting screwed by all his friends, that's how."

"Had you, in fact, had relations with any of his friends?"

"Yeah, most of them. That's why he did those paintings. They were good– very erotic– filthy, in fact. I think he sold every one of them. I tell you it's quite an experience to see yourself hanging on the wall of a gallery. There you are, larger than life, taking it from behind by one of your boyfriend's friends. He really knew me well."

"Isn't it true, Miss Dull, that my client never abused you or did anything to cause you to fear for your well-being?"

"No, it's *not* true. He did lots of things that made me fear for my well-being."

"Really? What, for instance?"

"Oh, I don't know– well, one time we all went out together– I think it was Cinco de Mayo or something. So one of his friends wanted to go to Abladape's on West Sweeny, which would have been okay with me, but Mark wanted to go to this little dive all the way down by the docks. He said they had authentic Mexican food there and that we'd love it. He said we'd have an evening we'd never forget. I was a little worried right off the bat, you know, because nobody goes down there after dark– not respectable people anyway. So we all piled into this guy's Vista Cruiser station wagon– that scared me, too, because it was just an old rust bucket ready to give up the ghost. Nothing worked on that thing. The radio didn't work, the windows didn't roll down, the turning signals were busted, the thing would stall at every light, it had no shocks. He had the hood tied down with twine. I wasn't sure we'd even get there. And I sure as hell didn't want to get stuck there if it died on us, you know? Anyway this place was this tiny, dingy, little, hole-in-the-wall dump. I thought I saw a cock-a-roach when we walked in, but I wasn't sure because it was so damn dark in there. I wouldn't be surprised if it turns out the whole floor was crawling with them. I swear I had the willies the whole time I was there. So, we order beers– sorry, *cervesas*– and I'm looking at the menu, which is a blackboard over an old refrigerator and Mark says forget about the menu. He says he's gonna order the house special. Okay, whatever. He says we're gonna flip over it. So the owner comes over and he orders 'pulmones burro'. The owner looked kinda surprised and he looked at all of us and sort of smiled. That's when I got suspicious. I asked Mark what 'pulmones burro' was and he just said not to worry about it and that it's a great delicacy south of the border. The guy brings the chips and these things are so greasy I swear you could practically see through them. They were like translucent with oil. So, I asked Mark how he heard about this place and he said he went to school with a guy whose family is part-owner. So, I asked him if his friend had ever eaten there. He said he grew up eating their food and what was I worried about? He said I was being a killjoy. He liked to accuse me of being a killjoy, but *he* was usually the one who ruined everybody's good time, because he always went too far. So, a woman brings out this platter– I don't know if she's his wife or mother or what– with this steaming pile of colorless stuff with cheese and onions and rice and some kind of chopped green garnish. So, I asked her what the stuff was and she just grins like an idiot and takes a couple of breaths like she's teaching a child-birthing class and says something like 'pulmones good' or 'very good' or something. I should have known right then, but I just thought Mexicans are quirky, you know? I mean, every culture has their pet expressions. I've never been overseas, so I don't know. Anyway, we start eating this stuff and it's really not too bad. It's a little chewy, but you could say the same thing about a lot of meats. The owner kept the beers coming and we kept up with him and we all had a pretty good time. When it came time to pay the check, it took us like half an hour to figure out who owed what, and it turned out he had overcharged us by twenty bucks! We tried to tell them that, but the guy wouldn't admit it, so we stiffed him on the tip. We gave him *nada*, as they say. Well, *that* was not the best idea, because the next thing we knew, this guy's whole family– his brothers, cousins, uncles, *tios*, whatever– comes downstairs and they start threatening us. So we managed to beat it out of there and get back to the car and the damn thing won't start! So the lunk-head who drove us there gets out and he's fumbling with the twine that's holding the hood down and the Mexicans are coming down the street from the restaurant and suddenly I feel really sick to my stomach and I can't get the stupid door to open because the handle falls off in my hand. The next thing I know I'm retching and somebody pulls me out of the car from the other side and the Mexicans are there and I throw up all my chunks of 'pulmones burro' and rice and beans and chips and beer. So the Mexicans almost step in it and they think that's really disgusting and they yell some stuff in Mexican and turn around and go back. The whole way back they're yelling curses at us, and Mark is yelling things like 'there's your tip, Pedro!' back at them. One of the Mexicans picks up a bottle and hurls it at us and just misses me, because I'm bending over to vomit, and hits the back window of the car and shatters it. Then one of the other guys with us, whose name is also Mark, he says *he* doesn't feel too good and the next thing we knew he was throwing up, too. What an evening."

"So, how did the defendant make you fear for your well-being?"

"What do you mean? Weren't you listening?"

Bright remained silent.

"He put all of us in extreme danger."

"By taking you down to that restaurant?"

"Yeah! And I'm not sure you could really legitimately call it a restaurant, by the way. If you read the transcript you'll see I avoided using that word."

"Did you feel that my client put you in this dangerous situation– and I do feel that you were in danger, by the way– did he do this on purpose to cause you harm?"

"Well, no, not really."

"Did he habitually put you in danger?"

"Habitually? Um, no. I can't say that exactly."

"Miss Dull, can you recall any other time that he put you in danger?"

"Well, there was the time that we went to Rosterdam Park we were climbing the rocks by the lake and he made me jump from one rock to another and I almost didn't make it. Does that count?"

"Sure, Miss Dull. That counts. Did you two split up because of how much danger he subjected you to?"

"No, it was a more conventional reason."

"You told us that my client took up with Miss Averdantis. Is that how you two finally split up?"

"Yeah. It's not a very exciting story, really. I mean if you're looking for some dirt, you'll probably be disappointed. We just sorta drifted apart, you know? A lot of couples drift apart. It's nothing new."

"Was there any other infidelity on his part?"

"I don't know. He never told me."

"Didn't you care? Weren't you curious?"

"I suppose not."

"No more questions."

13. Stanley Calvin

"Mr. Wynn, you may proceed with your next witness."

"Thank you, Your Honor. The State calls Calvin Stanley."

A man shuffled oddly up the aisle and past the swinging gate and approached the witness stand. The clerk held out the greasy-looking Bible and swore him in.

The man shuffled into the witness box and dropped clumsily into the chair, sitting with his legs splayed out.

"Mr. Stanley, please tell the court what you do for a living."

"I am retired now, but I used to be a performer."

"What sort of performer? Were you a singer or an actor?"

"No, I had a novelty act."

"What did you do?"

"I danced."

"I noticed that you walked stiffly, Mr. Stanley. Did you injure yourself performing your act?"

"No, I've always walked this way. I was born without knees."

"Born without knees? How could you dance, then?"

"Well, you see that's the point. People paid money to see me *try* to dance. I was a hit– at least for a while. I mean I was booked in all the swankest joints. I was very well-known on the circuit– from Boston all the way to Kansas City. I twirled and stumbled around the stage. The audiences really ate it up. They couldn't get enough of me. My act was known as "Stiff Stanley, The Kneeless Nijinsky." I pulled in some real bucks in them days. Real bucks, I tell you. And the dames– oh, boy, the dames!"

"Did you dance with a partner?"

"No, I always worked alone. I guess I just never found the right partner."

"What happened to that career, Mr. Stanley?"

"I guess I was sorta forced to retire."

"If you don't mind my saying so, you hardly look old enough to retire. In fact, you don't look a day over 55."

"I ain't. I'm 52."

"They say that the first thing that goes is the knees, but since that can't be true in your case, why did you retire?"

"Well, it's like this– I think the times have changed and people's tastes have changed. They were no longer lining up to see The Kneeless Nijinsky hobble and totter around the stage or try to do a soft-shoe. That, plus I had a little problem with my booking agent."

"Mr. Stanley, are you acquainted with the defendant, the so-called Mr. Mark Pitt?"

"I am."

"How well do you know the defendant?"

"I sorta know him very well."

"Would you say that you know him as well as one would know– let's say– a close friend, for example?"

Calvin pondered for a moment. "I'm not sure. I don't really have any close friends, so it's hard to say. I suppose I would say that I know Mark Pitt better in some ways. It's different."

"Mr. Stanley, did you know Mr. Pitt's now-deceased girlfriend, Evelyn Averdantis?"

"Yes."

"As well as you knew Mr. Pitt?"

"Yes, I did. Poor girl."

"Why do you say 'poor girl', Mr. Stanley?"

"Because of what he did to her."

"What was that? Tell the court. What did Mr. Mark Pitt do to poor Evelyn Averdantis?"

"He destroyed the poor girl. He took everything she had and used it and left her nothing. He performed unspeakable acts upon her person."

"How do you know he performed these unspeakable acts?"

"I saw him perform them. I saw him with my own eyes."

"You witnessed these acts?"

"Yes."

"What exactly were these so-called unspeakable acts? Can you describe them?"

"If I could, they wouldn't be unspeakable, would they?"

"No, I suppose not. Did Mark Pitt commit these acts against Miss Averdantis's will?"

"Sure. She didn't want him doin' that stuff all the time."

"Were they sexual acts?"

"Hard to say. Yeah, why not?"

"Can you describe them?"

"Yeah, sure. She was slender and had long, brown hair– that is, before he yanked it all. He was about five foot..."

"No, that's not what I meant. I meant can you describe the sexual acts that Pitt committed against Evelyn Averdantis's will?"

"Maybe not. I wasn't right next to them. D'you know what I mean?"

"Are you sure they were sexual acts?"

"Look, I know a sexual act when I see one. Sure, they was sexual acts. What do you call it when somebody makes you lie on your back and makes you put your legs behind your head? I call that a sexual act."

"Is that what he had her do?"

"He did lots more to her. I saw a lot of stuff going on there. He'd make her do stuff with other women. He'd put these great spotlights on her and make her squat there while he pleasured himself."

"You watched him do this?"

"Not exactly watched him, no. He'd back off, out of my field of vision, so I couldn't actually see him. But, what else would he be doing, huh?"

"Did you see Mark Pitt actually kill Evelyn Averdantis?"

"No, unfortunately, I did not. I never saw them during the daytime."

"Mr. Stanley, in your opinion, did the performance of those unspeakable acts– as you so quaintly put it– lead to the demise of Evelyn Averdantis?"

"I object, your honor. The witness is not a medical expert and is not qualified to say."

"Sustained."

"Okay, we'll leave it at that, then. Thank you, Mr. Stanley. Your witness, Mr. Bright."

Bright approached the witness. "What exactly did he take from her, Mr. Stanley?"

"Mark Pitt? Everything! He took her dignity. He took her– her self-respect. He took her confidence. He took– he even took her *hair*, for chrissakes! Poor girl."

"You must remain calm, Mr. Stanley."

"Do you know what he used to do to her?"

"No, what did he do to her, Mr. Stanley?"

"He'd– do things to her– late at night. He did things to her body. One time, he tied her up. He brought in somebody else and they both did things to her. Then they did things to each other, right over her! It was awful."

"Would they invite you to be there when these things were done?"

"Well, no, they wouldn't. Not really, anyhow."

"Not really? Were you present when these unspeakable horrors were performed?"

"Sure I was."

"There, in the room?"

"Um, no, not *in* the room. But, I was sorta close by."

"So, you didn't actually see these things you claim were done to Miss Averdantis?"

"Yes, I did."

"You just said you were not in the room. Was the door open?"

"The door? No, I doubt it. I don't know, really."

"I'm just a little puzzled, Mr. Stanley. How you were able to see these unspeakable acts when you weren't in the room and the door wasn't open?"

Calvin looked around the floor of the courtroom and didn't respond.

"Where exactly were you when you supposedly saw these so-called unspeakable acts? Were you perhaps on the roof of the building next door? Or on the fire escape? Where were you?"

Calvin shifted uncomfortably in his seat, but remained mute.

"You seem to be having a lot of trouble answering the question, Mr. Stanley– or should I say Mr. Calvin?"

"Stanley is fine."

"I'm sure it is. In fact, I'm sure you'd prefer it, wouldn't you?"

"Yeah, sure."

"And why is *that*, Mr. Calvin?"

"I– I don't get what you mean."

"I think you do. I think that every time I call you by your real name you bristle with fear. Isn't that right, Mr. Calvin? Isn't it true that the only people who call you by your real name these days are law enforcement officials?"

173

"Huh? No, that's not true. Well, maybe it's true. I don't know! You got me all confused. I can't think right. There's not enough room for my legs in this stinkin' box."

"What floor did the defendant and Miss Averdantis live on, Mr. Calvin?"

"I don't remember exactly."

"You ever take the elevator up to their floor?"

"I don't know. Maybe I did. I must've, because I have trouble climbing stairs."

"Maybe you did? You must have? Are you aware that the building in question has no elevator?"

"Huh? No, I didn't remember. I probably used the stairs every time. I don't know."

"What was the nature of your relationship with Mr. Pitt?"

"Huh?"

"The nature of your relationship. Were you on speaking terms with Mr. Pitt?"

"I can't recall if we ever really spoke to each other or not."

"Isn't it true that you were *not* on speaking terms with the defendant?"

"I don't know. Maybe I wasn't."

"Isn't it true that you were exaggerating when you said that you knew each other by sight?"

"What? Whaddya mean?"

"Isn't it true, Mr. Calvin, that my client and Miss Averdantis didn't know *you* at all, but that you knew them very, very well– by sight, as you say?"

"I told you I knew them by sight."

"You know a lot of people *by sight*, don't you, Mr. Calvin?"

"What's *that* supposed to mean?"

Bright went to his briefcase as Calvin was answering. Fishing through his files, he pulled out a newspaper clipping. He presented it to the witness. "Do you know what this is, Mr. Calvin?"

He stared at the clipping. "Yes."

"Can you speak louder, Mr. Calvin. I don't know if the court heard your answer."

"I said yes!"

"And what is it?"

"It's a newspaper article."

"What is the subject of the article?"

"It's– it's, um– it's about a crime."

"Come now, Mr. Calvin. There's no need to speak in such broad terms. Who's the article about?"

"It's about me."

"Is it an article extolling your talents as a stage performer?"

"It mentions that. It says in it that I'm a stage performer."

Bright approached the witness stand and got right in the face of Calvin. "No need to be shy, Mr. Calvin. You're famous! That article is about your sentencing for being the most notorious peeping tom that this great City has ever known, isn't it?"

Calvin sat quietly.

"This is an article about you, Mr. Calvin. You're a famous man– not for stumbling around in a grotesque parody of Fred Astaire or as a so-called Kneeless Nijinsky. No, your fame is based on the frequency and elaborateness of your escapades as a pervert, isn't it?"

Calvin looked away from the attorney. "I dunno. I guess."

"You were not exaggerating when you said you were well-known from Boston to– where was it? St. Louis?"

"Kansas City."

"Oh, yes. Kansas City." Bright reached into his file folder again. "As a matter of fact, I have another article– this one *is* from Kansas City– that also mentions your name. I must say that you get less-than-rave reviews for your work in this article. Maybe the crime reporter wasn't a fan of dance acts, eh? In fact, he doesn't even *mention* your dance act, unless you consider what he writes about how you dance around the truth. Here, Mr. Calvin, why don't you read this passage for us? This one that's marked in pencil."

"I object, Your Honor! Mr. Bright is torturing the witness. Mr. Stanley has paid his debt to society– many times, in fact. There's certainly no need to rub his face in the misdeeds of his unlucky past."

"Overruled."

"Here, Mr. Calvin. Let's hear about your unlucky past. Read the passage that's marked in pencil. Make it nice and loud– in your best stage voice."

Calvin took the clipping and, with a grim expression on his face, began reading from the article.

> Mr. Calvin was apprehended by police on August 11th, on
> the 800 block of Vista View Avenue in the commission of
> a lewd act. He was spotted by neighbors of the victim,
> Mrs. Abigail Montgomery, while apparently...

Do I really have to read this thing, Judge? I don't understand what this has to do with anything."

"Please read the rest of what Mr. Bright has marked for you to read, Mr. Calvin."

He looked at the paper again.

> ...peeking in at her through her kitchen window. Mr. Cal-
> vin, who gives his address as Pittsburgh, Pennsylvania, is
> a professional dancer performing nightly at the Bijou
> Theatre. He told police he was looking for his friend with
> whom he had taken a walk to "get some fresh air." Calvin
> claimed that the friend had, "suddenly dashed across the
> street, bounded up a front lawn and disappeared into one
> of the homes." He offered no explanation for why his
> friend would have abruptly dashed across the street, nor
> did he offer to name his so-called friend. He was unable
> to explain why his trousers and shorts were bunched

176

around his ankles during his search for the friend other than that his "belt had come undone." He did state to police that he looked through Mrs. Montgomery's curtains rather than knock on her front door because of the very fact that his trousers and shorts were bunched around his ankles and he didn't want to alarm her.

"What altruism you exhibited!"

Wynn rose to his feet. "Your Honor, haven't we heard enough? I don't see that this has any bearing on the case."

"Mr. Bright?"

"I'll move on if Mr. Wynn will allow me to place into evidence the twenty three other articles I have from such cities as Binghamton, New York and Cleveland, Ohio, among others, that all contain similar stories about Mr. Calvin."

"I'll allow that without a challenge, Your Honor."

"All right, Your Honor, I'll move on. What are you, Mr. Calvin?"

"I don't follow."

"I think you do. But, just in case you really don't follow, here's an example. I'm a lawyer. Judge Tuilgy is a judge. People are baseball players or fishmongers or housewives. What are you?"

"I'm retired."

"Evidently not. You're still practicing your primary vocation, aren't you? I mean, how did you see these so-called unspeakably horrific acts that my client committed if you are retired?"

"I *have* retired. I haven't danced in years."

"You may not be a famous kneeless dancer anymore. That much we can all agree on, but you're still practicing your avocation as an infamous pervert aren't you?"

"I'm not a pervert."

"You're not still doing this work?" Bright held up the newspaper clipping.

"No, I'm not."

"Then, if the door wasn't open and you weren't inside the apartment, you couldn't have seen these unspeakable acts, could you?"

Calvin looked at the district attorney, then looked down at his own lap, where his fingers were busy plucking at a loose thread. "No, I guess I couldn't."

"Why are you here, Mr. Calvin?"

"I thought maybe I could, you know, get my name in the papers again– for something other than just, you know, getting arrested. I haven't worked for years. I'm flat broke. I need a job."

"No more questions, Your Honor."

"Mr. Wynn?"

"No more questions."

"You may step down, Mr. Calvin."

From the Highbridge Morning Star:

> The trial of Mark Pitt, accused of murdering his twenty-seven year old live-in girlfriend, Evelyn Averdantis, is certainly beginning to live up to its moniker of Trial of the Century as it finished its third day of testimony yesterday. Lead prosecutor, Ambrose Wynn, husband of beloved celebrity Lynn Maguire, called five witnesses– six, if you count the seeing-eye dog that accompanied arts critic, H.B. Sweatclown in the witness box.
>
> The picture of Mark Pitt that is emerging from the testimony is of a cocky and callous young man, who took what he wanted, so long as it furthered his quest for the holy grail of the art world– fame and fortune.
>
> While none of the witnesses so far has actually provided a motive or even the means by which he was supposed to have committed this awful act, Wynn and his team are doing a fine job drawing an outline around Pitt's guilt in order to indicate its existence.
>
> As has been the pattern so far in this spectacle, these witnesses recounted tales of adultery, revenge, bizarre experimental operations, Norwegian cults, Eastern cults, voyeurism, casual sex and abstract art.
>
> Even the Ringling Bros. would be hard-pressed to provide as much variety and exoticism. The only things Pitt's trial is missing so far are the wild beasts, but who knows what Monday's session may bring?
>
> Pitt faces life in prison, if convicted.

14. Donna Laniny

"Call your next witness, Mr. Wynn."

"Your Honor, The State calls Donna Laniny."

A tall, stiff woman approached the stand. After swearing the oath, she sat in the box and flipped her graying blond ponytail back over her left shoulder.

"Miss Laniny– may I call you Donna, by the way?"

"May I call you Ambrose?"

"Miss Laniny, are you acquainted with the defendant?"

"Yes."

"And were you also acquainted with his victim?"

"Your Honor!"

"Sustained, Mr. Bright."

"Oh, yes. I'm sorry, Your Honor. Miss Laniny, were you also acquainted with *the* victim, Miss Averdantis?"

"Yes."

"What was your relationship to them?"

"I lived upstairs from them."

"How well did you know them?"

"I don't know what you are trying to insinuate."

"I didn't mean anything strange by that. I'm just asking if you were just neighbors or friends perhaps. Maybe you even socialized with them?"

"Me? Socialize with them? No, sir. I lived upstairs from them. And that is all."

"How long did you live upstairs from them?"

"I've been in that apartment for sixteen years."

"So, basically, the whole time that Mr. Pitt and Miss Averdantis were so-called tenants, then?"

"I've been in that apartment for fifteen years."

"I see. So, *not* sixteen years."

"What are you suggesting by that?"

"Well, you said you've been living in your apartment for sixteen years and then changed that to fifteen years."

"I've lived there for sixteen years."

"Sixteen."

"Yes."

"Okay. From your vantage point as an upstairs neighbor, what were you able to observe of the relationship and habits of the defendant and his girl-friend?"

"She worked, he didn't. She cooked and cleaned. He yelled, she whined. She'd get dressed up and he dressed like a bum. When they had sex she made a lot of noise– like a cat. They stayed up late at night. They had friends that came over and stayed in their apartment. Is that the kind of thing you need to know?"

"You seem to be a very observant neighbor, Miss Laniny."

"I had the advantage of spending a lot of time in the stairwell."

"How's that?"

"What I mean is that because I have to spend a lot of time in the stairwell, I get to know more about my neighbors than I would otherwise know. That's all I meant."

"I see. Actually, I take that back. I don't see. Why do you have to spend a lot of time in the stairwell?"

"I don't *have* to really, but I do."

"Why is that?"

"Because of the beast that lives there."

"Where?"

"In the stairwell between my floor and the door to the roof."

"Somebody lives there?"

Laniny chuckled. "You said 'somebody', but it's more of a some*thing* than a some*body*."

"This is that beast that Detective McKenna talked about at the start of the trial. What is it, a homeless person or something?"

"No, it has a home. It lives there. It's been there quite a long time– several years at this point. Let's see…" She counted on her fingers and mouthed some words to herself. "It's been there nine years this October."

"You haven't called the police all this time?"

"What are they going to do?"

"Well, they could take him away and put him in a shelter, for one thing."

"Ha! They can't get it. This thing runs up and hides. Don't you understand? If they come to take it, it'll just scamper up those stairs and disappear in the darkness at the top. It's not going to just sit there waiting for them."

"I'm not sure I understand this. If the 'beast', as you call it, scampers up to the roof, wouldn't the police be able to arrest him there?"

"It."

"What?"

"It– not him. No, they wouldn't be able to arrest it on the roof, because it doesn't go to the roof."

"Where does he– sorry, *it*– go, then?"

"I told you. It goes up and hides in the gloom at the top of the stairs."

"It hides in the gloom?"

"Yes."

"Is the light burned out or something?"

182

"Yes. The beast started hiding on the stairs not long after the light burned out. It's been there ever since."

"You said this so-called beast has been there for almost nine years?"

"That's right."

"Have you asked the super to replace the light in the stairwell?"

"Certainly I have. It doesn't make any difference."

"He won't do it?"

"No, he does it, all right, but the beast puts the light out right away. It wants to be able to hide in the gloom. I appreciate your concern, but there's really no point in even discussing it. It won't go away and it can't be scared away. It's unfortunate, because it used to be a nice building to live in."

"Have the other tenants complained about this– this beast?"

"I'm not sure anyone else has ever seen it."

"How can that be?"

"I told you, it hides in the gloom whenever anyone approaches. I've tried to sneak out to catch it unaware, but it always knows when I do that. It simply darts out of sight and up into the darkness. Honestly, I don't know why you insist that there's some way to handle this. There just isn't. Believe me, I know. I've tried now for almost nine years."

"I still don't understand completely. Has it ever threatened you?"

"Yes and no. It's hard to put into words. It's more of an implied threat. I know, for instance, that I can't move from my apartment. It won't let me."

"Have you tried?"

"Of course I have. I went so far as to rent a truck and packed everything up and whenever I brought boxes downstairs it somehow managed to go down and bring them right back up again. Then, while I was downstairs, it un-packed everything I had already packed. It just wouldn't let me leave."

"Have you thought about just leaving– moving out and going somewhere and leaving everything behind and having someone else get your stuff for you?"

"I can't do that."

"Why not? You could go somewhere and have a professional mover get your belongings."

"I can't. It would know. It would figure it out and find some way to stop it."

"How would it know?"

"I have no idea. It just does. It probably would figure it out before I even tried it. Really, Mr. Wynn, there's no point."

"Miss Laniny, is this beast human?"

"I don't know. I can't even get a good look at it. Based on its abilities and characteristics, I tend to think that it's not human. But, like I said, I haven't even gotten a good look at it– just fleeting glimpses as it scoots up those stairs. It's got powers that seem almost superhuman sometimes, but it's got the spite and pettiness and selfishness of a regular human. I don't know."

"No more questions."

"Mr. Bright?"

"Thank you, Your Honor. Miss Laniny, to the best of your knowledge, is it possible that the other tenants in the building also know about this beast of yours?"

"As far as I know, I am the only tenant who knows about it. I've mentioned it to other tenants over the years, but it seems to me that no one was very interested."

"Why do you think that is?"

"I suppose that it's because it stays up at the top of the stairs and they don't have to deal with it. I'm the only tenant that has direct contact with it."

"You say you have direct contact with it. Have you tried communicating with it? Do you ever have conversations with it? Anything like that?"

"No. Well, when I say I've had direct contact, I don't mean I've touched it, although it has brushed past me on more than one occasion. I mean, I'm really the only one so far who has seen it. And I have spoken to it, but it never responds. It just hides up there in the darkness, holding its breath."

"So, you *have* seen it. Can you describe it?"

"No, because I've just seen fleeting glimpses of it– you know, like a shadow moving swiftly up the stairs. It's dark. That's about all I can say, really. And it's big."

"Dark and big."

"Yes."

"Does it speak?"

"Not to me."

"To anyone?"

"I couldn't say. I only know it doesn't speak to me– or around me, for that matter. If you're asking if I *think* it speaks, I'd say no, probably not. I think it would have said *something* in the nine years it's been lurking in the stair-well."

"Miss Laniny, do you believe it is capable of violence?"

"I suppose we are *all* capable of violence."

"Do you have any reason to believe it is *not* capable of violence?"

"No."

"Has it ever tried to break into your apartment?"

"No, I don't think so. It's been in my apartment, but only when I had left the door unlocked and only when it was thwarting me from moving away."

"Do you believe that it would try to enter anyone else's apartment for any reason?"

"I have no idea."

"To the best of your knowledge, is it *capable* of doing so?"

"Oh, sure. If they left the door unlocked, that thing could easily get into any apartment. That thing is fast, remember. I don't understand why you're asking me all these questions about the beast. You don't think…"

"I'm just asking the questions, Miss Laniny. The jury will decide what to make of it all. What do you do for a living?"

"Me? I used to be an entertainer. I had a children's show on morning television."

"And now?"

"I, um, pick up some money, you know, doing odd jobs, here and there."

"You're no longer an entertainer?"

"No, that's all in the past now."

"So, what do you do for a living now?"

Laniny sighed and brushed off her lap. "To tell you the truth, I can't work anymore."

"Are you on disability?"

"No, not on disability. I *should* be on disability, but I'm not."

"Why is it you're not working, then?"

"I hate to harp on it, but it's that damn beast. Sorry, Judge."

"What does it have to do with the beast?"

"It won't let me work."

"What do you mean, it won't let you work?"

"It won't let me work. I can't hold down a job. I start working somewhere and before you know it, the beast fools with my lock and I can't get out the door in the morning. Then, once it's satisfied I'll be late for work, it will release the lock, but too late. I've lost many jobs that way and I've finally given up looking for work. What's the point? I'm sorry. I'm not mad at you. I'm just exasperated." Tears welled up in her eyes and she wept into her hands. She continued speaking through her sobs. "I just can't! I just can't! I don't know! I tried and tried! I just can't!"

"Please, Miss Laniny, pull yourself together."

"What for? What's the point? You have no idea! Oh, god! None of you can know! Look at me! Look what it's done to me!" She looked up from her hands, her face red and soaked with tears. "I used to be beautiful. You didn't know that, did you?"

"No. I'm sorry, I mean I..."

"That's okay. How could you? I'm not as old as I look, you know. How old would you say I am? Go ahead, guess. How old, eh?"

"Really, Miss Laniny, I don't think..."

"Oh, never mind. What's the point? I lost my composure just now, but I really have become resigned to my fate. I really have. It's not all bad. I take comfort in believing that this beast won't allow anything bad to happen to me– you know, *really* bad, like what happened to her."

"Miss Laniny, no one knows this beast better than you do. Do you think it's possible that this beast could have snuck downstairs and gotten into Evelyn Averdantis's apartment and killed her?"

"Why would it have done that?"

"Is it *possible*?"

She shrugged and turned her palms up. "Is it possible? Yes, I suppose it's possible."

"Thank you, Miss Laniny. No more questions."

15. Catherine Prawn

"Your Honor, The State calls Miss Catherine Prawn."

A voluptuous young woman wiggled her way to the witness stand and took the oath. She wore clothing that strongly suggested the details of her concealed anatomy. She carried a few extra pounds on her frame, and each of those pounds served to enhance her already-intriguing physique, at the same time testing the integrity of the material of her clothing. This fact did not go unnoticed by all present, and Judge Tuilgy was seen to sit up just a little straighter in order to pay closer attention to her testimony.

"Miss Prawn– may I call you Cathy?"

"If you have to."

Wynn smiled eagerly. "Cathy, I hope you feel comfortable and at ease as I ask you these questions. You'll let me know if you feel anything other than that, won't you?"

"Sure."

"Very good. Now, please tell the court what you do for a living."

"I'm a model."

"What sort of model, specifically?"

"A figure model."

"And I'm certain that you are an excellent model." Wynn rubbed his hands together. "Who employs you to do your modeling?"

She ticked off the employers on her fingers. "The Community College, The Fine Art Guild on M Street, the H.S.C.A."

"What's that? The H.S. what?"

"The High School of Creative Arts."

"Ah, of course. *They* hire you to model?"

"Why are you surprised? They have a great art program. I model there twice a week."

"As I understand it, you do your figure modeling in the nude. Is that correct?" There was a pronounced murmur in the courtroom– some audible oohs and aahs, as well.

"Yeah."

"I'm just– I don't know. I was thinking that it was sort of surprising, that's all. I just can't picture you posing in front of a bunch of high school kids while they just sit there drawing or painting."

"On the contrary, I think you *are* picturing me posing nude in front of a class of high school art students. I'll tell you one thing– they're a lot cooler about it than you are, Mr. Wynn. Speaking of which, you might want to take a cool drink or something. You're all red and sweaty."

"Yes, thank you. It's just that- um, it is a little stuffy in this courtroom. Miss– I mean Cathy, you listed several institutions that hire you to pose for artistic purposes. Do you also pose for private individuals?"

"Why? You thinking of hiring me?"

Wynn coughed and turned a slightly darker shade of red. "Why, no. That's not why I asked. I'm certainly not an artist. You'd be shocked if you saw my drawings."

"You'd be shocked if you saw some of my poses."

"I suppose I would…"

There was a long pause, during which Wynn seemed to go into a trance.

"Mr. Wynn?"

"Hmm? Oh! I'm sorry, Your Honor. I, um– it *is* hot in here, isn't it?" Wynn walked over to his table and poured ice water for himself. He gulped down half a glass before returning to the witness. "Miss Prawn, I'm a little curious about this modeling thing. I mean, it's not a profession I've had much experience with and I don't know much about it. You'll have to bear with me."

"That's all right, Mr. Wynn. I'm bare with a lot of people."

Wynn's face went blank again.

"That was model humor. You've heard of stand-up comedy. We have recumbent comedy."

"Yes, of course. I knew that. That's very funny. Do you cut-up while you're posing?"

"Most of the time we have to act like we have lockjaw or rigor mortis or something. Most art classes don't like the models to interact with the students. They can get distracted from paying strict attention to the body."

"I find that hard to believe."

"You seem to be having a hard time with this whole thing, Mr. Wynn. Believe me, it may be hard at first, but once you get used to it, it's not so hard anymore."

"Well, you must understand that most of us perform our jobs staring at paperwork all day. I spend most of my days reading and writing briefs."

"I work without briefs."

"Ha! You really are clever. It's no wonder they won't let you talk to the students. You'd have them in stitches."

"That's another thing that separates me from the artists."

"What's that?"

"While they're in stitches, I perform *without* a stitch."

"Ha ha!"

"No, seriously, the whole set-up is a model of efficiency. It's all pretty simple really. The pose is struck, the timer starts and the students race against the clock to come up with something resembling the human form."

"And do they?"

"Sometimes. Sometimes they make something that actually looks a little like me. Sometimes they draw something that, if it existed in the real world, wouldn't live very long."

"Do these so-called art students ever freak out when you drop your drawers?"

"No, they're pretty cool– well, when I say they're pretty cool, they may not be, but they are so worried about not looking cool that they play it as cool as they can. But, I don't just stand there on the model platform and drop my drawers, as you so bluntly put it."

"How does that work exactly?

"One place I work has a screen that I go behind and change into my robe. Then I come out from behind the curtain and get up on the platform and– *voila*! Creative Arts has a changing booth."

"Like Superman, eh?"

"If you insist."

"I meant like Superman changing in the phone booth."

"Yeah. Anyway, the model disrobes once he or she gets on the platform and the pose begins."

"So, there are men that do this sort of thing, too?"

"Are you pulling my leg?"

"That's the farthest thing from my mind."

"Somehow I doubt that my leg is the farthest thing. Yes, there are men who do figure modeling, too. There are more female models than male. There are just more jobs for women in this business."

"I can believe that. I mean, if I were faced with a choice of drawing you, for example, versus, let's say, Mr. Bright, over there, I'd pick you one hundred percent of the time."

"But, if you were doing a painting or sculpture of Hercules, I wouldn't fit the bill, would I?"

"Neither would Mr. Bright. I can tell you that I have no desire to depict Hercules, regardless of who is posing for it."

"Don't feel bad. There are a lot of guys like you in the art world."

"What do you mean?"

"Oh, you know, guys that dabble in drawing because it's the only chance they get to look at a young woman in the nude. Those are the types that don't have the guts to go to a sleazy girlie bar. Or maybe they don't have the money for a hooker. I don't know. All I know is that they're the ones that look at your breasts even when they're drawing your hands. It's a wonder the fingernails don't end up looking like nipples. It's pitiful, really."

"Oh, I don't know. I don't think there's anything wrong with appreciating an attractive female."

"There's more to modeling than just being an attractive female, you know. It's not just standing around, looking voluptuous and alluring. The model is an integral part of the creative process. Just like not everybody can paint or draw, not everybody can model– regardless of how stunningly good-looking they are."

"I'm sure you're right. Not everybody can sit still– even for five minutes."

"That's not the point. Look, a corpse can sit still for as long as you can stand the smell, but do you think a corpse makes a good model?"

"I don't know. I would think that it would."

"Nope."

"Why not? You can move it to any position and it never complains. I guess if it had rigor mortis, you'd have a helluva time bending it into a pose."

"That's not the point. A corpse is as creatively and interactively dead as it is physically dead. The best professional models participate in the creation of the artwork. They give something. They exude something through their gesture. It's an energy– a vibe– an attitude, maybe– that the artist senses and, in turn, imbues his or her work with. It's a collaboration. Do you understand?"

"It makes sense, the way you put it, but I'm not sure how you can capture a vibe on paper– unless you have one of those machines like a lie-detector machine. Those devices can detect the most nuanced electromagnetic impulses on the subject's skin."

"Good luck getting a lie detector to paint an image of Joan of Arc."

"No, that wouldn't be feasible. Still, how do you think artists can pick up on that sort of thing? Do you believe that artists are more sensitive? Do they have some kind of superhuman powers of perception? And, if they are superhuman in some way, why haven't they risen to the top and taken control of society?"

"First of all, I didn't say they are superhuman. Sure, it's possible that artists can use their perceptions more effectively to create great works, but it's also true that certain people use the same sort of sensitivities to heal the sick or teach children or nurture plants."

192

"Come on, Miss Prawn. You're not telling me that plants have an attitude or a vibe like models do, are you?"

"I don't want to get into that argument about whether or not you should be playing Bach records for your begonias. I only used that as an example, because some people have what you call a 'green thumb'. Well, what exactly *is* a 'green thumb'? Maybe it's the same as a good draftsman having a 'black thumb'. Are you following me? I have a friend who is a musician and he said that a model is like a musical composition. He also told me what the difference is between a model and a musical composition."

"What is the difference?"

"You can find bars in a musical composition, but you find models in bars."

"Ha ha! And in the old men's magazines, you could find bars on top of the models! You know, across the vital bits."

"You would know best about that. My friend said that a model is like a composition because a great musician can make great music from a great composition. A great musician can't make great music from a lousy composition. A bad musician can't make great music from a great composition. You see? It's like that with art. Without the artist or musician, it's just a pose or a composition– and maybe not a good one– but a composition is not music, nor is a posing model art. It's a collaborative effort."

"I think I see precisely what you mean. So now, are you, as a model, a composer of poses?"

"Maybe you could be an artist, Mr. Wynn."

"How's that?"

"To be able to see precisely, as you phrased it– to *really* see– is one of the keystones to drawing and painting."

"You mean other than just having keen eyesight, I take it?"

"To really see something exactly as it is, and not as you presume it is, is at the core of drawing the face or the figure."

"I'm not sure I would presume to draw *your* figure, Cathy."

"I don't know the word– maybe it's assume. What I'm trying to say is that people think they know what the human body looks like, but they don't.

193

When they draw it, they come up with a sort of schematic version. It's only through practice and observation that people can drop those pre-conceived notions and draw what's really there."

"Okay. Good. Now, Miss Prawn, you work for private artists as well as institutions, correct?"

"That's right."

"Have you worked for many individual artists?"

"I've worked for maybe twenty or twenty-five individual painters and sculptors over the years."

"Have you modeled for the defendant, Mr. Pitt?"

"Yes."

"What did you do for him?"

"I modeled for him many times over the last two years. He had me for eight or ten sessions. If I remember correctly, I did a couple of sessions where he drew me and then I posed several weeks for three paintings he did."

"What types of poses did Mr. Pitt have you take?"

"Uh, let's see. For the drawings, they tended to be the usual sort of twisting, standing poses and a few kneeling or reclining. The paintings were more unconventional."

"What did he have you do for the paintings?"

"What do you mean? What kind of poses?"

"Yes."

"They were more in the nature of what you might call overtly erotic."

"Weren't they, in fact, obscene?"

"I didn't think so. I guess if you're an old lady, you might think they were obscene."

Wynn pulled a few 8x10 photographs from his paperwork and showed them to Prawn. "Miss Prawn– Cathy– please take a look at these pictures. Is that you in those photos?"

"No. These are pictures of Mark Pitt's paintings."

"But it was you that posed for those paintings, is that correct?"

"Yes."

"This photo here has a female form, lying on her back with her legs spread. She's holding her legs up with her hands behind her knees. Is that correct?"

"Yes."

"You posed for that?"

"Yes."

"You don't consider that obscene?"

"What, the painting? Or the posing?"

"Hmm? Well, I suppose the painting."

"No."

"You don't consider the painting obscene?

"No, I don't."

"The pose, then?"

"Not that either."

"You mean to tell me that, if juror number three over there dropped down on the floor, naked, and held her legs back and apart like this," he pointed to the photo, "you wouldn't consider that obscene?"

"Who, her?" Prawn took a long at juror number three, who looked extremely uncomfortable. "I don't think she's do something like that– not here anyway."

"That's not the point. Just answer the question, Miss Prawn."

"I don't think it's nice to comment on her like that."

"Your Honor, can the witness be instructed to…"

"Mr. Wynn, can you use an example other than one of the jury to make your point?"

"Not as dramatically, Your Honor. Look, Miss Prawn, do you think that– let's see– if *I* were to get on my knees and... Never mind. Let's move on."

"Mr. Wynn, do *you* think it's obscene?"

"Me?"

"Yes. Do you think it's obscene?"

"I'm really in no position to comment. I'm the prosecuting attorney on this case. Cathy, if you don't consider this type of thing obscene, what *do* you consider obscene?"

"How much waste there is of the Earth's natural resources. Pollution. Mass starvation. War."

"What does that have to do with lewd displays?"

"You said obscene– not lewd. Of course it's a lewd display, but I still say it's not obscene. I don't consider anything I do with my body while I pose for artwork as being obscene."

"All right, let's drop this whole subject. It's going nowhere. You obviously have an odd take on what constitutes..."

Bright bounced to his feet. "Your Honor! It is not for Mr. Wynn to characterize Miss Prawn's standards about obscenity, regardless of whether *he* thinks they're odd or not. If the court were to hear some of Mr. Wynn's standards about various things..."

"That's quite enough, Mr. Bright. Let's not engage in a war of personal standards for obscenity. Do you have any further questions for the witness, Mr. Wynn?"

"Yes, Your Honor. Miss Prawn, as you have testified, you've posed for many artists in your modeling career. Would you say that the demands made upon you by the defendant, Mr. Pitt, were some of the most extraordinary demands made upon you?"

"No, not really. I mean, he's certainly not one of the most conservative, traditional artists I work with, but he's not the most outlandish either."

"There are artists who are even more outlandish than Mark Pitt?"

"Oh, yeah. Listen, I posed for an abstract artist who did these gigantic can-vases– I don't know if you really want to hear this."

"Miss Prawn, we must get all the necessary facts in this case and let the jury decide what the truth is in the end."

"Funny you should say that."

"What?"

"'In the end.' The reason I chuckled is that this artist I started to tell you about that artist who did these gigantic canvases– are you sure you need to know about this?"

"Yes, Miss Prawn. Please proceed."

"Well, this artist, who is *very* well known, though I'm not sure he'd want his trade secrets given out, so I won't tell you his name, he does these huge abstract paintings. The thing is, they're *not* really abstract. They're really figure studies– only you'd never know it. I think that's why he's so success-ful. What he does is take a body part and zoom in on it really close up and that's what he paints. So, he's got paintings of certain body parts or parts of body parts that are painted twelve feet by twelve feet."

"So? The artist Chuck Close does that sort of thing. What makes this guy's work so remarkable?"

"Chuck Close paints portraits. This artist paints body parts. Do you under-stand what I'm saying?"

"What do you mean, like feet and hands and the like?"

"No, like– do you really need to know this?"

"Yes."

"Like an anus or a nipple or a little toe or a, you know, vagina. The thing is he crops the image and plays with the colors a little so that you'd be hard-pressed to recognize that it *is* a body part. So, why I brought it up is that he works from live models– not photos– and he's switched now, but he used to use these magnifying visor things so he could get really close to the model's body part to see it close-up."

"When you say 'he's switched now,' what does he do now?"

"He uses this fancy closed-circuit camera system– like a TV– well, it *is* a TV, but it's not, you know, broadcast anywhere. It's just in his studio. So instead of having to constantly go back and forth between his painting and the model, he just stays up on the scaffold and looks into his TV screen, which he keeps up there with him. The camera part is rigged up with a special close-up lens so it stays in focus."

"Is the model in another room from where he is, then?"

"She could be, with the system he has, but she's still on the padded table he has in the studio. It's really the same as before except for the camera poked into your crotch or backside or armpit instead of him peering in. He still comes down for a look-see periodically, but it's a lot easier on his knees this way. It's quite a good set-up. He has this padded table that's made for massages. It's very comfortable. It's much better for the model and I think his paintings have gotten better."

"Why's that?"

"Mainly because he doesn't have to interrupt his work as much to climb down and look through his visor. The one bad thing for the model is that it used to be that you could move around more when he was up on the scaffold before he got this new system."

"Didn't it bother the model to have this creep sticking his face into their intimate regions?"

"Yeah, well, some of us wouldn't pose for him. It made some models really uncomfortable. He's not a creep, by the way. He's very considerate, very professional and he pays very well– especially since his paintings have gone way up in value. Believe me, I've worked with some *real* creeps. This man is no creep. I've modeled clothed for artists who did non-nude work who were some of the biggest creeps."

"Would you classify the defendant, Mark Pitt as a creep?"

"No. He's about average."

"What does 'average' mean in this context?"

"He's just average. I don't know. He tries to get away with some stuff, but he doesn't push it, you know?"

"He tries to get away with what? What did Pitt try to get away with?"

"You know, trying to squeeze more time from the pose, playing with the time. That sort of thing. You know, you'll hit the end of the half hour and he's saying, 'just a minute, I've gotta do one more thing'. That sort of thing. Some artists take advantage. They don't care that you're cramping up or your leg fell asleep or your shoulder hurts or whatever."

"Mark Pitt does that sort of thing?"

"No more than most. He always had at least some sympathy for the model."

"You say he had sympathy. Did he have more than sympathy?"

"What do you mean? What's 'more than sympathy'? D'you mean empathy?"

"Let me ask in a different way. Did you ever receive extra consideration from Mr. Pitt?"

"You mean like a tip?"

"Not a tip. I mean something *extra*."

"He usually had beers around. Snacks maybe. He did a drawing I particularly liked one time and he gave that to me."

"Did he expect anything in return for this drawing?"

"No, I don't think so. He just gave it to me."

"Mark Pitt, who sells his paintings for tens of thousands of dollars, just *gave* you a drawing? Just like that?" Wynn snapped his fingers.

"Yeah."

"Miss Prawn, do you really expect us to believe that he just gave you a drawing and expected nothing in return?"

"Well, it was just a thirty-minute sketch, you know? It wasn't any big deal. I just liked it, that's all."

"So, let me get this straight. He pays you money to pose for him. You get naked. He draws you for thirty minutes and then you say, 'gee, I like that', and he just hands it over?"

"Yeah, that's pretty much it."

"And he expected nothing else in return?"

"Like what?"

"Miss Prawn, when did Mark Pitt give you this drawing?"

"I don't remember. Maybe a year and a half ago. I don't know."

"Did Mr. Pitt sign his drawing?"

"Yes."

"Did he date it, as well?"

"Yes."

Wynn pulled a mailing tube from behind the prosecutor's table and extracted a drawing from it. He unrolled it as best he could and brought the curled gray paper to the witness stand. "Is this the drawing we are talking about?"

"Yes, that's the drawing."

"I ask you to look at the lower right corner of this drawing. What date do you see?"

"July 8th two years ago."

Wynn put the drawing back on the prosecutor's table and picked up some paperwork. "Miss Prawn, do you recognize this paperwork?"

She looked it over. "Yes."

"It's a report from a medical clinic at 1430 Concord Avenue, is it not?"

"It is."

"What is that a report of?"

"It's the report of a procedure."

"What procedure?"

"An abortion."

"What is the date of the procedure?"

"September 16th."

"On that report it states that you were eight weeks along in your pregnancy. Do you still maintain that you gave the defendant nothing in return for that drawing?"

"He would have given me that drawing anyway. That's just how he is."

"Ms Prawn, did you love Mark Pitt?"

Prawn hesitated, then silently nodded.

"You need to answer out loud, Miss Prawn."

"Yes, I love him."

"Would you do anything for him?"

"Anything?"

"Would you lie for him? *Have* you lied for him?"

"I don't know. I suppose I did lie for him."

"Would you lie to this court for him? Would you lie to save him from death?"

"I swore an oath, didn't I?"

"Yes, Miss Prawn, you did swear an oath. You say you've lied for him. What else would you do for him?"

"I don't know. I guess I'd do anything for him." Her eyes welled up with tears.

"And have you done 'anything' for him?"

"What do you mean?"

"Didn't Mark Pitt ask you to join him and Evelyn Averdantis in bed?"

"What?"

"Isn't it true that Mark Pitt asked you to join him and Evelyn Averdantis in bed? And we're not talking about a catnap here."

"Well, he, um…"

"Isn't it true that the defendant wanted you to participate in his insatiable quest– his unquenchable thirst, if you prefer– for perverse debauchery by having you and poor Evelyn Averdantis perform depraved sexual acts on him and on each other?"

"Depraved? He did kinda want, um, you know, to, uh…"

"Miss Prawn, isn't it a fact that Mr. Pitt beguiled you with his unnatural charm and coerced you into participating in shameful and indecent relations with poor Evelyn Averdantis?"

"Oh, God! Yes, it's true. It's true! I was coerced. I didn't want to do it. I was scared I would lose him. I would do anything for him and he gave me to *her*. Oh!" She sobbed into her hands for a moment while Wynn poured himself a glass of water and casually sipped it. When she composed herself, she continued. "You know, I've come to realize that I never had him to lose in the first place. Sure, he liked me. He was even attracted to me. But, he loved her and would find partners of all persuasions to satisfy her twisted nymphomaniac cravings!"

Wynn practically spit his mouthful of water. "Miss Prawn! Cathy! Please, just answer the questions put to you. We mustn't get off…"

"But, *she* made him go out and cast a net and fish for…"

"Really, Miss Prawn, you cannot offer such wild and random speculations. We must stick to the facts and not wander from them. I realize that you feel…"

"She was a piece of work, I tell you." Prawn was shaking her head as she spoke. "I know you're not supposed to speak ill of the dead, but…"

"Your Honor, I have no more questions."

"Mr. Bright, your witness."

"Thank you, Your Honor." Bright had a slight smile on his face as he approached the witness. "Miss Prawn, you said something to the effect that Evelyn Averdantis was a 'piece of work'. Can you elaborate on that?"

"I object, Your Honor. The witness is not a certified expert in such matters."

"Your Honor, the witness made a statement, which was allowed into the court record, and I am simply asking what she meant by that statement. Certainly Miss Prawn is an expert about what she herself has said."

"Overruled."

"Miss Prawn, can you explain what you meant when you said that?"

"She was just– how can I put it? She came from a really messed up background. She was rich and she thought the whole world revolved around her. She was always scheming and using people to get what she wanted. She didn't care about other people's feelings at all. I think she had psychological problems."

"Now, I have to object to *that*, Your Honor!"

"Sustained. Miss Prawn, please confine your comments to your experiences and refrain from speculating about such things as other people's health– mental or otherwise."

"Sorry, Your Honor."

"You may proceed, Mr. Bright."

"Can you give us some examples of how she schemed to get what she wanted?"

"Oh, I don't know. I never saw anything. I just saw how she'd make him do stuff and how she prevented him from realizing his dreams. She was afraid he'd leave her, so she tried to cripple him emotionally and financially."

"What did she do with his finances?"

"She made him buy her stuff– drugs, mostly. She was a junkie. It's funny she died bald, because she always spent a lot of money on her hair. She went to that awful salon to get her hair done by that tight-ass trophy wife hair stylist. I think she was making it with her, too. That woman didn't know the first thing about cutting hair. She was better off bald, if you ask me. She liked expensive kitchen gadgets. They had an electric knife. She bought expensive shower curtains."

"These encounters you had with the deceased and the defendant– how did those come about?"

"You mean our three-ways?"

"Is that what you called them?"

"That's what they were."

"Did the defendant just ask you outright if you wanted to have sex with him and his girlfriend?"

"No, it wasn't like that. I was interested in Mark. I sort of fell for him right from the start. I tried posing for him always facing him, so I could see him working. I loved watching him work. You know, he's very intense and he makes this little face when he looks at what he's done and he kinda purses his lips and it makes this dimple right here." She pointed to a spot on her cheek. "I never wanted to give him a rear view because I couldn't watch him work that way."

"So, you never posed facing away from him?"

"Oh, I *had* to, sometimes. You've seen some of the paintings. There are many rear views– especially the one he sold to Andres Palacios."

"Is that the one where you're holding your– your, um…"

"Yeah, that's the one. I didn't mind too much because I knew he was looking at me and that made me feel kinda warm and tingly. I liked sharing myself with him that way."

"Were those more revealing sort of poses your idea? Did you suggest them to Mark?"

"No, I never suggested anything to him. His paintings were all his creation– the concept, the pose– everything. I did whatever he wanted."

"Why'd you do whatever he wanted?"

"Well, he was paying me, for one thing. I trusted him. I felt safe with him. I guess I wanted to please him, too."

"Did he tell you that Evelyn wanted a threesome?"

"Not in so many words. He invited me to come over after one of the drawing sessions they held at a loft downtown. I foolishly thought his girlfriend was away, so I went. When I got there, she was there, already drugged-up, and they plied me with wine until I had no resistance left in me. I wanted Mark so badly, I would have slept with his grandmother if it would have helped me get him. Well, I didn't have to sleep with his grandmother, but I *did* have to sleep with Evelyn."

"It must have been awful for you– so demeaning."

"To be perfectly honest, she was– it was, you know, okay. It was better than I thought it was going to be. I was nervous as hell at first, but she made me feel really safe. That was a first for me. It dawns on me that I thought it was odd that she was living with Mark. She clearly loved him, but she– I don't know– I think she'd been hurt by men in her life, and I got the impression that she sort of felt safer with women. You know, I kind of blew up at her a minute ago. It's not fair. She wasn't a bad person really. She was a drug-addicted nymphomaniac, though. That part is true."

"Did Mark Pitt tell you to get the abortion?"

"No. I did that on my own."

"Why did you decide to get an abortion?"

"I didn't want my parents to find out."

"Do your parents know what you do for a living?"

"Yes."

"Your parents know how you make a living, but you didn't want them to know you were pregnant?"

"That's right. It would have broken their hearts to find out that I had gotten pregnant out of wedlock."

"Did you decide to get the abortion to please the defendant?"

"No, I'm not sure if that would have pleased him or not."

"Would he have wanted the baby?"

"I don't know. I suspect he would have been like he was with anything else. He wouldn't have cared very much about it if it didn't affect his art. He cares about his art more than anything or anybody."

"Speaking of his art, do you like his paintings?"

"Some of them more than others."

"Which ones do you like more?"

"I like the rear views better than the frontal views."

"I see. No more questions."

"Mr. Wynn?"

"No questions, Your Honor."

"You may step down, Miss Prawn."

16. Stanley Pitt

A baggy-eyed middle-aged man in a gray suit came forth and took the stand. He took the oath and sat down wearily, waiting for the questions from the prosecution.

"Mr. Pitt, how are you related to the defendant?"

"Sorry to say, I'm his father."

"When did you notice your son first exhibiting odd behavior?"

"I object, Your Honor. Mr. Pitt is not qualified to comment on the oddness of his son's behavior."

Wynn waved his arms. "What? It's his own son, for crying out loud! How could he not be qualified?"

"Your Honor, Mr. Pitt only had one child and cannot properly compare his son to any kind of standard. Therefore, he cannot be qualified to say whether or not his son is odd."

"Your Honor, the witness has lived his life in the world and participated in society. Surely he has seen and heard enough to be able to judge the behavior of his son and whether or not it's odd."

"Your Honor, it has not been established that the witness has seen or heard anything of the sort, and cannot be…"

"All right, Mr. Bright. That's enough. Your objection is overruled."

"Thank you, Your Honor. Mr. Pitt, when did Mark start acting oddly?"

"I guess it was right from the start that I noticed he wasn't acting in a way that you'd expect from a regular boy."

"What sort of thing did you notice him doing that made you sit up and take notice?"

"Well, for one thing, when he was just a little tike– not much more than one or two– he would want to draw all the time. We'd take him to the zoo and he'd want to draw the monkeys and the giraffes. I remember he especially liked to draw the rhino. Now, most kids will pick up a pencil and draw a monkey or two, but he'd sit down and draw those animals in their cages and with the vines or the phony tree stumps they put in there to make it look like a real habitat. Every blasted detail in realistic colors, too. His mother, God rest her soul, bought him crayons. She started out with the eight basic colors, but before long he had worked his way up through the sixteen and forty-eight and was using the box of sixty-four. That kid was so crazy he was asking me and the Mrs. If they made a box of a hundred colors! As if sixty-four wasn't enough for anybody! I told him there were no more colors to make. He didn't like that answer. He cried for hours when I told him that. You know, he was so crazy for details that, when he was four or five years old, he started drawing not only the animals in their cages, but also the zoo keepers and the people looking at the animals. Tell me, who does that? I remember one drawing in particular. Before I dropped it and it broke, I had a German-made stereoscopic camera that I used to take pictures with. You'd get the film developed and you'd get back these pairs of slides that looked 3D when you looked at them through the viewer. Remember those? Really neat stuff. Anyway, I was trying to take a shot of the tiger and he wouldn't turn and look my way, so I chucked a rock at him. Not real hard– just enough to get him to turn, so I could shoot his face, you know? So that night, Mark does a drawing of the tiger and there I am in the drawing, with the camera in my hand, throwing a rock at the damned thing. The little bastard got me in trouble with the Mrs. with that one. She didn't approve."

"Do you think he did that drawing on purpose to get you in trouble?"

"Damned right he did. He was always doing that sort of thing. We had a maid service that came in once a week to do cleaning and whatnot. I let the Mrs. hire her because she said she needed help around the house. Anyway, one day he comes up with this drawing of me and Gretchen– the maid, that is– kissing each other. The minute the Mrs. comes in the door, 'look, mommy! Look what I drew today!' The little bastard."

"Had you been kissing the maid?"

"Well, yeah, but not like you think. It wasn't like that at all. She was European. They're all huggy-kissy about everything. I think I might have just paid her for the month or something. I can't remember. Sure, she was young and pretty, but so are a lot of people. Can I help that? That's who the agency sent. What could I do about it? What was I supposed to do? Knock her down? Come on. Be reasonable. I let her kiss me, you know, to show her appreciation. Not *everybody* despises me, you know."

"Did your son continue to use his art to assail your character?"

"He never let up. His depictions of my so-called transgressions and misdeeds got more elaborate and scathing as time went by. He was pretty vicious. And he had the cleverness of evil."

"I object, Your Honor."

"To what, Mr. Bright?"

"The witness used the phrase, 'the cleverness of evil', which is inflammatory, but also meaningless. Can we have that stricken from the record?"

"No, Mr. Bright, I will not. If we had all meaningless phrases in this trial stricken from the record, we'd have precious little left over to help us reach a verdict. You may proceed, Mr. Wynn."

"Thank you, Your Honor. Mr. Pitt, how else did your son's evil cleverness manifest itself?"

"Well, he always favored his mother. I always thought it was unnatural for a boy to do that. That's probably the reason he ended up without a real job. I tried to get him into my line of work, but he was never interested in man's work. He wanted to draw and color."

"Did he do bad things growing up?"

"What do you mean?"

"Well, did he torture animals? Or maybe try to set fires? That sort of thing."

"Let's see." Pitt rubbed his rugged chin. "He, uh..." Pitt quit rubbing his chin and shifted in his seat. "One thing he was always doing was lifting up little girls' skirts and trying to peek underneath."

"And how old were these little girls when he was trying to do this?"

"Oh, I don't know– maybe ten years old or so."

"And how old was Mark when he did this perverted and malicious thing?"

"He would've been ten, too."

"Did he spit at people or pick fights at school?"

"Nah! Him?" Pitt chuckled.

"Did he disobey you or your wife in the home?"

"Not really. He was pretty obedient, actually."

"So, his malevolence mainly manifested itself in his vindictive artwork, then?"

"Huh?"

"His evil twisted ways were confined to his artwork, would you say?"

"Sure."

"What about when he got older?"

"What *about* when he got older?"

"Well, did he get more evil and twisted? Was his vile personality exacerbated by the putrid teen hormones coursing through his reptilian veins?"

"Not so much. He kept to himself. When the Mrs. died, he locked himself in his room and we didn't much deal with each other. He still kept up his attacks against me, though."

"How did he do that?"

"He did some paintings in high school that were real cruel. He did a series of paintings of me that showed me covered in garbage and eating garbage. In one painting he called *Karen*, I was painted as a dirty pig screwing this prostitute on top of a pile of garbage."

"He did this in an art class at school?"

"Yeah! Can you believe it?"

"What did you do? Did you talk to them at the school?"

"Sure I did. I went down there and spoke to the art teacher and the principal. That art teacher was a looker, I tell ya. Anyway, they weren't much help. They took his side against me. They said he was properly exercising his right to express himself. They said that they encourage the students to get it all out and work out their problems and stuff. I told them that I'm as American as the next guy, but the First Amendment ends when somebody gets attacked directly."

"What did they say to that?"

"They said he was just interpreting in artistic terms what I am– you know, what I do for a living."

"By painting you eating garbage and having carnal relations with a prostitute? How is that a legitimate exercise of the First Amendment?"

"I don't remember exactly how they put it, but that's pretty much what they said. I mean, I can understand him painting me that way."

"Why, for heaven's sake?"

"Well, 'cause I'm a garbage man, so it kinda makes some sense when you think about it. But, poor Karen! I never paid her one cent for– for, you know, anything. She was on welfare, she wasn't a whore, for chrissakes. She did have those stockings and short shorts, just like he painted them, but that doesn't make her a whore or nothing. Both times she was arrested they couldn't make the charges stick. She dresses like that because she just likes to look nice and attractive– for me, you know, to sort of get the juices flowing. And I'm not the father of any of her kids, by the way."

"So the school was no help?"

"No help? They gave him a damn award! They don't have a clue what it takes to be the father of a boy like that. That was not good. It gave Mark a swelled head. He was always doing art, but this thing they did gave him the idea that he could be an artist. It sorta put the official stamp of approval on it." Pitt mimicked rubber-stamping something in mid air. "They gave him a prize and he used the prize to buy art supplies. That was a dark day for everybody, I tell ya. I think they had as much of a hand in that Averdantis girl's death as Mark does."

Bright rose to his feet. "Object, Your Honor! No, wait! Never mind. That school had nothing to do with Evelyn Averdantis's death either."

"Whoa, wait just a second! Now I have to object, Your Honor."

"Why don't we just let both objections cancel each other out, huh?"

"Very well, Your Honor. I'm willing if Mr. Wynn is."

"Sure. Let them go."

"Praise the lord! You two finally agreed to something. Please proceed, Mr. Wynn."

"Mr. Pitt, what about Mark's relationship with other boys?"

"He wasn't queer, if that's what you're trying to say."

"No, I'm just trying to get the picture of how he got along with his classmates and friends from the schoolyard."

211

"Oh. Well, he didn't have lots of friends, I guess. He had some, I suppose. I think he had friends. I know he had some friends. I, uh– yeah, he had friends, I guess."

"Did he go out and play with other boys?"

"Yeah, I guess he must have."

"Was he picked on at school?"

"I guess he was. I don't know how much he raised his hand, but I'm sure he got his chance like anybody else."

"No, I don't mean did the teacher pick on him to answer questions. I mean did other boys pick on him and tease him or beat him up? You know, the school bully."

"I don't know. I don't remember him with any black eyes or broken bones or anything. I don't know. Maybe he was."

"Did he have trouble with any of his classes or subjects?"

"Did he have trouble with any of his classes…" He rubbed his jaw as he repeated the question to himself. "Did he have trouble with any classes… Hmm. Couldn't say. That was more the Mrs's. job than mine. I know he didn't have any trouble with arts and crafts. I can tell you *that* much at least."

"Did you two fight a lot?"

"Well, the Mrs. would step in and try to calm things down. After the Mrs. died, by that time we really didn't speak much anyway. I mean, we had some blow-ups, you know?"

"What did you fight about?"

"His artwork mostly. I didn't like the things he was doing– not just the stuff he did to attack me, but other stuff, too. He seemed to have the knack of doing artwork that upset people for one reason or another. I was against all that stuff. I didn't want him going out into the world and spreading that crap everywhere. I was against him going to college. I didn't want him learning more about art. I didn't want him learning more about *anything*, for that matter. He was too smart-assed for his own good already. He was born smart-assed."

"How did he go to college without your support?"

"I couldn't stop him. I kicked him out of the house, hoping that that would scare him off school and into a real job. He just took up with some other guys that were going to that school and I haven't spoken to him since. Nothing could stop him."

"How could he afford to go to an art college without your support? The tuition there is astronomical."

"He had lots of money for school set aside from his share when the Mrs. died. She left him money for college. She's as much to blame for him becoming a successful artist as anybody. She was a good woman other than that. She could cook– not fancy, but good, solid food."

"You said that nothing could stop him."

"Yeah?"

"Would it be accurate to say that he wouldn't let anything stand in his way in his quest for glory in the art world?"

"Sorry, that he wouldn't what?"

"That he wouldn't let anything stop him when it came to his art?"

"Yeah, that's about right."

"And would it be fair to say that the same applied to people, as well?"

"That he wouldn't let anybody stop him? Yeah, that's him to a tee."

"Even if it meant the horrible and tragic death of a young woman?"

"Sure, that's it! You got it!"

Bright leapt to his feet. "Objection, Your Honor!"

"No more questions, Your Honor."

"Mr. Bright, your witness."

"What about my objection?"

"Your witness, Mr. Bright." Tuilgy was looking at the handle of his gavel, picking at some old crud in the carvings with his fingernail.

Wynn sat down with a big grin on his face. Bright let out a sigh, then made his way to the witness stand.

"Mr. Pitt, has your son ever physically harmed anyone, to the best of your knowledge?"

"You mean before this girl? No."

"To the best of your knowledge, has he ever threatened anyone with bodily harm?"

"No."

"No more questions, Your Honor."

"You may step down, Mr. Pitt."

"That's it?"

"Yes, you may step down now."

Pitt started to rise, but was reluctant to completely let go of the chair. "You sure? I can probably say more about him."

"Thank you, Mr. Pitt. You may step down."

"Well, you guys know where to find me."

"Thank you, Mr. Pitt."

From the Highbridge Morning Star:

> The Trial of the Century of Mark Pitt, accused of murder-
> ing his live-in girlfriend continued yesterday with the tes-
> timony of three key witnesses for the prosecution. Am-
> brose Wynn, spouse of the incomparable Lynn Maguire,
> who is appearing nightly at Club Utopia on Cord Street,
> elicited some damaging testimony from Pitt's upstairs
> neighbor, and from a young and comely nude figure
> model, and the defendant's father. The victim, Miss
> Evelyn Averdantis, was found completely devoid of any
> hair on her body or head.
> While the upstairs neighbor would seem to be the likeliest
> of the witnesses to have seen or heard the activities of Pitt
> and Averdantis, it was the young and lovely nude model,
> Cathy Prawn, and the defendant's own father, Stanley
> Pitt, who struck the most telling blows. Miss Prawn spoke
> of unrequited love and the unwanted abortion of Pitt's
> baby, as well as cruel and demeaning treatment while she
> was in his employ.
> Stanley Pitt recounted tales of his son's single-minded
> pursuit of his artistic urges and how Mark Pitt used his art
> skill as a weapon to destroy the happiness and welfare of
> those who loved him best.
> Although Dick Bright is acquitting himself quite well in
> defense of his client, he is clearly fighting an uphill battle
> to spare Pitt from facing what seems at this point to be an
> inevitable life sentence.
> The trial continues the day after tomorrow with the prose-
> cution expected to wrap up with one more psychologist.
> Prosecutor Wynn had wanted to question an inhabitant of
> the top floor of the building where Pitt and Averdantis
> lived and where the murder took place, but attempts to
> subpoena this person have been unsuccessful. The defense
> has announced that it will call only three witnesses. It re-
> mains to be seen whether Mark Pitt will take the stand in
> his own defense or leave his fate in the hands of others.

17. Dr. Odile DePew

A very thin woman in a gray suit, which hung on her as if on a clothes hanger, was called to the stand.

"Your name is Odile DePew?"

"That's correct."

"What is your occupation, Dr. DePew?"

"I am a research psychologist at the State Home for the Insane."

"What are your qualifications in the area of your research?"

"I have a Ph.D. in Insanity from Highbridge University and a Ph.D. in Business from Wharton."

"So, it's safe to say that you are not only an expert in sense, but also dollars and cents. Is that correct?"

"That's correct."

"Now, what we are interested in here, I think, has more to do with your expertise in the area of sanity. How many years have you been working in your field, Doctor?"

"Roughly, twenty-three years. Some rougher than others."

"What experiences have you had in the field of insanity?"

"I worked for three years as an assistant to Dr. Heinrich Mueller, a name some of you might recognize from your basic psychology courses."

"Oh, yes, absolutely. He was one of the most influential minds in the study of– and treatment of– insanity in the entire 20th century, wasn't he?"

"Correct. Until he was torn apart by a group of his patients on Christmas morning nearly twenty years ago, he was *the* most important man in his field. Needless to say, that was one of the rough spots I spoke of a second ago. You never want to see that kind of thing, believe me, Mr. Wynn. And to have it happen to someone who– well, let's just say that Dr. Mueller and I worked very closely." She sighed. "Very closely, indeed. Oh, well. It's some comfort to know that he died doing the work he loved so much and was so committed to."

"After you left Dr. Mueller's employ, where did you go?"

"I moved to Germany and worked with a team of researchers who were experimenting on– or rather, treating experimentally– a group of youths who were suffering from extreme paranoia and self-destructive tendencies."

"How'd that turn out?"

"Very well, actually. We feel we cured three or four of them and neutralized the rest. It was all very progressive and avant-garde, but we felt it was successful. I don't know if anyone else felt that way, but with these kinds of things you have scientists lining up on both sides of the issue as if they're playing dodge ball. Men can be quite childish, as I'm sure you know."

"Yes, indeed we can. How long were you with that group?"

"About a year. After that, I came back to the States and took a position at St. Bridget Academy for the Incurably Demented. I spent five years there."

"What did you do there?"

"Mainly administrative work. There wasn't much psychology happening at St. Bridget's. We spent a lot of time filling out reports and documenting disciplinary actions. We did have an art program there. We had art classes and put on theater productions."

"How'd you manage that?"

"It was hard, but so was everything at St. Bridget's. We did *Guys and Dolls* and were forced to use a patient who was wearing a strait-jacket cast as Sky Masterson. The guy did all right. He had a beautiful singing voice, but the love scenes were less romantic than they might have been otherwise. And then you had to kind of *imagine* that he rolls the dice that decide his fate and the fate of all the other hoodlums. The art classes were a real problem."

"What was the problem there?"

"You must keep in mind that these patients were really extreme. They preferred to paint and sculpt with their own feces rather than using the paints and clay that we provided. What a mess, and what a smell! Oh, lord! They did do some beautiful work, though– some very elaborate and delicate designs. One patient liked to sculpt wild animals and he did some marvelous figurines of elephants and bears and something he called a dik-dik, but we couldn't convince him to use clay. Needless to say, we could not keep that artwork. I think we burned it all or flushed it down the crapper. I can't recall which."

"Doctor, are you trained in art therapy?"

"Yes, one of my degrees is in art therapy."

"As a trained art therapist, do you look at artwork done by lunatics in order to decipher their neuroses?"

"Yes."

"What sorts of things do you look for in the artwork to determine insanity?"

"There are many factors in examining patients' artwork. Insanity can manifest itself in many ways."

"Give us some examples."

"Okay. For one thing, the subject matter can raise red flags about a person's mental state. If you're looking for an example, I've seen artwork by the dangerously insane that depicted body parts."

"You mean, just the body parts and all disconnected from the body?"

"Yes, exactly. Sometimes they're shown as having been hacked or ripped off the body, lying in pools of blood. Sometimes they are just separated from the body– not cut or ripped off, but just scattered about or grouped together in some sort of impossible assemblage."

"Is one type more dangerous than the other?"

"No, you pretty much have to watch out for all of them. We learn in the trade to never turn your back on a nut. Even the nicest of them will hit you over the head with a chair or push your head through a window if you give them half a chance. One second they're smiling or acting catatonic, then, *wham!*" She mimed getting walloped over the head.

"What else do you look for, Dr. DePew?"

"Lurid colors. Color use tells you a lot about a patient's mental and emotional state. The most worrisome colors are the bright and cheery ones."

"Why's that? I would assume that the cheery colors would be used by happy people."

"Mr. Wynn, *nobody* is happy when they're in the asylum– least of all the patients. Bright colors are used by patients when they are trying to fool you into thinking they're happy and harmless. Those patients are scheming against you and are hoping you'll let your guard down. We treat patients that produce that kind of artwork with extra brutality and diligence until they start using more muddy and depressing tones. The dark and dreary colors are just more honest."

"Any other signs that you look for in the art of the demented and danger-ous?"

"We do. Here we enter the rarified air of professional art therapy and psy-chology. We examine the quality of the line and gesture. We look for bro-ken lines, jagged lines, patients who press very, very hard with the imple-ment, whether it be a crayon or pencil or brush. Obviously, if the patient presses so hard that they break through the paper or canvas, we know we have a problem with aggression and frustration. Jagged, broken lines are good strong indicators of extreme psychosis. Rapists, pedos– that's what we call pedophiles over at the institute– and serial killers all have, at one time or another, used broken or jagged lines in their drawings and paintings."

"Anything else you look for?"

"The real deal breaker, if you will, is disproportionality."

"What's disproportionality?"

"Disproportionality is the technical term we use to describe when a patient depicts objects way out of proportion when compared with other objects in the artwork and compared with reality. To give you an example, let's say a patient draws people with large heads and tiny, wormy, little bodies. That would indicate extreme emotional problems. We've seen many people with severe problems like that. Not many of them can function in society for very long."

"But, Dr. DePew, I've had to research art to some extent in my preparation for this case, and I see a lot of art that exhibits these symptoms. And yet you just assured me that these types rarely last in society."

"That's true. That's because it's in the art world itself that these tormented souls are welcomed and encouraged. Their success in– and support from– the art world almost always ensures that they will never get the help they need."

"So, what you are saying is that the art world is a hotbed of neuroses and psychoses?"

"Well, I wouldn't call it a hotbed, exactly. It's more like a sanctuary, really."

"Tell me, Dr. DePew, have you had the opportunity to look at Mark Pitt's artwork?"

"Yes, I have."

"Tell the court what you were able to learn about Mr. Pitt from looking at his so-called artwork."

"I was able to learn a lot about him from his artwork, but I also want to mention that I learned at least as much from my interviews of him."

"Did you speak with him at length?"

"Yes, I met with him at length and on several occasions. I felt it was necessary given the complexities of the case. You understand."

"Certainly. So, Doctor, what is your professional assessment of this so-called man?"

"It was worse than I had anticipated. He is suffering from what we at the Home call a 'Level 6 Psychopathy'."

"What is that, Doctor? It sounds quite serious."

"It is. A 'Level 6' is almost the most severe form of social maladjustment and delusion. It is one level below what we term 'total insanity'. In other words, he can just barely function in the society of mankind. He is obsessed with the notion that he must interpret things and translate reality into painted imagery. He is overwhelmingly preoccupied with sexual thoughts and urges and he has no compunction about indulging his desires with any-one who does not have the willpower to resist his urging. His warped and diseased mind has co-mingled his strange and misguided urges into what you see when you view his artwork. He is, in my professional opinion, a dangerous creature who should be hanging in the gallows rather than in the top galleries in town."

"Thank you, Doctor. No more questions, Your Honor."

"Mr. Bright?"

"Thank you, Your Honor. Dr. DePew, would you say that Rembrandt was a nut case?"

"I don't know. I've never had the opportunity to interview him."

"You've had the opportunity to see his paintings and etchings. What do you deduce from those?"

Wynn rose calmly to his feet. "Your Honor, Mr. Rembrandt is not on trial here."

"Your Honor, I am attempting to frame the witness's testimony, which condemned my client, into a broader a historical context."

"You may proceed, Mr. Bright."

"Thank you. Doctor?"

"What do I deduce from Rembrandt's work? I'm afraid I've never examined his work in the context of my profession."

"In what context have you viewed Rembrandt's paintings?"

"Why, in the context of an art appreciator, of course."

"So, you *can* view art in that context?"

"Of course. I'm a member of the Museum of Fine Art. Of course I can view art that way. What sort of person do you take me for?"

"So, setting aside my client's supposed lunacy, can you…"

"I never called him a lunatic, Mr. Bright. That's not a term we at the Home like to use in public. It has negative connotations."

"True. You did not call him a lunatic. Anyway, setting his diseased and warped psychosis aside, what do you think of his artwork?"

"I'm not qualified to judge the artistic merits of a piece of art. That's not my field."

"So, Doctor, if you can't tell a fine painting even if it ran up and bit your behind, how can you discern the difference between an involuntary jagged line and a sophisticated deliberate artistic expression?"

"I don't know what you're getting at."

"I see artwork by great artists in the museums that use the sort of irregular lines and distortions that you just described as the product of a psychotic mind. Why would the museums of the world be representing the life work of a legion of crazies?"

"Mr. Bright, have you or anyone you've known ever owned a Volkswagen?"

"Yes, I did."

"The Volkswagen automobile is the product of the psychotic mind of Adolph Hitler. Does that mean it shouldn't be in the showroom or on the roads? No, of course not. But, I bet you'd agree with me that Hitler shouldn't be allowed to tool around Highbridge in one of his Beetles."

"I would agree with you. That being said, I don't think Hitler actually sat down and drew the design for the Volkswagen himself."

"He was an artist, though, wasn't he?" She smiled a victorious grin.

"Have you ever studied his artwork?"

"No."

"Then how do you know he was a madman?"

"Because of what he did!"

"What did Mark Pitt do?"

"He's on trial for murder."

"I asked what did he *do*?"

"As I said, he's on trial for murder."

"Did you see him commit this so-called murder?"

"No, of course not. I hadn't met him then."

"To the best of your knowledge, did *anybody* see him commit this so-called murder?"

"From what *I* know, no. I guess no one did."

"Was Evelyn Averdantis even murdered?"

"I'm no expert in that field."

"So, you deduced that Mark Pitt was a madman based on examining his artwork, but that Hitler was a madman based not on his artwork, but on his deeds?"

"Yes, I guess I did."

"So, you can diagnose people as crazy whether or not you ever meet them or even see their artwork?"

"I didn't diagnose Adolph Hitler, Mr. Bright."

"No, but you agreed with others' diagnoses without examining any material. Do you tend to do that, Dr. DePew?"

"Hitler is a well-documented and thoroughly studied historical figure, so it's different."

"Are you saying that you can properly diagnose people based on what you read in a history book?"

"No, but given Hitler's deeds and what was written about him, I can make what is probably a fairly accurate diagnosis."

"What about other artists throughout history? Are they all murderers?"

"That's a silly question. No, of course not."

"Why? Because they were never tried for it?"

"Yes, that's one reason."

"So, if Vincent Van Gogh had been tried for murder, you would say he was a murderer?"

"If he was convicted, I would."

"Same thing with Mark Pitt?"

"Yes, of course."

"So, if Vincent Van Gogh would have been convicted, you would say he was a murderer, because he had been convicted, and not because his art-work exhibited any signs of psychosis, correct?"

"I see what you're driving at." She smirked and nodded her head. "Yes, Mr. Bright, having nothing to do with my diagnosis."

"So, what exactly is your diagnosis of Mark Pitt's mental state worth, Doctor, if *you* don't even put much store in it?"

"Mark Pitt is a very dangerous man, Mr. Bright– very dangerous. He's very clever and seductive."

"Seductive?"

"Huh? Yes, he's, um, seductive." She blushed deeply. "Maybe seductive is the wrong word."

"I find that an interesting choice of words. Maybe it's *not* the wrong word. Why did you call him seductive?"

"I didn't mean to call him seductive. I must've meant he was, uh, tantaliz-ing. No, that's no better. Look, I don't know what I meant. You've got me all confused with all this talk about Adolph Hitler and Vincent Van Gogh. I don't know if I'm coming or going."

"Did you really need twelve interviews with my client before deciding he was a dangerous psychopath, Dr. DePew? I mean, after all, you were able to condemn every other artist to the trash heap of psychopathy just by glancing at a few of their paintings." He stared at her for a long time. "Why the twelve interviews?"

"Uh, sometimes you just have to have more contact before deciding what to think about a particular subject."

"What sort of contact, Doctor?"

"I don't know what you mean."

"Don't you? What sort of examinations did you perform on Mark Pitt, Dr. DePew? No answer? Let's tackle this thing from another angle, then. You met with my client, who, by the way, volunteered to meet with you and complete your battery of tests so that he could clear his good name. Is that accurate?"

"Yes, from what he told me, he did it voluntarily."

"Where were the first two meetings?"

"At the Home, of course."

"They took place on March second and March fifth, correct?"

"Yes, I believe that is correct."

"And they took place at 10:00 A.M. and 10:45 A.M., respectively. Is that correct?"

"Sounds right. I can't recall exactly."

"These interviews lasted each approximately eighty to ninety minutes. Is that correct?"

"I believe so."

"And where were the next ten meetings?"

"Where were they?"

"Correct."

"You want to know where they were?"

"Yes. Where were they?"

"Um, well, you see there was a problem at the office at the Home– I couldn't seem to schedule a good time– well, so anyway, we had to hold the meetings somewhere else– other than the Home, I mean. And what with one thing or another we picked a suitable alternative for the meetings. That way we could continue what we had begun and, you know, I really wanted to make sure we left nothing, you know– that I had done all I could so there would be no doubt. It is a murder trial after all."

"So, where were these meetings held?"

"I, uh, well, I had to hold them at an outside venue."

"Which was where?"

"At 1410 Aqua Boulevard."

"And what is your connection to that address?"

"It's, uh, my apartment."

"And why couldn't you hold them at the Home for the Insane?"

"It was just easier."

"Do make a habit of that?"

"What?"

"Having raving lunatics at your apartment for interviews?"

"Not really, no. I have all my materials there and everything, so it seemed, you know, the best solution under the circumstances."

"Why was it okay for this man, whom just a few minutes ago you called a madman and very dangerous, to come to your apartment on ten different occasions? And why were his visits scheduled for late evening hours?"

"Well, like I said, the regular office at the Home– well, there was some sort of scheduling problem or something. And I work, sometimes until seven or seven-thirty, so it just made sense to schedule them late."

"What about the one on March twentieth?"

"What about it?"

"That was a Saturday."

"Yes."

"You met with my client at 10:45 P.M. that night."

"Oh, that. I had tickets to *Fiddler on the Roof* that night. I couldn't meet earlier."

"Did you consider that someone might look askance at a meeting with a young, male subject at such a late hour and in your apartment?"

"I suppose that a person who was unfamiliar with the situation *might* get the wrong idea– if they were so inclined. It seems you took it that way."

"How is anybody supposed to take it? Have you ever done this with any of your other subjects, Doctor?"

"You mean meet at my apartment? Or meet very late?"

"Both."

"I've met with patients very late before. I used to work the graveyard shift at the Home, so I met with patients at all crazy hours of the night."

"In your apartment?"

"No, not in my apartment. That was unusual. But, I told you there was a problem with getting the office."

"Yes, you did tell me that. But, you couldn't remember the exact problem, correct?"

"Correct. Look, you are acting like there was something– like I did something wrong. Let me remind you that I am a professional. I am highly respected in my fields of insanity and art therapy and I don't appreciate your endless badgering about this blasted meeting time. Have you ever dealt with insane people, Mr. Bright?"

"I don't treat screwballs locked up in asylums, if that's what you mean. But, then I don't meet with young people of the opposite sex in my apartment, late at night– if they're clients or witnesses, that is."

"Well, I don't normally, either."

"What sort of examinations did you give the defendant in order to determine his degree of psychopathy, Doctor?"

"Um, the standard tests and forms. I believe you have them in your possession."

"Yes, I have a copy of the paperwork here." He picked up a file folder and leafed through the paperwork within. "If you don't mind an observation, Doctor, it seems to me that the report in this folder is not complete."

"You should have everything that Mr. Wynn was given."

"Yes, I do. It's just that it seems to me that this report represents only a few hours worth of work with the subject."

"I don't– I'm not following you, Mr. Bright."

"Well, I have here in this folder about a dozen similar reports, made by you for other subjects that we pulled out of the Home's files. These dozen or so reports were pulled at random and were prepared for a wide variety of patient types, and all within the last eight months."

"Yes?"

"It's just that each of these reports is about the same as the one you prepared for my client, but we checked the records at the Home and, in every case, you spent no more than three hours with the patient. So all of these reports, added together, represent less time spent than the one report you prepared for Mark Pitt. Can you explain that?"

"As I said, Mr. Bright, since he was accused of murder, I wanted to make extra certain of my findings."

"That's what I thought at first, but in these dozen reports, we found five other patients who were accused of murder, too. So, I was compelled to change my mind and attribute the extra time you spent in your apartment, late at night with Mark Pitt to something other than professional thoroughness and consideration for his precarious legal position." He paused and looked at her. "Do you care to offer another explanation?"

"Some patients' cases are not as clear cut as others?"

"Is that a question? Tell, me, Doctor, do you really think he's a psychopath? Or was it something else?"

"Like what?"

"Like revenge, perhaps?"

"Revenge for what?"

"For breaking off an affair? The jilted woman thing?" Bright went to his briefcase and pulled out a sheet of paper. "I have in my hand a sworn statement from a Mr. Ted Bosch. Mr. Bosch, you may know, lives at 1410 Aqua Boulevard, on your floor, Dr. DePew. He works for the Transit Authority as a supervisor, so his hours are erratic. On this particular morning, the 23rd of March, which corresponds to the day after your seventh meeting with the defendant, he states that he saw the defendant, whom he recognized positively from photographs he was shown by us, leaving your apartment at 4:20 A.M.. He states further that Mr. Pitt exited the apartment, made eye contact with him, winked and smiled, as he put it, conspiratorially. He goes on to say that the two rode down in the elevator together, during which time, Mr. Pitt engaged Mr. Bosch in conversation. Mr. Pitt stated that he was, quote, worn out, and asked Mr. Bosch if he had ever had an older woman."

Wynn jumped up at the prosecutor's table. "Your Honor, it is hearsay, what this streetcar conductor– or whatever he is– claims he heard from Mark Pitt."

"Overruled. Continue, Mr. Bright."

"Thank you, Your Honor." He looked back at the paper. "So, he asks Ted Bosch if he'd ever had an older woman. After confirming that Mr. Pitt was referring to sexual congress when he used the word 'had', Mr. Bosch replied that, as a matter of fact, he had. Mr. Pitt then observed that, quote, older women seem to have an endless appetite for sex. Mr. Bosch then offered his considered opinion about the pleasing looks of his neighbor– that's you, Ms DePew. It seems you have admirers. Mr. Pitt then replied that, while he thought it was great sex, if he had to perform like he did that night, more than once every few days, he'd soon be joining his poor girlfriend, who had recently died. Mr. Bosch expressed concern for the young man, wondering how he would get through the day's work after such a strenuous night. Mr. Pitt explained that he does not work regular hours, because he is a famous artist, about which Mr. Bosch congratulated him, stating that he always wanted to draw pretty pictures, but that he had no talent for it. At this point, the two men were already in the lobby and their conversation came to an end as they bid each other goodbye. Dr. DePew, is the part about the defendant leaving your apartment at approximately 4:20 A.M. on the morning of March 23rd correct?"

Dr. DePew had turned a deep crimson color and was wiping her forehead with the heel of her hand. "I don't know what to say. I think it's pretty obvious at this point that I was not really working on my report while I was meeting with Mark all those times. He's a very attractive young man, you know. Mark and I clicked immediately, the first time we met. I think he knew it, too."

"Did he make the first overtures?"

"Ha! No, he didn't. Poor guy. No, I resolved during that first meeting in March that I would have him. I pulled out all the stops for our second meeting– the whole nine yards, you know? You may not realize it, but I can still turn heads if I want to. I know I'm not young anymore, but I've kept myself in shape and my skin is still soft and firm. So, I got my hair styled and bought a new dress– a little too provocative for the office, but nothing, you know, cheap-looking. I got myself a pair of dark red pumps to match my lipstick and wore my best French perfume. I'm sure he noticed, but he was probably scared that my coming on to him might have been part of the test, so he played it cool. That's when I decided to get him to my apartment."

"How'd you do that?"

"I told him what I told you, that the office couldn't be scheduled."

"Did he believe you?"

"Did you? I don't think it mattered that much to him. I knew he hadn't had a woman since his girlfriend died, so I figured he needed me as much as I needed him. I like to believe that he wanted to come to my apartment, you know, for me– not because he thought I might give him a better evaluation in my report." She looked at Mark Pitt. "The report was the farthest thing from my mind when I invited him and the farthest thing from my mind when we broke it off. I merely used the report as the excuse to keep seeing him– at least I used it as long as I reasonably could. I had already completed it anyway."

"You had?"

"Certainly. It took me only two hours to complete it after my evaluation."

"But, I don't understand."

"What don't you understand?"

"Your report– you basically call him a raving lunatic in this report."

"So?"

"Well, why did you have him come to your apartment?"

"For the sex. I told you Mark and I clicked immediately."

"So, you didn't give him a terrible report in order to get back at him?"

"Of course not. That would be unprofessional."

"No more questions, Your Honor." Bright shook his head the whole way back to his chair.

"Mr. Wynn?"

"No more questions, Your Honor."

"You may step down, Doctor."

18. Dr. Marcus Dalrymple

"Your Honor, the prosecution rests."

"Very well. Mr. Bright, call your first witness."

"Yes, Your Honor. The defense calls Dr. Marcus Dalrymple to the stand."

An old man approached the stand to be sworn in. He was bent with age and his skin was wrinkled and gray from decades of smoking.

"Dr. Dalrymple, how are you acquainted with the defendant, Mark Pitt."

"I was the Pitt's family physician."

"How long have you known Mark Pitt?"

"All his life. I delivered him."

"Were you his doctor throughout his childhood?"

"Yes, and into his teen years."

"How would you describe him?"

"You mean physically?"

"His character. Would you say he is an unusual person in any way?"

"Well, yes, I suppose I'd have to say that he is unusual."

"In what way is he unusual?"

"He's an artist, so he is– how can I say this?– different, in a way, from the rest of us."

"Would you say he is a dangerous person?"

"No, certainly not."

"Would you say he is unpredictable?"

"No, I would say the opposite, in fact. I'd say he is *very* predictable."

"How so, Doctor?"

"Well, you have to know him. He always had an odd way of seeing things. He'd notice things that other children didn't notice– or, if they did, they never said anything about them. He did, though. He was always saying the craziest things. He's a smart boy. He sees things in ways that others don't. He's very perceptive that way. So, if you know this about him, you can predict that he will come up with something seemingly out of left field, but right on the money. His mother was a lot like that, too."

"Tell me, Dr. Dalrymple, did he take after his father at all?"

"Oh, yes. He has a manner about him that is irresistible to the ladies."

"I didn't take the elder Mr. Pitt to be much of a ladies' man."

"Um, no, Stanley Pitt is not a ladies' man. My mistake."

"You knew Mr. and Mrs. Pitt well?"

"I was their physician for two years before Mark was born. I treated the young couple for any number of ailments. I treated Mrs. Pitt for headaches. I treated Mr. Pitt for pneumonia. As I said, I delivered Mark and treated him through all the usual childhood diseases and two broken fingers."

"How old was he when he broke his fingers?"

"Two or three, if I recall. Mr. Pitt slammed the car door on his fingers. Poor kid. I suggested that he take up drawing to help his dexterity after the splint and cast were removed. Mrs. Pitt liked the idea. Mrs. Pitt was a special woman."

"In what way? Do you mean how much she supported her son's creativity?"

"That and other things."

"You sound very fond of the late Mrs. Pitt."

"Yes, indeed. That's where Mark got his good looks, you know."

"Really?"

"He sure didn't take after his father."

"I haven't seen any pictures of her, so I couldn't say."

"You're missing out, my friend. She was quite a beauty– quite a beauty. She was taken from us far too young." He sighed.

"Were you her physician when she became ill– I mean her final illness?"

"No, I wasn't."

"Why not?"

"I just wasn't."

"Did you have a falling out?"

"Not with her."

"With Mr. Pitt?"

"You could say that."

"About her treatment?"

"You could say that, too."

"I'm not sure I understand your meaning, Doctor."

"No, I suppose not. Let's just say that Mr. Pitt and I were not on the best of terms."

"Why not?"

"Mr. Pitt, in my opinion, did not treat his wife with the level of considera-tion that befitted her. In turn, Mr. Pitt resented my opinion. Eventually, Mr. Pitt grew to resent much more than just my opinion."

"Did you try to take an active part in their relationship?"

"I did."

"Did he feel that you were meddling?"

"To put it mildly."

"What did Mrs. Pitt think?"

"That's for Mrs. Pitt to say."

"She's deceased."

"Yes, I know. I went to her funeral. Even Mr. Pitt could not keep me away. I owed *that* to her, at least."

Wynn rose to his feet. "Your Honor, this is all very intriguing and melo-dramatic, but I fail to see what this testimony has to do with the death of Eleanor Averdantis. Sorry– Evelyn Averdantis."

"I agree, Mr. Wynn. Mr. Bright, if you can't tie this testimony in with the case before us, I will be forced to ask you to move on."

"Yes, of course, Your Honor. Please bear with me another moment and it will become quite clear to you."

"Very well, you may proceed, but make it quick."

"Thank you, Your Honor. Dr. Dalrymple, have you stayed in touch with Mark Pitt since you last treated him."

"Yes."

"For medical reasons?"

"No, I retired from medical practice a number of years ago."

"Do you stay in touch with many of your former patients?"

"No, I don't."

"Why Mark Pitt?"

"I just felt that it was something I wanted to do."

"Are you concerned about his health?"

"No, no, nothing like that. As far as I know, he's in the best of health. He's a fine, strapping young man."

"Why, then?"

"Oh, I don't know. I think he's a fine fellow and he's becoming quite the famous artist, you know."

"And that's the reason you follow him– because he's a fine fellow and a well-known artist?"

"Sure. Why not?"

"Are you sure there's no other reason?"

"What other reason could there be?"

"I don't know, Doctor. I could think of one or two. I'm asking *you*, though."

"I don't know what to tell you."

"How about the truth, Doctor? When Mrs. Pitt died, she left a certain sum of money for the welfare and education of her son, Mark. That sum was placed in a trust fund and managed by Furst Savings and Loan. Seven years ago, when the fund was nearly tapped out, a sudden influx of cash was deposited into that fund by an anonymous person. You following me so far, Doc?"

"Yes, I think so."

"Okay. Now, we did some checking around and we found the most intriguing coincidence. Do you want to know what that is?"

"I suppose you'll tell me."

"Yes, I will. On the same morning that this mysterious $7,200 deposit showed up in Mark Pitt's trust fund, an identical withdrawal was made on another account in that same bank. I'll give you three guesses who it was who withdrew $7,200 from his account on that same day."

"I suppose you mean me?"

"Yes, I do, Doctor. Do you want to explain that coincidence?"

"It's just that– a coincidence. Nothing more."

"Come now, Doctor. You swore an oath."

"I don't know what you want of me."

"Did you deposit that $7,200 into Mark Pitt's trust fund?"

"All right, I did."

"Why did you do that?"

"I like the kid. I told you that. He's a good, talented young man. I want him to succeed– that's all. Look, if it were up to his so-called father, Mark would be a garbage man or something instead of a thriving artist. I just wanted to give him a fighting chance. You can understand that, can't you? This world can destroy a person, you know. I've seen it a thousand times in my many years of practice. I've seen the young shrivel up and die like raisins. I've seen drunkenness and drug addiction. I've seen obesity distort and destroy people. I've seen depression poison the mind and bodies of the ultra-sensitive. I've seen teenagers' lives ruined by unwanted pregnancies. I've seen the trust of the children of those teenagers betrayed by their parents. I've seen women, who would make wonderful mothers, unable to produce babies. Sometimes because they are barren, but sometimes because their resentful and vindictive husband has sperm that is as weak and as useless as *he* is. Sperm that is stingy and devoid of feeling and…" He stopped suddenly. "I'm sorry. I got myself upset."

"That's quite all right, Doctor. Tell me, who is this person whose sperm is so weak and useless?"

"Huh? Oh, I, uh, I was just speaking in general terms. I didn't mean anybody in particular. I just meant in general, you know, that they're weak and useless."

"Are you certain, Dr. Dalrymple, that you didn't mean one particular person? Perhaps someone you knew and treated? Perhaps the husband of a woman whom you held in very high regard? Perhaps even more than high regard? Perhaps even held in your arms? What about it, Doctor? We're talking truth here."

"Ha! What about it? Oh, hell! I suppose it won't make any difference now, will it? Of course I held Mrs. Pitt in the highest regard, as you put it. I loved the woman with all my heart. I still do, and she's been dead so long now that she's probably just dust in her grave. I'd do anything for her. All she need do is wish it– just *wish* it– and I'd make it happen. If she had wished that cur of a husband of hers dead, I would have killed him. The only reason he's still walking around today is because she loved him. How she could love him is beyond my ken, but love him she did. Never has there been a creature less deserving of love than he is, but he had the love of the most exquisite woman that ever existed. How's that for irony, Mr. Bright? I'll tell you something else that's ironic. That scoundrel did everything in his power to subvert my– that boy– and prevent his becoming an artist, but instead, he gave Mark the flame he needed to strive against all adversity. Mark could see the power his art had over him and he set his sights accordingly. That monster couldn't stop us, no sir."

"Us?"

"What? Uh, yes, us."

"When did you start hating Stanley Pitt?"

"Let me say that, from the start, I never like the man."

"Yes, but your level of dislike is unnaturally high. When did that start?"

"Around the time that Mark turned two."

"Who started disliking whom first?"

"I suppose he did."

"Do you know what precipitated it?"

The Doctor shifted uncomfortably in his seat.

"Doctor?"

"I guess I do."

"What was it, Doctor?"

"I told you already that his sperm was weak and useless."

"What does that have to do with anything?"

"Everything. Nothing. I don't know. Does it really matter now?"

"Doctor, my client, of whom you are so fond, is on trial here. Yes, it matters. What does Stanley Pitt's sperm have to do with this?"

"Mr. Stanley Pitt was incapable of producing a child."

There was an audible hum in the courtroom.

"If what you say is true, then how did he end up with a son?"

"In the usual fashion– only he wasn't the father."

"Who was?"

Dalrymple groaned. "Forgive me, Darla."

"I'm sorry. What did you say?"

"Please! I promised I would never say anything about it. I gave my word, Mr. Bright."

"You also swore to tell the truth here."

Dalrymple rubbed his palms nervously up and down his knees. "Do you believe that it might save Mark from a terrible fate, Mr. Bright?"

"I can't promise anything, Doctor. But, it just might make the difference, and you do realize that you swore an oath to tell the *whole* truth."

"Yes, I know. I should never have… I should have done the honorable thing and committed suicide."

"Well, you didn't. So, who was the father? Was it you, Doctor?"

"Yes, it was me. He knew it, too. He found out when Mark was two. That's why he started hating me. That's why he punished her. That's why he tried to ruin Mark's life. Mark was named after me, you know."

"Did Mrs. Pitt pick that name?"

"Yes. She wanted to honor her love for me."

"We had Stanley Pitt right here on this witness stand and he said nothing about this."

"Can you blame him? He's embarrassed by it. He thinks he's such a he-man, tossing garbage cans around and driving ten-ton trucks. He could never admit he isn't man enough to produce a child."

"You never married, Doctor?"

"I had never loved anyone– that is until I met Mrs. Pitt. She was the loveliest woman this world has ever known. I don't know why she married that man. He had about as much love in his heart as he had sperm in his testicles. At least he didn't beat her. You have no idea how many hours of my life I wasted praying for a fatal disease to strike him down. I used to be a devout man, Mr. Bright. I lost my belief that there is a god, because Stanley Pitt would have died if there was one– not Darla. Darling Darla, who lies in the ground like a buried treasure while he frolics on the surface and poisons our world with hate and spite. It's just not right. It's him that should be dead and entombed– not her. Not Darla."

"Not to change the subject, but were you acquainted with the deceased, Miss Averdantis?"

"No, I was not. But, one wonders whether any run-of-the-mill bastard child of the Averdantises could ever be quite good enough for Mark Pitt. Mark is going places, Mr. Bright. He'll make his mark in the world. You'll see."

"Thank you. No more questions, Your Honor."

"Your witness, Mr. Wynn."

"Thank you, Your Honor. Dr. Dalrymple, you have a very high opinion of your son, do you not?"

"I don't think it's unwarranted."

"Oh, don't get me wrong, Doctor. I agree that he will certainly make his mark. In fact, he may already have made his mark. That's what we are here to determine. I wonder, though, what you would be willing to do to help your son to make his mark in the world. Tell me, have you talked to your son about his career and his future?"

"No, I haven't."

"Have you talked to your son about the things in life that can prevent a man from achieving his dreams?"

"No."

"Are you familiar with the story of Samson and Delilah, Doctor?"

"I am. That's the story where Samson gets his hair cut by Delilah and he loses all his strength."

"And what lesson would you draw from that, Doctor?"

"I don't know. I never thought about it, really. I guess the idea is that Samson shouldn't have fallen in love with Delilah, because it led to his downfall."

"What about Odysseus?"

"What about Odysseus?"

"Well, he was heading home from the Trojan War and what happened to him?"

"He met up with a Cyclops and got most of his men killed."

"Aside from that."

"You mean the Sirens?"

"No. Guess again."

"It's been a long, long time since I read the Odyssey, Mr. Wynn."

"All right, I'll tell you. What delayed him for ten years or more from getting back home to his beloved wife was a dalliance with Circe. All those years while he was under her spell his kingdom, such as it was, was going to hell in a hand-basket. His wife was having the hardest time fending off the suitors and his son was being plotted against. And his dog– well, we won't go into that. Did you feel that the Odyssey made some valid points about the human condition?"

"Yes, I would say so. I suppose that's why they still assign it to school kids."

"So, you feel that a man can be prevented from reaching his goals by the pull of a relationship with a member of the opposite sex?"

"I suppose that could happen."

"If you saw that happen to someone you cared very much about– someone who meant the world to you– would you want to warn them not to get side-tracked and bogged down in such a relationship?"

"I guess I would."

"When you saw Mark Pitt take up with this latter day Delilah– this 20th Century Circe– did you tell him to kill her?"

"What? No!"

"Are you sure you didn't call him up and advise him to do away with her, so that his career wouldn't suffer?"

"I didn't."

"Didn't you provide him with a cocktail of drugs that you prescribed, using your years of experience as a doctor, that you knew would leave no detectable trace in Evelyn Averdantis's body?"

"No! That's preposterous!"

240

"Is it, Doctor? It seems to me that you would do absolutely anything to ensure that your boy would stay on the fast track to success and glory as the biggest and brightest art star that Highbridge has ever known. Isn't that true?"

"No, it isn't. You've got me wrong."

"Do I? Who was Evelyn Averdantis to you, Doctor? She was dragging Mark Pitt down, slowing him up, distracting him with her wiles. Wasn't she?"

"No. I don't know. I didn't know her. Maybe she did. I don't know."

"Maybe she did what, Doctor? Maybe she subverted your son? Maybe she intended to make an honest man of your fruitcake artist progeny? Maybe she wouldn't sacrifice everything so that he would float to the top of the art world's cesspool. Is that why you plotted with him to dispose of her? Is that it, Doctor?"

"No! No! That's not true! I would never do such a thing!"

"I wonder. No more questions, Your Honor."

"You may step down, Dr. Dalrymple."

"Your Honor, you've got to understand…"

"You may step down, Doctor."

19. Dr. Opici Varlata

"The defense calls Dr. Opici Varlata."

A Slavic-looking man approached the stand to be sworn in. He was wearing a light gray suit and brown shoes.

"Doctor, thank you for taking time out of your very busy schedule to come here to enlighten us about this important issue."

"Sure, no problem."

"Dr. Varlata, what is your current occupation?"

"I am a psychologist. I specialize in psychological issues related to what we in the industry term 'creative types'. This is a category of people who can usually be found populating the theatre, the literary arts, the visual arts, sometimes the musical arts, and, occasionally, jobs such as architect."

"Where were you trained?"

"I received my degree from the University of Prague."

"And where's that?"

"In Prague."

"Where?"

"Prague."

"Ah, I see. Um, Doctor, how long have you been practicing?"

"Thirty-two years. Twenty-two in the United States."

"Where were you for the other ten?"

"Prague."

"I see. And, for those of us who are not as familiar with Prague, Prague is not in the United States, correct?"

"That's correct."

"Just to clarify for those few who may not know, where is Prague exactly?"

"In Czechoslovakia."

"Thank you, Doctor. Now, Dr. Varlata, we have had testimony in this case from more than one so-called expert on the psychology of artists and the extreme danger they supposedly pose to our great society. Can you tell us exactly why we should believe you instead of these other doctors?"

"Mr. Bright, I am Czechoslovakian."

"Yes?"

"Czechoslovakia is in Europe."

"Yes, it is."

"Do you not recall your Psychology-101 textbooks? Europe invented psychology. As a matter of fact, we not only invented it, but we produced some of the most psychologically twisted men in all of history. Psychology is in our blood, Mr. Bright. We live and breathe the human psyche. It permeates our day-to-day existence. You'll find it in our motion pictures and our fine art. You'll even pick up traces of it in our writing. This is in direct opposition to the American sensibility, which avoids psychological questions and replaces the human psyche with action– mostly violent action– as if the human being was an insect reacting to the enemies in its environment. The flawed hero of European culture is turned into the robotically efficient soldier ant, with a heartless exoskeleton of gun metal gray, in your American culture."

"So, what you're saying is that, as a European, you have an inherently better understanding of the human psyche?"

"That is correct."

"I object, Your Honor! It is patently absurd for a European to waltz into this American courtroom and make wild claims that Europe has a better understanding of anything– except, I grant you, chocolate and Swiss watches, and maybe German optics. What gives this so-called witness the right to…"

"I understand your point, Mr. Wynn. Nevertheless, I will allow the witness to express his opinion on the matter. You may proceed, Dr. Varlata."

"I don't wish to insult the American understanding of the human mind, but Europe has a fifty-two hundred year head start on America, and one of the ways that head start is most apparent is in psychology. I mean, look at Adolph Hitler, for example. I doubt America will produce an Adolph Hitler anytime soon."

"Let's hope not, ha ha!"

"Yes, well, Hitler did do an awful lot for the German economy. He took a country, which was on the brink of total collapse, and in a few short years..."

"Killed ten or twelve million innocent people."

"I've never said that his techniques for stimulating the economy were holistically sound."

"Now, you've made a career studying the relationship between the artist and society, haven't you?"

"It has been a large part of my work, yes. I am fascinated by the complex love-hate relationship that exists between artists and the State. I'm also interested in the relationship that exists between artists and the general public, which tends to appreciate art– whatever that means– but usually from a safe distance. It is a cautious relationship. The general public is afraid of art unless and until that art can be completely comprehended by the public."

"Why do you think the public is afraid of art?"

"The public does not understand how artwork comes to be. They suspect that some form of magic is involved– some great dark power, perhaps, that is summoned in the dead of night to serve some mysterious purpose. The public believes this claptrap because they are unskilled in art. One common belief is that art can contain magic powers. Can you imagine? It's the 20th Century and people still believe in magic! I'm not talking about a squatting native somewhere deep in the jungle. I'm talking about a cab driver or a window washer or a congressman. Even paleontologists believe this stuff."

"What about the relationship between the State and the artist?"

"I object, You Honor!"

"On what grounds, Mr. Wynn?"

"It is irrelevant to this trial."

"Your Honor, Mr. Wynn has called several State-certified experts to testify how crazy and dangerous my client– and all artists– are. I think it's at the heart of the case."

"I disagree, Mr. Bright. Objection sustained."

Bright looked like he was bursting to say something, but merely turned a ruddy color instead. After a long pause and a deep sigh, he turned back to his normal complexion and to the witness. "Okay. Now, Dr. Varlata, you were given full access to the defendant, Mark Pitt. Did you conduct a psychological evaluation of him?"

"Yes, I most certainly did."

"How much time did you spend with him?"

"Oh, let's see. All tolled, I'd say approximately four hours."

"And you didn't see him at your apartment, right?"

"What?"

"Never mind. What sort of tests did you employ on Mark Pitt?"

"I used a battery of tests that we use on everyone that we evaluate. It's a carefully crafted, clever and economical approach to zeroing in on the subject's deepest psychological recesses. I treated him just like any other– why did you ask me about my apartment?"

"No, no reason. Really, it was unimportant. Don't worry about it. Go on– continue. You were saying you treated him just like other patients?"

"Yes. Well, yes and no. I mean that many of the people we evaluate are not, strictly speaking, patients. They're just people that we evaluate– no different from you or me."

"Why would you evaluate a normal person? Don't they have to be considered a raving madman to be evaluated?"

"No, not at all. Despite the extra expense, it's imperative that we evaluate everybody, so that we have a good measure of how normal, sane people score on these tests. How can you say that someone is *in*sane if you don't know exactly what *sane* looks like, right?"

"Makes sense. So, Doctor, what did you find out about Mark Pitt?"

"He scored very strongly in the range of sanity. I have an expensive chart that may better illustrate what I'm talking about." The clerk dragged out the easel. "Can I get up, Judge?"

"Certainly."

Varlata climbed down from the stand and walked over to the easel. "If you look here, this area that I'm circling with my hand, this is sanity. Okay? Now, just to give you a frame of reference, this gold star here is where former Mayor Drayton placed after his set of examinations. This gold star here is Bishop La Farge. This here is the well-known actress, Lillian Gish. This one down here is a fellow named Oscar Tulley, who operates the newsstand next to the subway entrance outside our building. You can see that these people scored quite solidly in this gray area denoting sanity in one form or another. Well, Bishop La Farge was somewhat close to the far end here, but still."

"Where did Mark Pitt end up on this chart?"

"Right...," he pointed to the exact middle of the gray area on the chart, "...here. Smack dab in the middle. Mr. Pitt scored very solidly sane."

"Thank you, Doctor. You can retake the stand. Doctor, does that mean he would not commit a murder?"

"Of course not."

"Of course he wouldn't commit a murder?"

"No, of course it doesn't mean that he wouldn't commit a murder."

"But, you said he scored very solidly sane."

"Yes, that's correct. Let me explain something. Sane people kill, too. I will give you a startling little statistic to ponder: Nearly two thirds of the total number of murders committed in Highbridge last year, were committed by perfectly sane people– people just like you or me or Mr. Pitt over there."

"But you could draw the conclusion that he would be less likely to commit murder than someone who is less sane, correct?"

"Not necessarily. There are a lot of raving sickos out there who wouldn't harm a fly. On the other hand, there are perfectly sane Mafia hit men, who kill more people than you can shake a stick at. They make excellent money, too. Sometimes I question my own sanity when I think about how little I make compared to the criminal element– and I'm including politicians in that mix. I'm only half-joking. No, I must advise caution when making assumptions about sanity. If you want to go by just numbers, here's another startling statistic: The thirty-seven percent of murders that are committed by what we call other-than-sane people is committed by fifty-two percent of the total adult population. Now, this number excludes people who are under the age of sixteen and older than eighty-five. We excluded them because we determined that the very young and the very old are atypical adults. It's not just Mafia hit men who make money from murder, by the way. Inheriting property is another way that people gain assets from murder."

"Dr. Varlata, sanity aside, did you find anything in his psychological profile which would tend to bolster the view that Mark Pitt is no more capable of murder than your average person?"

"Oh, sure. His response to various key questions indicated a personality, which, though single-minded, is somewhat compassionate. He scored relatively well in reluctance to do harm, for instance. You'll notice in section seven, page forty-seven, that his response to the scenario in which we give him the choice of breaking a baby's legs or deafening a middle-aged hotel employee, he made *no* clear choice. That is a strong indicator that he is reluctant to do harm– even though, according to the details in the scenario, one of the choices would have clearly been advantageous to his career path and the other would have been a boon to his love life."

"Would you say that a person who gave answers like his is a likely candidate to commit a murder?"

"I would say the opposite. He would not likely commit a murder unless it was a crime of extreme passion. In this regard, he is the quintessential artist personality. It's this inability to be entirely ruthless that essentially handcuffs the artist and relegates him to the lowest income levels in society. That is what eventually forces the artist out of the field and into more lucrative endeavors, such as janitor or clerk or warehouse worker. It's a matter of survival, you see."

"Doctor, a lot has been made about Evelyn Averdantis's corpse being virtually hairless. Did your testing of Mark Pitt touch on that at all?"

"Not as such. I was not aware of this anomaly. Now that you brought that up, though, it brings to mind a curious response to question...," Varlata flipped through his copy of the evaluation, "... sixty... two. Yes, here it is. To the situation presented, in which an ostrich is threatening a baby squirrel, whose nest is constructed inside a priceless antique cabinet, the choices presented to the subject are as follows: Let the ostrich attack the squirrel and risk the cabinet being irreparably damaged. Distract the ostrich by plucking its feathers, probably saving the squirrel's life and preserving the cabinet from damage done by the ostrich, but risking damage done by the squirrel. Reason with the ostrich, offering him a reasonable alternative to attacking the squirrel. Attack the squirrel yourself, removing the incentive for the ostrich to attack the squirrel and possibly minimizing the damage to the priceless antique cabinet."

"Which did he choose?"

"He chose plucking the feathers. Curious, eh?"

"What conclusions did you draw from that answer?"

"Well, none really at the time. That was one of several questions on this test that are designed to challenge the subject without providing any really useful psychological information to us. They have no bearing on the score or on the sanity index."

"Why have a question like that on the test? Isn't it just a waste of time?"

"We have nine such questions on this particular test. No, a question like that can be quite useful if it causes the subject to react violently or causes the subject to blank out and go catatonic. So, unless that sort of thing happens, we don't care which answer they pick. That being said, I wonder now if his response might have had some significance after all. Hmm, we'll have to take a look at that. I'll write that into next quarter's budget."

"Dr. Varlata, did you make any useful evaluations of my client's reaction to the death of his girlfriend?"

"No, not really. Do you think that might've been useful?"

"I don't know. I just mentioned it, you know, because it might give some insight into whether or not he's a viable suspect. I mean, if he's maybe faking being upset or doesn't seem to care at all– that sort of thing."

"I must admit, the thought never crossed my mind. I'll certainly look into such a thing for the future, though. I'm a little concerned that adding more questions will affect the price of printing the tests."

"Thank you, Doctor. No more questions."

"Your witness, Mr. Wynn."

"Thank you, Your Honor. Dr. Varlata, from which university did you earn your degree?"

"The University of Prague."

"And what degree did you earn from that institution?"

"Both my Bachelor's and my Masters. I got my PhD elsewhere."

"And, Doctor, what subject is your degree in?"

"Economics."

"Economics? What gives you the right to practice in the field of psychology, Dr. Varlata?"

"Economics was my major. I minored in psychology, and I passed my psychology exams."

"So, you don't even have a degree in your so-called field?"

"That's correct."

"Doctor, can you tell me how a person who is not qualified can practice in a professional field?"

"If you think I'm not qualified, you are mistaken."

"Your degree is in *economics*, Doctor! If you were a medical doctor– god forbid– you would be thrown in jail for what you are doing."

"I'm not a medical doctor. But, since you brought it up, I know many medical doctors who have murdered patients through their ineptitude. These men are my colleagues, and they are all men who have medical degrees from the top medical colleges in the world. That piece of paper didn't keep those poor victims alive, Mr. Wynn. I am qualified to do what I do. I passed the exam. I am a professional. I don't have an axe to grind. I don't sleep with my subjects. I don't try to *cure* my patients by ripping out the part of their soul that is their avenue to universal connectivity, and sometimes their only hope of emotional survival. I am a champion of that part of mankind that sets us apart from the machine."

"Universal what? What the heck are you talking about?"

"Universal connectivity is what the human species has all but lost in this organized and mechanized society we have created and shackled ourselves with. It is that part of us that is a part of everything. It's there, whether you are aware of it or not. You can't see it or touch it or measure it. You can detect it by the absence of some key things that usually replace it."

"Like what?"

"A sense of time. Time is a human construct. It doesn't exist in nature. When you are experiencing universal connectivity, you lose all sense of time. There are other things, the absence of which means that you are experiencing universal connectivity. Artists experience it when they are really into their work. They lose track of time and need very little food or sleep."

"What kind of voodoo is that? Ha! You make out like these ne'er-do-wells are a bunch of shamans or something."

"Take it or leave it, Mr. Wynn."

"So, with your degree– I mean your *real* degree– how come you don't turn this great discovery of yours into some kind of miracle cure for the economy, huh?"

"I'm working on it."

"Really? Hmm. Maybe, while you're at it, you can cure the common cold, too! Ha ha!"

"Funny you should say that, because productive artists and writers and such are sick only a fraction of the time that most people are."

"I'd be impressed, Dr. Varlata, except you've proven that time doesn't exist, haven't you? So, how can you possibly make such a claim?"

"Maybe I should rephrase that. They are sick much less frequently than creatively inactive people."

"Listen, Doctor, why don't you just fess up and come clean and tell us you're making all this mumbo-jumbo up, eh? I mean, we have a murder trial happening here, in case you haven't noticed. We don't really have time to lollygag around with crackpot theories about why artists are so spacey."

"It's obvious you don't know any artists, Mr. Wynn, or you'd..."

"Oh? I hate to interrupt you, Doctor, but I've known artists in my life– and one artist very, very well indeed. One of my ex-wives was a potter. I had to put up with her and all that went along with her so-called craft. So, before you paint me with too broad a brush, consider *that* fact."

"Well, I take it back, then. You have known artists very well. Whether or not you understand anything about them is another matter entirely. You did say she was one of your *ex*-wives, correct?"

"What the hell do you know about me or my marriages? You think that because you're a European, you can come into an American courtroom and insult this City's leading prosecuting attorney and we'll just say, 'thank you, sir. Please say something else derisive, sir.' Well, it doesn't work that way. You'll find that I have an unending capacity for duking it out with recalcitrant witnesses and wise guys from *The Continent*."

"That must be your particular flavor of Universal Connectivity, Mr. Wynn."

"What does that mean?"

"If you have an, as you put it, unending capacity for doing something or performing such a feat that would normally make someone tired and frustrated, that must be the thing which connects you to the universe and gives you access to that limitless energy supply."

"Are you saying that I've made an art out of prosecuting cases?"

"In a sense, yes. It's obviously your calling."

"Maybe your theory makes sense after all, Doctor. Nevertheless, it seems to me that this battery of tests you administered to Mark Pitt amounts to nothing more than a pile of cheap paper. How can a professional psychologist draw *any* conclusions from this zany hodgepodge of improbable scenarios?" Wynn rapidly leafed through the pages. "Ostriches and squirrels– escalators that change direction while you're on them– singing corpses– arrgh, this is a bunch of crap! How do you answer that, Dr. Varlata?"

"I know my business, Mr. Wynn– just as well as you know yours– and I know how to elicit responses to get at the subject's deepest personality traits. Of course the scenarios are improbable– perhaps many of them are absurd– but it is the response that reveals all. The scenario is merely a tool. Your response to the scenarios reveals quite a lot about you, you know."

"Oh, let's not go there, Doctor. I could easily claim that these scenarios say a lot about you, too– and not all of it is complimentary, I assure you."

Bright rose to his feet. "Your Honor, while Dr. Varlata seems to be quite capable of holding his own in this encounter, it seems to me that the court would best be served if we called off this sparring match at this point and moved back to the murder trial. It is clear that Dr. Varlata's expertise is above reproach and, while his European techniques may seem strange to our American sensibilities, it is a highly regarded tool in diagnosing mental disorders and measuring sanity."

"That was very eloquent, Mr. Bright. I'm sure Judge Tuilgy is deeply impressed by your little soliloquy, but that doesn't change my conclusion, namely that this report is so much trash and Dr. Varlata is a glorified bean counter with some kind of Freudian complex that makes him imagine himself a psychologist."

"Gentlemen, please refrain from sniping at each other. I do agree, Mr. Bright, that this childish bickering between Mr. Wynn and your witness must end. Mr. Wynn, do you have any specific questions to ask the Doctor regarding this case?"

"Yes, I do. Dr. Varlata, what about the homosexuality factor?"

"What is that?"

"It's fairly common knowledge that most artists are homosexuals. So, I was wondering if you detected any homosexuality levels in the defendant."

"No, I didn't detect anything like that."

"Wouldn't a closeted homosexual, who despised his girlfriend and wanted her dead so that he could pursue his cravings for sodomy, be capable of murder, Doctor?"

"I suppose a person who is like what you have just described might be capable of such an act. Yes."

"Have people killed for that reason?"

"I don't know. It sounds a little fantastic to me."

"Oh, come now, Dr. Varlata. You deal in a wild forest of demented human degeneracy. Surely this little hypothesis is not too hard to imagine."

"Maybe for you."

"Do you want to have at it again, Doctor?"

"Please, gentlemen. When you're in my courtroom, you will conduct yourselves with at least some semblance of maturity and civility. Any more questions, Mr. Wynn?"

"I guess not, Your Honor."

"Any more questions, Mr. Bright?"

"No, Your Honor."

"You may step down, Dr. Varlata."

20. Art Prodigy

"The defense calls Mr. Art Prodigy."

A skinny man walked to the stand to be sworn in. He was dressed in old, paint-stained corduroy pants and a white dress shirt, which was yellowed and also paint-stained.

"You are Art Prodigy?"

"I am."

"Tell the court Mr. Prodigy, how you know the defendant, Mark Pitt."

"Well, I am his best friend."

"How long have you known Mark Pitt?"

"Eight years? Seven years?"

"You tell me."

"I don't know. Let's say seven or eight."

"In those seven or eight years, what sort of relationship do you have with the defendant? Do you guys do things together? Do you socialize together?"

"Yeah, we do things together. We've gone out to parties and clubs. We've gone to a ballgame or two. We got to go to the basketball finals two or three years ago– no, two years ago. That was a blast. This other friend of his who was a drug addict and I think is dead now, he gave Mark tickets. We were down in the lower section behind the visitor's bench. That was wild. We won the game 106-105 on a last-second shot by Tuttle. Maybe it was 116-115– no, it was 106-105. Anyway, I think it was Tuttle that got the winning basket. No! I remember now, it was Hamilton, and the final score was 102-101 or something like that. I'm pretty sure we won by a point. Anyway you could probably look it up."

"Would you consider yourself a close friend of the defendant?"

"Well, yeah, I'd say so. I mean, we hang out and talk about stuff, you know. He hasn't let all this success go to his head. He's still okay, you know what I mean? I mean, he's not too good for his buddies, you know, like some people get when they hit the big time. I've known people who get like that. They don't even want to be seen with the old crowd. It's like they never came from anywhere– like they popped up outta nowhere– poof, here I am, Mr. Fancy-pants, woohoo, look at me, I'm God's gift to the world. You know? But, Mark is cool. He's not like that. Of course, he's not a millionaire yet either. Maybe you have to make a million before you start acting that way. I don't know. I'd say the odds are against him, though, 'cause there aren't many millionaire artists out there. Don't get me wrong. I like Mark's work, but he's never gonna make a million dollars painting crotches and asses... I don't think. Right now he's making money, but maybe the pool of collectors for that kind of art is limited, you know? I'd think he'd have more luck selling breasts. But, then again, there are a lot of artists doing breasts, so there's more competition. I suppose he's gotta do what he's gotta do, whether it's crotches and asses or feet or spleens or tonsils or whatever. He just got lucky I guess, you know, with the stuff he's doing. Also, he got lucky with that Bettnasser guy. I didn't envy him for that really, 'cause I think that guy was trying to, you know, get Mark, in *that* way, you know? But, still, it paid off and the guy ended up dead and that was the end of that. Not that he doesn't have his troubles now, but that was a big relief."

"What was?"

"Bettnasser dying when he did. He was causing Mark a lot of stress, coming on to him. You know he was an old queen. When Mark found out Bettnasser died, we went out and celebrated at Argyle Lounge. We got plastered."

"Did Mark Pitt ever talk to you about his female acquaintances?"

"Well, sure. What do you want to know?"

"Specifically about his relationship with Evelyn Averdantis."

"Yeah, he talked about her a lot."

"Did he love her?"

"I guess so."

"He didn't say?"

"Well, Mark's not the type of guy to wear his heart on his sleeve. He might have loved her. I don't know. I know he was more serious about her than any of the others. I mean, they had their ups and downs, you know, but they lived together for a few years. That can put a lot of wear and tear on a relationship. They almost broke up a few times."

255

"To the best of your knowledge, did the defendant ever threaten Miss Averdantis?"

"Like how?"

"Oh, you know, threaten to do her bodily harm or kill her. That sort of thing."

"You mean tell *her* that? I'm not sure."

"Had he threatened her in conversations he had with you?"

"Well, sort of, I guess."

"Did he or not?"

"I guess not. I mean, he said some stuff, but it was his usual over-the-top B.S., so I don't think he meant it."

"What did he say?"

"Well, he said he was going to kill her and freeze her."

"What? Why would he say that?"

"He was doing some preliminary drawings for a painting and she was modeling for him and he said she could never keep still for five seconds. So, he said he was going to kill her and pose her and freeze her body so he could get some work done. I'm sure he was kidding. He said he saw it in a horror movie on TV."

"Anything else?"

"Well, I thought he was kidding when he said he was going to make his brushes from her hair. That turned out to be true. He did start making all his brushes from her hair. At first, he just made them from her head hair, but he got better at it and made fan brushes, pinstriping brushes, fine detailing brushes– all with her hairs. He developed this system where he used different hairs for different brushes. You know, like her head hair for one type and her eyebrows for another. He used her– well, you get what I mean."

"Certainly. Did the defendant mention anything about her being ill or feeling sick in the days before she died?"

"Well, no, I don't think so. I saw her a couple of times that week and she seemed fine to me. I mean, it was hard getting used to her not having any hair, you know what I mean? But she *acted* normal. She wasn't a real bubbly type of girl anyway, you know. I mean, I liked her okay, but she acted like she had the weight of the world on her shoulders sometimes. She wasn't always a lot of fun to be around. She was quiet and I thought a little secretive, you know? She was sort of a homebody, you know? She didn't like going out with us. If she had her choice, she'd just want to stay home every night."

"Did she stay home every night?"

"No, that's the funny part. We'd go out sometimes and leave her there at the loft, then we'd come back and she wouldn't be there. It didn't happen all the time, but it was kinda strange."

"Did she ever say where she had gone?"

"Not to me. She didn't usually answer questions about herself. From what little Mark said about her, it seems she had been kicked around the block a few times in her life and I kinda got the impression that she was sorta tired of it all, in a way. I don't know. It was like she didn't care."

"Did she strike you as a suicidal person?"

"I object, Your Honor. Mr. Prodigy could not possibly be qualified to assess the victim's propensity for suicide."

"Sustained."

"Let me rephrase the question, then. Did she ever mention, while she was in your presence, anything about killing herself?"

"Well, no. She never really talked about much– at least while I was around. She acted sort of disinterested, you know what I mean?"

"What about the defendant using her hair for his brushes? Did they talk about that in your presence?"

"Funny thing– that was the one thing that seemed to animate her. She wasn't much into anything else, but she seemed one hundred percent behind the hair thing. I think it was somehow at least partly her idea. You know she did care about his art. I think she always believed in him– that he would make it in the art world some day. He was just like me before he met her."

"How's that?"

"Well, he was going nowhere. He couldn't get any galleries to pay attention to him. His work wasn't all that great back then, either. He was doing similar stuff, but– I don't know– it just didn't have the mastery that he's become known for."

"What made the difference?"

"It was when he started painting with the brushes he made from Evelyn's hair."

"Are you saying the brushes made the difference?"

"Well, yes and no. I mean, I tried to do a couple of paintings with his brushes and I didn't see any improvement at all. In fact, I thought the brushes were really hard to use. You know, human hair, to be honest with you, sucks if you're using it for oil paint. I don't know about watercolor. Maybe it works better for that, but for oil paints it's really bad."

"Then, how could his painting have improved?"

"Beats me. But, it *did* improve– drastically. I could only think of one thing."

"What is that?"

"I know it sounds stupid, but I think it was because it was *her* hair, given to *him*, for *him* to make paintings with. D'you know what I mean? I mean, it's like it won't work for anybody else. It's like magic or something. Or like a garage door opener, you know? It only works with that one garage door. Her hair would *only* work for him. I know it's stupid, but those brushes are terrible. Believe me, I know. But, you give Mark those brushes and he can whip off a really beautiful painting with them." He shrugged and smirked.

"How can something like that work only for one person?"

"A friend of mine said he thought it was magic."

"Like black magic?"

"Yeah, maybe, or maybe some kind of Eastern discipline. I don't know what he meant exactly. I was talking to my mother about it once. She thought it was love, believe it or not. I mean, my mother can be a little odd about a lot of stuff, you know, the way mothers can sometimes be. But, maybe she's right. What else would explain it?"

"No more questions."

"Mr. Wynn, your witness."

"Thank you, Your Honor. Mr. Prodigy, tell the court, if you will, what your given name was."

"Bruce Farmer."

"Why did you change your name, Mr. Prodigy?"

"I wanted a name I could use to promote myself as an artist."

"What was wrong with Bruce Farmer?"

"I didn't think I'd be able to market myself as easily with a name like Farmer. Once I came up with Prodigy, I felt I had to change my first name, too. It seemed to me that Art Prodigy was more in keeping with the personality of an up-and-coming art star."

"And are you an up-and-coming art star?"

"Well, I've sent my slides to several of the big galleries in town. A few times, actually."

"Have you had any major exhibits?"

"I was in a show at Palettable Art last September."

"A solo exhibition?"

"Well, no. That one was a group show."

"Any other shows?"

"Well, not as such."

"What do you mean, 'not as such'?"

"I mean no. It's not like I haven't had any shows. It's just, you know, that I haven't had any real big shows. Not like, you know…"

"Not like Mark Pitt?"

"Well, that's not what I was gonna say, but you're right. Not like Mark."

"You wish you'd have shows like him, I bet. Did you graduate from college, Mr. Prodigy?"

"Yeah, I have a BFA from Pratt."

"Where's that?"

"New York City. It's an art school– a good one."

"Okay. When you graduated from Pratt School, did you think you'd be living exactly the way you are now?"

"What do you mean?"

"I mean, floundering in entry-level jobs in warehouses and art supply stores. Isn't that what you've been doing these last several years since you graduated?"

"Well, yeah, I guess."

"Would you say that the level that Mark Pitt has achieved in his art career is about where you thought you might be– and wanted to be– by this time?"

"Yeah, I suppose so. Sure."

"Mr. Prodigy, regarding the art world, do you think that the best artists always float to the top, so to speak?"

"Ha! No, I don't think so."

"Do you think that the art world is one of those realms where *who* you know counts more than *what* you know?"

"Well, yeah. I mean, even in Mark's case, you know, with the brushes he made from Evelyn's hair, he might not have made it big without old Bettnasser's help."

"I see. Hmm. Are you a believer in the old adage, 'one hand washes the other', Mr. Prodigy?"

"I don't know what you're getting at, Mr. Wynn."

"Well, let's say, for instance, that you wanted a favor from somebody. You would expect to offer your services to the other person, correct?"

"I guess so, yes."

"And vice versa. If someone wanted you to do a favor for them, they would expect to have to do something for you, correct?"

"Yeah, that makes sense."

"So, my next question is, what did Mark Pitt, who is now in a position in the art world to help his old buddy, offer to you in exchange for your favorable testimony?"

"What?"

"I'll make it plain for you, Prodigy. What is he going to pay you for the load of B.S. that you dumped on this courtroom here today? What did the defendant promise you if you got up here and twisted the truth and made up stories about how lovey-dovey he and his victim, poor Evelyn Averdantis, were? Eh?"

"He didn't do that. Do you think I'd sit here and ignore my oath and lie about him and Evelyn just so I could get a show or something?"

"Yes, I believe you did just that."

"What do you take me for?"

"I take you for a scoundrel, Mr. so-called Art Prodigy. Come now, you know you're not fooling anybody in this courtroom. You and Mark Pitt are hardly friends anymore are you?"

"Sure we are. We're friends."

"You *were* friends with him. That much is true, but only that much. Isn't that right, Mr. Prodigy?"

"No! I mean yes, that is true. I mean we've been friends a long time. We're still friends– *good* friends."

"Are you? I'm not so sure. I'm not so sure that you're not really just one of the old ne'er-do-wells that Pitt cast off like some old snake skin. Most of those old friends faded away into the past, didn't they? But, you stuck around like a sea gull behind a ferry boat– hoping for some discarded scraps to be tossed overboard so you could swoop in and snatch them in that nasty little beak of yours. You lurked just beyond the tree line, like a jackal hoping for a discarded bone to gnaw on."

"That's not true."

"No? Haven't you been looking for ways to continue in his presence, hoping for someone to notice you and hoping against all odds for someone to give you a show in a real gallery?"

"No."

"Haven't you ignored countless friends and family members and gallery owners, who have all told you that you just don't have what it takes to make it in the art world?"

"No."

"You haven't ignored them?"

"No, I mean I have what it takes to make it."

"Then, why haven't you, Mr. Art Prodigy? Why are the doors slammed in your face each time you knock? Could it be that it's *who* you know? Did Mark Pitt promise you a show somewhere if you came through for him in this murder trial? What did he promise you, Prodigy?"

"He didn't promise me anything."

"Did you like Evelyn Averdantis?"

"Yes."

"A lot?"

Prodigy hesitated.

"Did you like Evelyn Averdantis a lot?"

"I don't know."

"You don't know if you liked her a lot?"

"Well, I don't know how much a lot is, you know?"

"Did you want to sleep with her?"

"I don't know."

"Come on, Prodigy."

"All right, yeah, I guess so. Everybody did."

"But, we're not talking about everybody here, Prodigy. We're talking about you. You see, I'm still trying to figure out why you tried to stay friends with Mark Pitt. Isn't it true that for years Pitt wouldn't even give you the time of day?"

Prodigy rolled his eyes and looked up into the upper left corner of the court-room. "I guess so."

"Then, it must've been something other than his good company that kept you sniffing around the campground. Was it the chance at success or something else?"

"Sure."

"Sure, what? Success or something else?"

"Judge, is he allowed to just keep asking me this stuff over and over again, or what?"

"Yes, he is, Mr. Prodigy. Please answer the questions put to you."

"Jeez. What was the question?"

"You didn't care about the art, did you?"

"Of course I did."

"Isn't it true that what you really cared about more than anything else was Evelyn Averdantis?"

"Why would you say that? So what if I did care about her? Is that a crime?"

"No, but if you knew something that would lead to the conviction of Mark Pitt for her murder and didn't reveal it here, that *would* be a crime. If you made a deal with Pitt to receive some sort of consideration for leaving out crucial facts from your testimony, that would be a very serious crime. I think you're a scavenger. I think now that Evelyn's dead and you can't have her, maybe you figured you'd put the squeeze on Pitt and get *something* for yourself– even if it isn't Evelyn. Is that it, Mr. Prodigy?"

"Don't call me that. I hate the way you say my name. *Mis*-ter Prodigy. It sounds derisive."

"It is." Wynn waited a moment. "You didn't answer the question, *Monsieur* Prodigy. You like that better? Eh?"

"Did you ask one? You know, everything you say sounds more like a statement than a question."

"Should I take that as a yes?"

"Should you take what as a yes? I don't even know what you're talking about."

"I think you do. In fact, I think you know *exactly* what I'm talking about."

"That's nice."

"Your stalling for time won't work. No savior is going to swoop out of the sky, crash through the ceiling and whisk you away. We'll stay here all day if we have to."

Bright perked up at that. "Your Honor, I'd rather not listen to several more hours of this sort of questioning, if it please the court."

"Mr. Wynn, much as I hate to do so, I agree wholeheartedly with Mr. Bright. Can you bring this to some sort of fruition or curtail it now?"

Wynn clenched his right fist. "Certainly, Your Honor. I suppose I can end the questioning here. I think the courtroom has gotten a pretty vivid picture of what sort of man Mr. Prodigy *really* is. No more questions."

"You may step down, Mr. Prodigy."

"Call your next witness, Mr. Bright."

"The defense rests, Your Honor."

"Mr. Bright, is the defendant declining his right to answer the charges?"

"Yes, Your Honor."

From the Highbridge Morning Star:

> Testimony wrapped up yesterday in the Trial of the Century of artist, Mark Pitt, accused of murdering his live-in girlfriend. As expected, the defendant did not testify in his own defense. Ambrose Wynn, whose wife is whiskey-voiced singer, Lynn Maguire, finished sketching the character of Pitt with the help of the last in a series of psychologists– this time with a lurid twist befitting the character of this trial. Pitt, who has emerged as a sex-crazed predator, finagled his way into Dr. Odile DePew's apartment and ravished the woman before bragging about his exploits to a total stranger as he left the building.
>
> Wynn seemed quite satisfied with his prospects as he rested his case and public defender, Dick Bright, took over. In a final extraordinary twist, it was revealed by defense witness, Dr. Marcus Dalrymple, M.D. (retired), who was the Pitts' family physician for many years, that he himself is the natural father of Mark Pitt. Needless to say, those present in the jammed courtroom were astounded at this revelation.
>
> Mr. Bright called a psychologist of his own, European-born Dr. Opici Varlata, who attempted to frame the defendant in a somewhat more sympathetic light. His testimony was tarnished however when it was revealed that his doctorate is in economics and not psychology.
>
> The final witness was a fellow-artist and former friend who goes by the name Art Prodigy, who offered some poignant moments when he spoke of the victim, Evelyn Averdantis, whose nude body was found lying in a bathtub last Spring. He testified that the woman seemed tired of the struggle of life and of supporting her boyfriend, Mr. Pitt, while he spent all of his time coloring pictures.
>
> Closing arguments are expected this morning in this unprecedented legal battle between the State and the rogue painter. Pitt faces life in prison, if convicted.

21. The Prosecution– Closing Argument

"Mr. Wynn, are you prepared to deliver your closing argument?"

"I am. Your Honor." Wynn stood at the prosecutor's table and gathered his thoughts and mustered his powers for his final attack. After waiting a few extra seconds for the gravity of the situation to sink into the jurors' minds, he lifted his head and began to speak. "Ladies and gentlemen, you have heard days of testimony from many different witnesses. Some of the witnesses knew the defendant or his victim personally. Some of the witnesses were called upon to provide a framework– or context, if you prefer– within which you can more clearly discern the true character of the so-called man, who is on trial for this awful crime. You have heard testimony from highly-trained professionals, who were summoned into this situation because the silken tongue of Satan can weave a cocoon of lies that can fool even the cleverest of us sometimes. These professional psychologists and forensic experts were brought into the court because someone had to cut through that cocoon and bring the truth into the light of day.

"The art world is a very strange realm indeed. Most of us have never had any experience of it. It contains mysterious practices and peculiar, unwritten rules. It is populated by human beings for the most part, but these human beings are not like you and me. They think strange thoughts and have a language quite apart from the English that we speak. They work with special substances and manipulate exotic compounds. They're motivated by bizarre psychosexual urges and they interpret the world in the most disjointed and abstracted ways. They look at people like you and me and they don't see people the way we do. They see lines and colors, light and shadow. Who knows what seeing people like that does to a person's soul? Does it rob them of their humanity? Does it make them heartless and brutal? Can they love? Is there any room for compassion in that encyclopedic carcass of tone and volume and gesture? That's all they care about, you know. You look astonished. It's true. You've heard testimony about how inhumanely they treat their models– asking them to hold painfully contorted poses for countless hours while they practice their wicked craft. What does that mean for us– society at large? What did it mean for Evelyn Averdantis? Poor Evelyn Averdantis, who gave *everything* to Mark Pitt, including her hair, for chrissakes! Did he care?" Wynn gestured with a sweep of his arm toward the defendant. "Yeah, I guess he cared, all right– about getting rich and establishing himself as an art star. He got rich doing his art thing with her eyebrows and pubic hair and long, beautiful head hair. Now that he's established, does he still need her? Would he still want her around? Wouldn't she just get in his way? He obviously had an insatiable appetite for women. That's been demonstrated here in this trial. Was he tired of her? Did he want to move on to someone more voluptuous? That curvaceous young

Catherine Prawn was waiting in the wings. She was so enthralled by him that she would have offered him anything he wished. All he needed to do was ask. And that was when he didn't have quite the fame and fortune that he has today! There's a lot for you to consider.

"We heard from the defendant's own father that art was always most impor-tant to him. He was always oriented that way. Perhaps he was born that way. Who knows? I'm not sure science has found an 'art gene', so to speak. I'm certainly not implying that we should shun Mark Pitt just because he's an artist, but we do know that, from a very young age, he used art– almost as a weapon– to hurt his father. His father was clearly just trying to do his best for the boy and his mother. And, remember, Mark Pitt was not even this man's son! You have to wonder about such a person. Most people, when they think about art, think about pretty pictures of mountains and flowers and sunsets. Most of us don't think of art as a weapon to be used to inflict emotional harm on someone. Clearly the defendant has had a much different view of art than we do. When he was a child, he used art in an Oedipal way, to dethrone his father and usurp his natural position. Well, we all know what happened to Oedipus, don't we? Unfortunately, here in America, we can't crucify Mark Pitt like they did to old Oedipus, but we *can* mete out justice another way. It's your responsibility to do that. You must convict this man before he destroys another life. He destroyed his fa-ther's happiness. He destroyed a stalwart teacher's otherwise good year and scarred him for life, such that the poor man felt compelled to transfer out of that school, because he could no longer teach in the same school within which he had suffered so much humiliation. The toll is astounding. He messed up the lives of two level-headed young ladies, a rival artist, a homo-sexual millionaire gallery-owner and an old and dear friend and fellow-artist, whom he tried to bribe into testifying favorably. He even seduced a trained professional psychologist into a sordid May-December tryst, though, thankfully he was too late to stop her from properly vilifying him in her evaluation. No one stopped him when those misdeeds occurred. Along comes Evelyn Averdantis– sweet, young girl– oblivious to this psychotic's maniacal tendencies. No one warned her. No one was there. Now she's– well, you know the rest, ladies and gentlemen. And she had to be laid to eternal rest as bald as Yul Brynner." Wynn bowed his head solemnly, and shook it slowly and gravely.

"You have the reports. You have the facts. It has been shown to you, quite clearly, how dangerous this– this *art star* is to our otherwise fine society. I implore you to perform your duty, unpleasant though it may seem. It is the humane thing to do. It really is. Think about this frightful little scenario: What if Mark Pitt is allowed to roam the City, free as a bird, for another fifty or sixty years? I shudder to think of how many good, decent people he will destroy with his so-called artistic talents." Wynn paused and nodded repeatedly as he gazed at each of the jurors. "Think about *that* when you retire to deliberate." Wynn returned to his seat.

22. The Defense- Closing Argument

Bright rose to his feet and strolled into the center of the courtroom, facing the jury. "Ladies and gentlemen, you are charged with a very important task here today. The task is not, as my famous adversary, Mr. Wynn, has stated, to protect society from a crazy maniac who is cutting a swath of destruction and death like some sort of abstract-expressionist tornado. No, it is to exonerate a man who has lived his life much the same as any other man with the lone exception that he can be labeled an 'artist'. Science is now attempting to ascertain whether or not a person is born an artist or becomes an artist by choice. I'm sure some of you have artists in your lives– perhaps even close family members. I think we all know that having an artist in your family can be difficult given the culture we live in. It's a little different for our counterparts in foreign countries. Europe, I know, has a very enlightened and liberal attitude toward artists in general and one could say that they sometimes even encourage that sort of thing. I know that's hard to fathom, but if any of you has traveled to Europe, you know I speak the truth. Now, with that being the case and taking what my opponent believes, you would think that Europe would be experiencing a catastrophe of biblical proportion. Well, they're not." Bright pounded his fist on the short wall in front of the jurors, keeping time with the words. "Don't– believe– every– thing– you hear!" He walked away a couple of steps.

"Accusations have been leveled at the defendant sitting there. Has the prosecution proven *anything* in this case? Let's look at it for a moment. And when I say let's look at it, I mean let's *really* look at it– the way young Miss Prawn described how good artists really look at the human figure, the way they see what's there instead of their preconceptions. One thing the mighty Mr. Wynn has proven is that there are a lot of people who are willing to make accusations. That's one thing. Another thing Mr. Wynn has proven is that there are a lot of experts who have a lot of fairly extreme theories about people. I guess I'm kind of naïve about people. I don't tend to think everybody is crazy. Lord knows what some of these so-called doctors would say about the twelve of you if they got *you* to take their tests. Didn't you worry about that just a little when you heard them categorize Mark Pitt as the worst kind of miscreant? I did. What would the good Dr. Bitsch say about *any* of us if we had to answer the question about who our favorite tyrant was? Poor Mark Pitt was unlucky because he was forced to take these awful, damning tests. He was unlucky because and he just happened to be in a park– alone– when his girlfriend chose to die in her bathtub. Only maybe it wasn't luck." He wagged his finger in the air, then placed it under his lower lip. "Maybe– just maybe– Evelyn Averdantis waited until he *was* out of the house to let herself die. Maybe she didn't want him to be there. He certainly would have tried to revive her if he had been there. 'Why *certainly*?' you might ask. Simple– he loved her. He needed her. He succeeded with her in his corner and because of her. Sure, he might continue to succeed– even

269

without her by his side– just because he's built up a kind of momentum and established a reputation. But, his success was assured with Evelyn by his side– loving and supporting him spiritually. The problem for Evelyn was that she was just tired. She was tired of a mother who squashed her creativity because it was too messy to deal with. She was tired of trading her body for drugs– drugs that she took to smooth out the rough edges of her loveless upbringing. She was tired of being hit on by her bosses. She was tired of loving a boyfriend who didn't have the manly courage to even utter a peep of protest when she found a real man at a gallery opening one night. Yes, a real man, who was the first man to fight for her. It seems appropriate that she found this man at an exhibit depicting the horrors of human experience. Amid the screams and cacophony of suffering she and Mark fell in love. But that doesn't change the fact that she was tired. Her final grand sacrifice that ensured his success was the sort of thing she had hoped she could accomplish in her life. She really made a difference for him and his art. And then she said farewell.

"You may have been convinced– as someone alleged– that Mark Pitt just wanted to use Evelyn Averdantis to achieve his goal of becoming an art star. If you believe that, then answer this in your own mind: How could Mark Pitt know when he met Evelyn Averdantis that she would eventually find the missing piece to the puzzle for him? *She* was the one who approached H.B. Sweatclown and was given the secret of the magic of her hair– the Pavitra Bala. Mark Pitt didn't send her to him. She went to Sweatclown all on her own. And, if he had killed her, why would he wait so long from the time he became a successful and famous artist before doing it? It makes no sense. Why would he have to kill her? Sure they had squabbles, as most couples do, but there was no testimony to the effect that Evelyn Averdantis would have made it impossible for Mark Pitt to break it off with her– *if* he'd wanted to.

"Mark Pitt was painted in lurid fashion as a crazed and evil demon by the prosecution. If I recall, Mr. Wynn said that the defendant was looking for any opportunity to leap out of his seat and tear all of you to pieces. Well, either he just didn't get the opportunity during this trial or he's really not the crazed and ferocious beast that Mr. Wynn wanted you to believe. Ask yourselves how such a crazy character could possibly commit what would have to be an absolutely perfect murder? What expertise was he supposed to use in order to commit this perfect murder? Mark Pitt was an excellent art student, but the prosecution failed to establish that he had acquired *any* expertise during the course of his life that could have been used to kill someone and leave not a trace. Anyway, he had no motive. Again, I didn't hear anything from the prosecution witnesses that would lead me to believe that there was any enmity other than the typical squabbles that couples have with each other.

"No, it just doesn't add up. No motive, no expertise, no cause of death." He ticked the points off on the fingers of his left hand. "There wasn't the possibility of collecting any kind of life insurance on her. They were never married. No– no evidence, no conviction, ladies and gentlemen. I would go so far to say that the inestimable Mr. Wynn failed to make a case against the defendant at all– weak or otherwise." He paused a moment. "Certainly not for murder. He did prove one thing beyond any trace of doubt. He proved that Mark Pitt is an artist. No one disagreed with that fact– not the people who knew him or the critics or the psychologists. Even his father confirmed it. I am certain that you will do the right and just thing and acquit Mark Pitt of all charges. I thank you, and I thank you on behalf of Mark Pitt."

Bright walked back to the defense table.

The So-Called Trial of the Century

From the Highbridge Morning Star:

> The jury heard the closing arguments in the Trial of the Century today. Mark Pitt, accused of murdering his live-in girlfriend, Evelyn Averdantis, never took the witness stand in his own defense– a tactic by Dick Bright that drew praise from legal experts who have been paying close attention to the proceedings.
>
> Whatever testimony Mr. Pitt could have offered in his own defense would have been unlikely to completely undo much of the damage done by numerous psychological experts and character witnesses brought to the stand by Ambrose Wynn, lead prosecutor and husband of statuesque recording artist, Lynn Maguire.
>
> The closing arguments held no particular surprises. Wynn hammered home his assertion that Pitt is a crazed maniac and that he used up and threw out the victim. Bright cautioned the jury to think for themselves and not to believe the extreme evaluations of the psychologists.
>
> After the jury heard Judge Tuilgy's instructions and the court adjourned, Wynn fielded questions on the courthouse steps, denying rumors that his marriage to Ms Maguire is on the rocks. Wynn insisted that the only thing on the rocks is the rye whiskey that was waiting for him across the street at O'Toole's Bar and Grill. Wynn praised his adversary, Mr. Bright, with whom he had numerous heated exchanges during the trial, and said that he thought that a bright future awaited him. This remark brought guffaws from the crowd of reporters who have been packing the courtroom since day one.
>
> The jury has been sequestered during the trial in order to avoid exposure to the deluge of press that this trial has generated. Several of the witnesses have already signed lucrative deals with publishers for their version of the story, which has captivated this City for more than a week. One witness, a curvaceous nude model who goes by the name of Cathy Prawn, has agreed to pose for one of the leading men's magazines for an undisclosed sum.
>
> It is impossible to predict how much time the jury will need before it can reach a verdict. One of the major difficulties facing the jury is how much weight should be given to the psychological experts' testimony. It's likely that those arcane reports will largely be ignored by the blue-collar jury, many of whom seemed at times to stare blankly into space while ten-dollar words flew back and forth.

The So-Called Trial of the Century

Much has been said and written about the sociological ramifications of this trial, which has been followed closely on one side by a loose association of advocates for arts education and funding, and on the other by high-powered organizations who are concerned about preserving decency and morality. It remains to be seen if the outcome of this trial means that any cultural shift one way or the other is in the cards.

From the Highbridge Morning Star:

Judge Tuilgy declared a mistrial in the so-called Trial of the Century today when the jury came back without a verdict after six days of deliberations. Hopes for justice dimmed over the last few days when it became clear that the jury was either deadlocked or, as some legal experts have come to believe, completely baffled. Numerous times the foreman requested transcripts of testimony and subsequently each time the foreman sent back messages that they were farther from a verdict than when they began.

This trial, in which some of the great questions plaguing Western Society could have been resolved, turned out to be a baffling and a futile exercise in pointless verbal acrobatics and macho gamesmanship. What at first had promised to be one of the landmark events in the history of jurisprudence ended up an expensive circus, with everything but the elephants– and far too many clowns.

Reporters swarmed all over the key players in this cheesy vaudevillian melodrama, but Ambrose Wynn, who is currently embroiled in a messy divorce from the darling of Cord Street, Lynn Maguire, had no comment. Neither did Dick Bright, whose stock has certainly risen with the news of this non-verdict. Mark Pitt, who was not heard from during the trial, was whisked away through a side door into a Cadillac Fleetwood limo. Only Stanley Calvin, the so-called Kneeless Nijinsky, was there and eager to speak, trying to kick-start the moldering cadaver of his once-vital dancing career.

The So-Called Trial of the Century